WOLF WARRIORS II

THE NATIONAL WOLFWATCHER COALITION ANTHOLOGY

EDITED BY

JONATHAN W. THURSTON

A THURSTON HOWL PUBLICATIONS BOOK

ISBN 978-0-9908902-8-7

WOLF WARRIORS II: THE NATIONAL WOLFWATCHER COALITION ANTHOLOGY

A Thurston Howl Publications Book
Published by Thurston Howl Publications
thurstonhowlpublications.com
Nashville, TN

Mailing address:
439 Lemont Dr
Nashville, TN 37216

jonathan.thurstonhowlpub@gmail.com

Cover image by ------

Edited by Jonathan W. Thurston.

Printed in the United States of America
10 9 8 7 6 5 4 3 2 1

ACKNOWLEDGMENTS

"The Montexan" by Alan Good. Copyright © 2015 by Alan Good.

"The Greatest Gift of All" and "In Winter" by Alanna Khubieh. Copyright © 2015 by Alanna Khubieh.

"In Passing" by Amy Hakanson. Copyright © 2015 by Amy Hakanson.

"Full Moon" and "Lone Wolf, Pack Wolf" by A.M. Duvall. Copyright © 2015 by A.M. Duvall.

"Startle Wolf" and "Wolf Host" by Anne Walsh. Copyright © 2015 by Anne Walsh.

"Celebration" by Autumn Beverly. Copyright © 2015 by Autumn Beverly.

"Dissipation" and "St. Francis and the Wolf" by Chelsea Dub. Copyright © 2015 by Chelsea Dub.

"Silent Willow" by Chiara Renda. Copyright © 2015 by Chiara Renda.

"The Appearance of Grace in Our Lives" and "Miracle" by Chris Albert. Copyright © 2015 by Chris Albert.

"A Pup's Nose" by Christian Esche. Copyright © 2015 by Christian Esche.

"Dog Days" and "Echo" by Dana Sonnenschein. Copyright © 2015 by Dana Sonnenschein.

"Let the Wolves Run Free" by Ratty. Copyright © 2015 by Ratty.

"Wolf in the Snow" and "A Wolf's Plea" by Dawn Sharman. Copyright © 2015 by Dawn Sharman.

"The Line" by Forest Wells. Copyright © 2015 by Forest Wells.

"Growing Gray" by Hannah E. Christopher. Copyright © 2015 by Hannah E. Christopher.

"The Beast of Minnesota" by Hemal Rana. Copyright © 2015 by Hemal Rana.

"Kai," "Little Red Cap," and "Were Dance" by Isis Raye. Copyright © 2015 by Isis Raye.

"Luna" by Jason Limberg. Copyright © 2015 by Jason Limberg.

"Ahuli's Orange Eyes," "Alpha Netar," and "Unalii in Fall" by Jay Huron. Copyright © 2015 by Jay Huron.

"The Hunter" by Jenny H. Thornton Woodley. Copyright © 2015 by Jenny H. Thornton Woodley.

"Canis rufus," "Howl of the Southeast," and "Persistence of a Species" by Jeremy Hooper. Copyright © 2015 by Jeremy Hooper.

I dedicate this book to my family of friends who have supported me this year: Debbie, Dustin, Kelsey, Angel, Alli, Hollyann, Ken, Hype, Taka, and Shoji. I also dedicate this to the menagerie of animals who now reside at my home in Nashville: my ever-loyal Temerita (a dog who still insists she is a cat), Kitty (she's a cat), Piper (she's an evil cat), Bugsy the adorable bunny, Archimedes the snake (just Archie for short), and Venaticus, the tarantula that wants to eat all the other animals.

CONTENTS

BOARD OF DIRECTORS AND CONTENT PROVIDERS FOR THE NATIONAL WOLFWATCHER COALITION

National Wolfwatcher Coalition Board of Directors

Nancy Warren, Executive Director and Great Lakes Regional Director
Daniel Sayre, Southwest Regional Director
Janet Hoben, Southeast Regional Director
Dr. Chris Albert, DVM, Veterinary Consultant to NWC
Cheryl Kindschy, Social Media Outreach Director
Candice Copeland, Social Media Outreach Director
Kat Brekken, Eco-Education and Tourism Director, Yellowstone
Brandi Nichols, Yellowstone Adviser

Content Provider Volunteers on Facebook Page

Dr. Chris Albert, DVM: Great Lakes
Daniel Sayre: Southwest, Mexican Gray Wolves
Cheryl Kindschy: Southwest, Letter to the Editor Team
Janet Hoben: Southeast, Red Wolves
Mitch Rand: Red Wolves
Candice Copeland: Yellowstone, Grand Tetons, Colorado and Utah, Pinterest, Twitter
Michelle Roberts: California and Alaska
Genevieve Jaquez-Schumacher: Washington and Oregon
Eileen Sutz: Wolf topics

LETTER FROM THE NATIONAL WOLFWATCHER COALITION

Five years ago a group of friends had a vision—to form an organization that speaks solely for the wolf. What emerged was the National Wolfwatcher Coalition.

Our statistics speak for themselves: More than thirteen million hits on our website www.wolfwatcher.org; over 785,000 likes on Facebook, with posts reaching nearly one million advocates; over 1,600 supporters follow us on Twitter and Pinterest.

We have extended our reach around the world with friends in many foreign countries including France, England, Greece, Germany, Italy, Mexico, Canada, Ukraine, New Zealand, and Australia. The mission of the National Wolfwatcher Coalition is straightforward: to educate and advocate for the long-term recovery and preservation of wolves utilizing the best available science. We believe in using peer-reviewed data and encourage comments on wolf-related affairs following the principles of democracy.

We have no membership dues. We do not sell or share our mailing list. We do not send out solicitations begging for money. We do not mail you merchandise you did not request, and we do not inundate your inbox with emails. We have an electronic newsletter that we send out when we have important information to share, and if you no longer wish to receive the alerts, it is easy to unsubscribe. We rely on social media and supporters who seek us out for information.

The National Wolfwatcher Coalition is an all-volunteer organization. None of our board members or volunteers receives any compensation. They work out of their homes, donate their time, energy, and talents to educate and advocate for wolves. We do not maintain an office which helps to keep expenses down nor do we maintain a facility with captive wolves.

A core group of volunteers works every day on behalf of wolves. Our volunteers are scattered across the country but work on issues in every region where there is a current population of wolves. Our goal is to find middle ground and encourage the use of non-lethal methods to resolve conflicts.

Volunteers attend meetings, hearings, and workshops and participate by providing testimony on a variety of topics including delisting, hunting, and trapping regulations. Volunteers scour the newspapers, publications looking for articles to share; we have a letter-writing team that submits letters to the editor. If you would like to volunteer, complete the volunteer form found at http://wolfwatcher.org/connect/volunteer/

We are able to advocate for wolves because of the generous donations from our supporters and through the purchase of merchandise available for sale at our website store. There are many other ways you can support us. Every eligible purchase you make through smile.amazon.com will result in a donation to us. All you need to do is select National Wolfwatcher Coalition on your first visit to smile.amazon.com (the settings you created on amazon.com remain the same). Shopping through Pinterest www.pinterest.com/NWCmedia/ benefits us as well.

Mountain Artwear www.themountain.com/wolves/ will donate $1 to us for every wolf shirt you purchase and as an added bonus; you will receive a 15% discount, with code NWC15, for any wolf product.

This financial support has allowed us to foster relationships with other like-minded organizations. We wish to thank Jonathan Thurston for putting together this anthology and donating the proceeds to the National Wolfwatcher Coalition. And of course, special thanks to all who submitted art work, poetry, prose, and stories. This anthology would not have been possible without your contributions. Your dedication to helping wolves is truly appreciated. These are critical times for wolves. The century-old fears, myths, and hatred toward the wolf still exist today. Wolves are now a hunted game animal in every state where they have lost their federal protection. Wolf policies allow for liberal killing of wolves involved with conflicts. With today's anti-wolf political climate, it can sometimes be discouraging, but we are a strong pack. We will not give up the fight for wolves, not today, not tomorrow, or the next day. And, with your continuing support, we can ensure future generations will hear wolves howl.

Board of Directors
National Wolfwatcher Coalition

INTRODUCTION

Wolves walk a fine line, between angels and demons, between dreams and reality, somewhere between the world of light and the world of shadows. There are those who would kill them for their strength and those who would tame them for their beauty. Even scientists today dispute how dangerous wolves truly are. One of the only things we can accurately say about all wolves is that they have been a part of our history, literature, and culture since recorded time. Inherent in this dualism, this walking alongside humans even as they dodge our spears, bullets, and traps, wolves are fighters: they are warriors that stand dignified against a raging war of corrupt politics and hatred rooted solely in myths.

For authors like Jack London and Ernest Thompson Seton, the wolves' midnight howls were enough voices to prompt them to action, to preserve the forest warriors. However, in today's society, the wolf's voice has become mute. Gunshots ring across the fields, and their echoes linger, howls unheard. Through this silence, people have arisen to help give wolves their voices back. Some of these people have contributed to this very anthology, but make note that even these contributors mark only a small percentage of the warriors that speak for wolves. Warriors that are wolves and warriors that speak for wolves work together, creating one enormous pack, the titular Wolf Warriors.

Like the wolves, our Wolf Warriors from everywhere. As wolves have appeared in the myths and legends of pre-colonial America, Europe, Russia, China, Egypt, and Japan, our Wolf Warriors come from every walk of life. The wolf is an animal of the world. It is with this concept of the world-wolf that I have collected wolf-related submissions from around the world this year to create the volume you now hold in your hands. People feel a certain affinity toward this beauteous animal across all the nations, and that affinity links us all, creating a community of wolf lovers all around the world. We are as diverse as the wolves to whom we have become so attached.

In 2014, I discussed with the National Wolfwatcher Coalition's Southeast Regional Director Janet Hoben the possibility of creating a charity anthology for the NWC, allowing people to submit art, poetry, essays, and short stories. I had not expected it would actually receive over two hundred submissions and eventually become an Amazon best-selling anthology for over a month. For that collection, we were honored to receive contributions from the best-selling and award-winning authors David Clement-Davies and Catherynne Valente.

In all honesty, Thurston Howl Publications had not intended to do a second volume of *Wolf Warriors* for at least another year. However, a series of ecological and political events prompted me to speak again with the National Wolfwatcher Coalition regarding an immediate second volume. *Wolf Warriors II* has mostly new authors and artists with a few from last year's anthology. At the end of the collection, you will find a list of our wolf veterans, those who were published in the previous volume as well as this one.

The editing committee has been more selective this year in terms of acceptance of submissions. As such, this is a much shorter volume. We also accepted works that were beyond our length requirements, allowing us to publish longer works. A final comment is that we are also publishing an art book of this year's and last year's artwork, tentatively titled *Pack Animals* to be released as a companion series. This is slotted for release in December 2015.

I already left a dedication at the beginning of the book, but I want to thank a few for the production of this book. Thank you eternally to the lovely lupine lady Candice Copeland, my secretary and the Social Media Outreach Director for the NWC, for all of the hard work and dedication she put into the scores of emails and lists I asked her to compile. A salute to the National Wolfwatcher Coalition for continuing to educate. A salute to the many contributors of this anthology. And, of course, a final salute to you the reader.

As you begin this book, I ask that you close your eyes every once in a while and just listen. In this book are connected the voices of around fifty individuals across the globe who are just hoping that you can hear their howls. They howl for freedom. They howl for love. They howl for someone to just hear them. They howl to the future.

Jonathan W. Thurston
Editor

AHULI'S ORANGE EYES, ALPHA NETAR, & UNALII IN FALL
JAY HURON

Jay mostly photographs in the Tri-Cities area of northeast Tennessee, but occasionally gets out to some of the surrounding areas in North Carolina and Virginia. He enjoys taking pictures of urban environments, events, and his family (pretty much anything, really), but his true passion is for nature, wildlife, wolves, and landscape photography, loving to get out and hike and bring back beautiful photos to show you!

Ahuli's Orange Eyes. Photography.

Alpha Netar. Photography.

Unalii in Fall. Photography.

THE APPEARANCE OF GRACE IN OUR LIVES & MIRACLE
CHRIS ALBERT

Chris Albert became a wolf advocate at the age of 8 after reading horrific stories about wolves. She explored a career in wildlife management but ultimately decided to become a veterinarian. She has learned over the years that wolves (and other wildlife) will thrive when those who have to live with them understand their value, so she works hard to educate farmers and hunters and children on the role and value of wolves in the ecosystem.

The Appearance of Grace in Our Lives

I entered the veterinary exam room somewhat absentmindedly, but exclaimed a jovial hello with delight when I saw John, one of my all-time favorite clients, with his hound dog Belle.

In a world of hunting where people often didn't treat their dogs so very well, John was different. He always made sure they were up to date on routine care, fed them quality food. He even got their teeth cleaned! The dogs lived in the house and were loved as family. But all that had changed when John's wife got sick. A lingering illness bankrupted them, and by the time she died, his visits to my clinic had drifted off. He kept his dogs, probably feeding them when he himself went hungry, but he just couldn't keep up their veterinary care.

I was hoping John's visit signaled better times, but he didn't look so happy. He was about 65, grizzled face, thin body, in a white t-shirt and jeans. The lines on his face were more deeply etched, his hair gone completely silver now, and he had a sad, defeated look about him.

"It's so good to see you, John. What's up?" I smiled.

"Belle's not doing well," he said, acting almost embarrassed. Clearly, he wanted to say more, but stopped.

I examined Belle. I remembered her from a decade ago, a beautiful brindle Plott Hound. Swellings in throat were immediately apparent. They were lymph nodes, and as I checked the less obvious places for lymph nodes, they were swollen all over.

"You're right, John," I said softly. "Her lymph nodes are swollen all over, and that probably means lymphoma, a form of cancer."

"Can you give me some pain medicine for her?" he asked, somewhat urgently.

It was an unusual request. Dogs with lymphoma don't particularly hurt; they're just tired. As they get very sick, they sometimes have trouble breathing, but pain isn't a big problem. I explained this to John, mentioning chemo, which I figured he couldn't do, but assuring him that steroids would do better at managing her symptoms than pain medicine.

John sighed, looked at me sadly, and began the real explanation for his visit.

"Hard times have gotten harder, Doc," he started. "Hounding season is here, and I have heard that the state of Wisconsin pays up to $2500 for a dog killed by a wolf. The hunting and trapping blogs say it's a 'good way' of getting paid for unwanted dogs.

"It doesn't seem quite right..." he continued somewhat angrily. "With all the things that need attention, why is there money for this? But...there is, and $2500 will be enough for me to eat and care for my dogs this winter. I haven't been able to find work in a long time. I know Belle is dying, but I also know that if we asked her she would help out if she could."

"To get that money" I said carefully, "you will have to turn Belle loose in known wolf territory. The wolf pups are still young, the parents will protect them: they will tear her apart. She may die a painful and lingering death, and all by herself."

John's eyes met mine. "That's why I want the pain medicine," he said.

Wow. I thought. *Talk about an ethical dilemma.*

"Let me give this some thought," I answered.

It took me two days to come to terms with the request. In the end, I decided that my duty was to Belle, to keep her from suffering as best I could. I called John and told him I would prepare a shot for him to give.

Two weeks later, John came to the clinic again. This time, he was a totally different man, upbeat and cheerful, with a skinny new hound by his side, wagging her tail. I waited for his story.

"Well, Doc," he said, "it didn't go at all like I planned." He shook his head and chuckled. "Right now the wolves are at rendezvous sites. I looked up the caution areas and took Belle. I gave her the pain shot you gave me and looked into her eyes…but I couldn't do it: I couldn't turn this friend that had been there through thick and thin out into the woods to be killed like that. I just sat there and bawled."

John looked sheepish at this point. He was not usually the kind of guy that would admit to bawling. "Then maybe a miracle happened," John continued, his face reflecting the wonder he felt. "As I sat in the car on that gravel road, I saw movement in the bushes. Out crept this dog, tail between her legs, cowering. Maybe she looks like a hunting dog, but she says she's not. I guess that's why she was dropped off for the wolves to tear up for that easy money. It ain't right," he shook his head sternly. "So I opened the car door, she hopped in, and Belle and I took her home.

"Belle died later that night. She was ready. I am really glad she died warm, and comfortable, with her family right beside her. I am really glad I didn't leave her for those wolves to tear apart. I'm even glad that those wolves didn't have to do that – defending their puppies and all – I don't blame them for killing dogs that are a threat to their young 'uns."

I went to examine the new dog, who hadn't stopped wagging her tail.

"What's her name?" I asked

"I call her Grace…" he smiled, "…because she has brought me grace. My wife's death was making me a bitter old man. Then suddenly this week, I was grateful for so many things: doing the right thing by Belle and finding this dog that I needed as much as she needed me. Then, miracle of miracles, I even got a call out of the blue – a friend asked if I could come work for him part time! I think we're both going to be okay now!"

It was my total pleasure to agree.

Author's note: this story is fiction. However, it COULD be true. Veterinarians often face ethical dilemmas as outlined in the story. Wisconsin does, indeed, pay up to $2500 for hunting dogs killed by wolves, and the blogs do boast that turning a dog loose in wolf country is a good way of "getting rid of a useless dog." If wolves are hounded during puppy season, they are just defending their young. Anti-wolf folk often trumpet that wolves are killing pets, but the only dogs killed are the ones purposely released into known wolf territory.

Miracle
(Inspired by So Yapo Timke)

Eleven-year-old Jonathan loved being the first one up in the quiet before dawn. He slipped on jeans, his old gray Mariners sweatshirt, ran his fingers through his tussled brown hair, and slipped downstairs. At the front door, he put on his boots and stepped outside to the cool morning air of the family's sheep farm...to tragedy.

The tragedy wasn't immediately apparent, for the wolves had come upon the unprotected sheep in the fields farthest away from the house. But even as he walked to check on his beloved "Snow," the foundation ewe of *his* herd, something knotted his stomach. Something wasn't right.

And then he spotted them – scattered, silent, torn young ewes on the hillside. ALL of them? Five...six...seven...eight...yes, all of them.

Filled with rage, and sadness, and shame that he hadn't thought to move them inside last night, Jonathan moved from body to body, hoping someone had been spared, weeping when he came upon Snow.

It was at this moment, in the midst of all this death and pain, that the tiniest miracle began to happen.

The stage had been set for this miracle a month or so earlier. There was a new girl at school, Laura, petite and blonde, who wore sensible clothes like T-shirts and khakis, and had a quiet, sad, older look about her. Jonathan learned that Laura had lost her dad, and felt an instant bond, since he had recently lost his mother.

At first, the children didn't talk much, but in moments when the memory of the lost parent came and overwhelmed one of them, the other was there, with a quiet look and a soft, brief touch that said, "I understand your pain, your pain is real, I am here to hold it with you"...until the moment passed. They had shyly exchanged phone numbers, and sometimes called to talk.

Laura's mother, Jan, was new in town, working on non-lethal deterrence of wolves in Washington's sheep country. The people of the town were mostly polite, but they were also sheep farmers. They knew how to keep their flocks safe: shoot the wolves. This newfangled concept of deterrence was untried, untested, took a lot of time, and the sheep farmers responded to the opportunity with "thank you very much, we'll manage our own affairs." What did this petite blonde woman know of farming life? It was just easier to shoot wolves.

Still, it was Laura whom Jonathan called when he finally got back to the farmhouse. Within a half hour, Laura and Jan were standing in the farmhouse in the gray light of dawn, with Jonathan and his dad, Mark.

It was very awkward.

Laura's face was drawn with genuine sympathy, and she moved to touch Jonathan's hand as she had done so often before. Jan, also, had the same expression, and the same touch. "These are friends," Jonathan thought.

Mark, on the other hand, was not so sure. His expression showed the craggy lines of worry and loss, more worry, more loss, and distrust. He would not have called a wolf sympathizer to his farm at this time, but his son seemed to find solace in these people, so he kept his mouth shut, lips pursed.

"May I help?" Laura's mother asked quietly.

"What do you have in mind?" his dad answered, a bit roughly.

"First I would remove the carcasses and secure the rest of the flock," she answered in a take-charge voice. "Then I can do an analysis of your farm, and we can install the best non-lethal deterrents for your situation."

She looked at Jonathan's dad with calm assurance: "I know you want to kill them, but likely you won't get the actual perpetrators, and more will come."

"This way will be better."

Mark sighed. Another time he would have blown up and sent Laura and Jan packing, but the miracle was growing in strength: because Mark was worn down from the loss of his wife, the worry over his son, and now the threat to his livelihood, he just sighed. At least the first two suggestions sounded good.

"No promises," he answered.

"Tend to the live ones first," Jan suggested. "Can we move them closer to the house for now?"

Mark nodded, whistling for Scout and May, the border collies, to go out and gather the flock. The four worked in silence, opening gates, body blocking stragglers. Clearly, Jan and Laura had been around sheep.

By the time that task was done, the truck had come for the carcasses. "This woman has resources!" Mark thought, with arched eyebrows. Though Jan was petite and blonde, she could fling an 80-pound ewe without much trouble. Jan noticed Jonathan wince when they got to Snow. "This one is special," she told the driver, and then to Jonathan, she said, "We can do more later, cremate and give you ashes back, or bury her." Jonathan had a vision of his mother and his face crumpled, but there was Laura and her soft touch.

"These people are friends," he thought again.

"Why did they kill ALL of them, and not even eat them?" he asked bitterly.

"Surplus killing is about opportunity, not bloodthirstiness," Jan explained. "Left to their own devices, and without interference, they would have come back and fed on these animals until they were gone." When people come upon many animals killed like this, they have, just in happening upon the kill, interfered with the wolves' return. Experienced wolves have learned not to return to a kill found by humans.

After this full morning's work, the mood had shifted. Now these were fellow farmers helping out, and it was time for breakfast.

"I'll need to walk the perimeter of the farm," Jan announced.

"How about we ride?" Mark countered, smiling for the first time. This woman and her daughter had put in half a day's hard work already, and showed no sign of stopping. They had earned his respect.

Jonathan took his cue and slipped off to catch and saddle up four horses. Laura came with him.

"Mom thinks this may have been the Huckleberry pack," she said quietly as they prepared the first horse. "The alpha female was shot in August. Mom says that's as hard on the wolf family as it was for us to lose Dad."

"Wolves aren't people," Jonathan said, more harshly than he had before, shutting Laura down.

But as the four mounted up and rode the farm's perimeter, a third small piece of miracle was forming in Jonathan's mind: Could it be that wolves mourned their mother? He felt an ache so strong he could hardly breathe. Could wolves feel that? He didn't know.

Laura dismounted at an area of many tracks. "They came in here, possibly just traveling to the creek," she pointed. "Perhaps, they came upon your sheep, and it was an opportunity they couldn't resist. "

"The wolves will need safe passage to the creek," Jan added. "Can we fence off this corner for them?"

"Fence off a corner of perfectly good grazing land FOR the wolves?" Mark asked incredulously.

"If their needs are met, and you make it aversive to hunt sheep, you will have the best protection ever. They will establish a territory here and keep out other wolves. Predators that know the rules are wonderful deterrence to other predators."

"We can help," she added.

"And you need dogs. Great Pyrenees for the close guarding of the flock, Anatolian Shepherds as perimeter guardians. Those can be here next week. We will pay for them. Until then, we will provide range riders."

Mark's dad pursed his lips again, but nodded, for the first time.

Over the next few months, he found himself nodding more than he thought he would.

Many changes happened on the farm that fall and winter. Most importantly, there were no further livestock losses. Due to the diligence of the family and Jan, there were no wolf losses either. There were frequent wolf tracks along the new perimeter fence, and Laura and Jonathan even saw the Huckleberry youngsters a time or two; the young wolves, like the young humans, managing to thrive despite the difficult loss of a parent. Jonathan found himself thinking about wolf families more and more.

Sometimes neighbors had predation events, and Mark was able to interject with "We had a problem last fall, but we did some things that helped a lot. I can give you a number….."

In the spring, Jan and Laura came with a special gift of eight lambs! One looked particularly like Snow.

"I know the individuals aren't replaceable" she said, "but I think these guys will do okay here now."

Jonathan was thrilled. Who doesn't love baby lambs! And he was happy for the new friends in his life, the change in his father's look as the farm began to thrive again, even for the glimpses of young and healthy wolves.

"Will you call her Snow?" Laura asked quietly.

"No," Jonathan answered. "I think I'll call her Miracle.

ARIZONA SUN, THE ENCHANTER, & WAR PAINT
MARTA ANNA PODOLSKA

Marta Anna Podolska (born in Gdańsk, Poland) is a self-taught artist currently working as a graphic designer and 2D and 3D animator in Germany. She has been drawing since the very moment she could grab the first pencil. Wolves are her favorite animals with which she became especially interested after visiting the West Coast of the USA where the Native American spirit (with great respect d of wolves' role in it) is present to this day. She loves traveling and getting to know foreign cultures and languages. Great animal friend, very fond of dogs. Her preferred media are pencil, charcoal and watercolors.

Arizona Sun. Pencil, color pencils, and watercolor.

The Enchanter. Charcoal and watercolors.

War Paint. Digital painting.

THE BEAST OF MINNESOTA
HEMAL RANA

Hemal Rana is an avid reader and an aspiring writer from North Jersey. Some of his favorite books includes Watership Down, It, the Magic Tree House series, *and* A Song of Ice and Fire. *"The Beast of Minnesota" is his very first published work, and he hopes to get more of his writings published in the near future. Hemal is currently a freshman at Rutgers University.*

The beast looked over its fallen prey in satisfaction. The prey was much larger than the beast. It was stronger. It was muscular. It had antlers. But nonetheless, the beast took its prey down in record time. It was faster. It was determined. It had sharp teeth.

The beast circled its fallen prey. The prey bled heavily from its various wounds, and its breathing slowed. The prey wondered how it allowed this to happen. It thought about how the beast came out of nowhere. How it wouldn't give up. Now, the prey just wished for the pain to go away.

The beast then stopped. It moved toward its fallen prey and looked into its eye. The dying prey looked back. There was a message in this stare. It was a message of understanding. In their silent conversation, the beast told its prey that it didn't die for nothing. That its meat would be used to feed the beast's pack. The pack will thrive thanks to the prey's sacrifice. The prey understood this and then closed its eyes for the last time.

Once the prey's breathing stopped, the beast began to feed. But it stopped when it heard something. Something was there. The beast didn't know if this something was friendly. The beast thought about making a run for it. But then, the beast heard a loud sound and then yelped in pain.

"Woo-hoo! Mike check this out! I got it in one shot!"

A man named Mike ran up to where his friend was standing and then saw what his friend got in one shot. He frowned and shook his head. He said to his friend, "Man, what'd you go kill Balto for?"

"Because the little beast killed Bambi's mom."

"I'm pretty sure that she didn't have antlers."

"Whatever. I was just doing the forest a favor and ridding it of a carnivorous monster."

"A ranger told me that those carnivorous monsters are a dying species."

"Makes sense. My grandpa told me about a hunter he knew whose specialty was killing wolves. This guy used traps, guns, poison, and a whole bunch of other nasty stuff. The hunter told my grandpa that killing wolves has sort of been an American tradition. Their population has been declining since colonial times. I'm surprised myself that there're still some of them left."

The two friends then walked up to the site of the killings. The corpses of the wolf and the deer were already starting to rot. The snow around them was red. Mike then asked his friend, "Would your grandpa be proud of this?"

"I guess so."

"I don't know about you Jim, but I don't feel like driving an entire species into extinction."

"Don't be so dramatic, it's just one hound. Anyway, let's head back before the game starts. I'm not going to miss the Vikings winning the Super Bowl."

"Me neither. Tomorrow we're eating dolphins for breakfast!"

The two went back the way they came, laughing and making jokes at Miami's expense. The corpses of the animals were left where they were.

Sometime after the men left, another beast arrived. This beast was not looking for prey to hunt. It was looking for its friends. Finally, the beast picked up its friend's scent and followed it. The beast would have been happy to see its friend, especially after a long, unsuccessful hunt. But when the beast found its friend, there was no happiness.

The beast circles its friend and the fallen prey for a while. Then it went up to its friend to check. No movement. No heartbeat. No life. The beast was horrified. It asked itself how it allowed this to happen.

The beast then lied down next to its dead friend. The beast put its muzzle into the deceased's fur. The beast whimpered in sorrow. The beast said goodbye.

BLUE MOON & LOST GIRL
SHANNON BARNSLEY

Shannon Barnsley is a writer, poet, and folklore devotee from New Hampshire, currently living in Brooklyn. She holds a degree in Creative Writing/Mythology & Religion from Hampshire College. Since graduating, she has been found giving tours at an 18th century Shaker village museum, translating British English into American English for an independent publishing company, and wandering the woods of New England with her ferocious yorkie mix. Her first book, Beneath Blair Mountain, *was published by 1888 in fall 2015. This is her second time contributing to a* Wolfwatcher *anthology, and she is happy to do her part to help the wolves that inspire her.*

Blue Moon

Every new parent complains. They aren't sleeping or never get to go out on dates anymore or can't get a moment of peace to take a bath or read something past a kindergarten reading level. Certainly, my exhaustion and frustration are nothing new. Still, as I stand here amidst the clawmark and spackle decor of my kitchen, sponging steak juice off my t-shirt, I can't help but think I have it a little harder than the other moms and dads at the playground.

For one thing, I doubt any of them have to leash their newborn. Their pixie stick addict four-year-old, maybe, but I've yet to see one of the moms at the mall with her six-month-old on a lead. I also doubt that any of the other moms keep flea and tick medication in their diaper bag or have to hide their own medicine in a silver box.

I often think of how much easier my life would be if I had never met Fritz. But how was I to know any of what would happen? I was just a crusading college drop-out looking for a crusade. He was an animal rights activist with a spare couch for me to crash on before a protest. We were young, we were naive, his roommate had already passed out drunk on the couch I was supposed to be sleeping on, and the rest was history. Somewhere between dodging tear gas and baking gluten-free, vegan brownies, we fell in love.

Three full glasses of wine and one full moon later, my fate was sealed.

I went home early from work one afternoon, complaining of nausea. Next thing I knew I was waking up handcuffed to the radiator. I could tell by the fluffy blue trim that they were my roommate's handcuffs. Apparently, I had tried to bite her. Sure, I'd been known to give a roommate or two a love nibble, but literally going for the jugular wasn't the kind of thing I went in for.

Fritz never told me he was a werewolf (who would?), but his roommate had mentioned it once or twice before passing out on the couch. I hadn't given his drunken ramblings any credence then, but when I was fired from my volunteer position at the animal shelter because I nearly ate one of the angora rabbits, I knew something was up. Perhaps Fritz and I had gotten a little too intersectional with our animal and human rights activism.

The next week went by in a flurry of steak-tips, vomit, and Craigslist ads for new roommates. Finally, I gave in and consulted the almighty oracle of fertility, found in her shrine at Rite-Aid, where many a desperate pilgrim would pray for good news. Unfortunately, the EPT gods did not look kindly on me that day. Instead, only the little plus sign stared coldly back at me.

Had this been before the rabbit incident, I probably would have gone straight to the nearest abortion clinic. However, when they found out I was in my first trimester of an unplanned lycanthropic pregnancy, I knew I would either wake up to a thorazine drip and some padded walls or in the pentagon as a classified science project.

Fritz was several states away and, not knowing his last name, I couldn't track him down on Facebook. It seemed the wolf was in the cradle and the silver spoon, and my little boy blue would be howling at the moon alone.

I spent much of the next month holed up in my room with spare ribs and chocolate sauce before realizing my new love of red meat had burned through my savings. I could no longer avoid reality, even if reality had strayed into speculative fiction. So, this wasn't exactly what I'd had in mind when I took some time off from college to find myself. But, hey, I had always fancied myself a champion of the misunderstood and the historically marginalized, and the mythological were about as underrepresented as it got.

I wasn't sure as to the endangered species status of the American werewolf, but, not knowing its natural habitat, the least I could do was give my lupine spawn a stable home life. So I got a job as a secretary at a human rights organization and started taking night classes in veterinary science. Then I called my mother, put my shower registry on the Pottery Barn website, and had several layers of reinforced steel added to the soundproof walls of the nursery.

I always hoped Fritz would somehow stumble across my registry and the caribou-flavored baby food or shepherd boy mobile would tip him off. It's not that I was hankering to play house with Lon Chaney Jr. or anything, but, like any parent, I wanted the best for my little wolf cub. Someone who could tell me the proper diet for a ten-week-old gray wolf or how much tranquilizer I could safely administer once he hit his terrible werewolf twos would have been a godsend. Then again, the Audubon Society opening up a daycare might have been just as good.

Sometimes I remember that innocent night (and less innocent morning) with Fritz and wonder where I would be right now if I had joined the Peace Corp instead, or simply found someone at the protest with an unoccupied couch. Still, raising a werewolf as a single parent has to be more interesting than whatever I might have done.

Not to mention little Julian Peter is certainly giving Mommy an edge on the other veterinary science students. My mysteriously acquired first-hand experience recently landed me a paid internship at a wildlife sanctuary in Canada. Canada has good schools, right? And free range elk. I've been meaning for Julian and I to go full paleo.

Even as I surrender my last clean t-shirt to the meat-soaked martyrdom of motherhood, I can't complain too much about how things turned out. I may be exhausted, overwhelmed, and tired of having to steal kennel cough and rabies vaccines from the local vet, but there are moments where I know I'm lucky. After all, when all the other moms and dads are being awoken in the night by a crib inmate's tantrum, I'm crawling eagerly into bed, knowing that my "The Sounds of Yellowstone" CD has once more successfully lulled Julian to sleep.

Besides, once in a blue moon, when I'm looking at the tiny paw print in Julian's baby book or watching his feet twitch while he's dreaming, I'm pretty happy with life's unexpected twists. But, so help me, if I ever get my paws on Fritz, I'm neutering him.

Lost Girl

<u>1</u>

They always talk about the girls who get lost
The ones who lose their way
wandering off, straying too far
from the paths their mothers
laid out for them—
one that leads to the only fate they had ever imagined
from girl to mother to grandmother
Bread and jam and the path
and the promise of a cottage and comfort
all she had to her name—

The girls who stumble, who fall,
who go wrong, who get lost
who get stolen and spirited away
The girls led astray by men who ran with wolves
and some who were only predators
Outlaws and thieves, poets and rebels
Men of the forest
and huntsmen in fair trade pelts trying to be.
Some with nooses closing around their necks
Some with only hemp

Girls left out of the family Christmas card,
whose transgressions are glossed over at get-togethers
and discussed at length by others on the car ride home
A warning to other girls
stay on the path
with its ivy-covered cottages and ivy league prayers.
Girls on milk cartons and the eleven o'clock news
and the cork boards in the grocery stores and post offices.
The ones pricked by push-pins
and behind glass.

They don't mention the girls
whose mothers gave them freedom and courage

and all the secrets of the forest
instead of a path that only led one way
even if they insisted it wasn't set in stone—
Dirt or cobble, it only bends toward what they know
and where they've already been.
Girls with moonlight in their hair
and cool water on their lips
that shout and sing and speak bluntly.

They don't mention the wolf girls
The ones who ate venison with berry-stained fingers
instead of bread and jam with silverware.
The women of the woods
who ran wild in forests and streams
without thought for cottages or paths
or grandmothers who judged you by the path they walked
once upon a time
still expecting you to
though the woods had changed
and now it was overgrown.
Anyone would get lost trying to follow it.

But it's the scarlet cape, I'm sure.
Your Rose Red wardrobe and your fairy tale degree.
You'll never get a cottage and a huntsman like that.

2

They don't mention the girls who stumble,
who fall for the promises when the woods get cold,
who go wrong,
who find themselves lost in the woods they knew
A new cottage complex cutting through their forest
(though they never finished it
after the housing bubble popped).
When lost and exposed we seek a hollow to protect us
So you made yourself hollow too.

The ones who once felt
the sting of burrs and brambles
but now are numb to the pinpricks of blood
The silent cry of a caged wolf
written on your arm
The ones whose eyes are dull,
their expressions tame
as they smile behind glass,
picture frames matching your decor.
A wolf necklace from that craft fair up north
the only sign of the wild woman you were.
The one your mother bought you
back when she loved you
for the person you were going to be
instead of worrying about the one you wouldn't.

Back before you started feeling small,
feeling weak
Weighing every failure,
every step farther you should be
down the path you forgot you weren't ever meant to walk.
Until they convinced you
your degree was the stuff of fairy tales
better to let your passions burn low
and bury them both in a mirrored box.

Fairy tales don't pay the bills
and Jack and Jill went broke
trying to tumble after dreams.
Wolfsong doesn't put bread and jam on the table.
But you never wanted jam and bread anyway.
You grow weak and anemic
without the meat that sustained you
that made you strong and spirited and alive.
That made you a wolf.

You look in the mirror and see
neither the fairest in the land
nor the fiercest in the forest.

Once a wolf, now just a lost girl.
What big dreams you had.
All the better to fail me with, my dear,
your grandmother echoes.
But the woods are silent.

3

The huntsman said he loved you and maybe he did.
Maybe the silver bracelet and the silver-tongued words
that weren't the only thing on his lips
still meant something today.
But then so did the girl he kept wanting to rescue
from her manic pixie self
a basketcase of gluten-free bread and organic jam
tamer than you were but somehow wilder now.
The one in the red cosplay cape
with the silver piercings.
The memory of her an axe to your heart.
Though it's her doe eyes he thinks of,
not the heart he ripped out,
even if he once called you his queen.

He thinks about saving her
while you scramble to save silver dollars
But it's never enough to save you from the debt
or be a salve for your stolen dreams
the stories ripped raw from you
as your pelt was torn away
to cover someone else's dreams,
the binding for someone else's fairy tales,
as you struggle to bind your wounds,
salt tears burning,
the only thing the stories promised that's still true.

You cry over chipped cups and "magic" pasta pots
and recycle the milk cartons someone else left out
herding silverware into the dishwasher like a good girl

the huntsman snoring in the other room.
You're dog tired and your hands shake
putting away the apples
from the grocery store.
You feel shut off, dead inside,
asleep
behind a wall of glass.

A lifeless pelt beside the huntsman
who once loved your fierceness, your wild side.
You were a wolf once
You roamed where you pleased
with no destination in mind
but now never wander past
the grocery store or the post office.
A medical bill and a student loan statement
cover your degree
a silver medic alert bracelet
replacing your lover's tokens.
You should have known
Silver was always going to be the death of you.

It's your eleventh hour, but the news doesn't care
And no one will put up pictures and amber alerts
for the girl lost somewhere inside you.
You cry for her, but she can't hear you
and neither can the wolves
Your lips speak only words that are all too human
and frailer lies,
the truth lost in the woods you can't find your way back to.

CANIS RUFUS, HOWL OF THE SOUTHEAST, & PERSISTENCE OF A SPECIES
JEREMY HOOPER

Jeremy Hooper is a graduate student at the University of Tennessee, Chattanooga, where he's studying the relationship between humans and coyotes in the city of Atlanta, Georgia. He has been involved with the Red Wolf Species Survival Program since 2008 through his work at the Reflection Riding Arboretum and Nature Center in Chattanooga. Jeremy's goals are to improve relations between humans and predators through research, education and partnerships.

Canis rufus. Photography.

Howl of the Southeast. Photography.

Persistence of a Species. Photography.

CANIS RUFUS GOES TO TOWN & RIDDLES
LUDLOW

Ludlow (the nom de plume of Ned Mudd), resides in the jungles of Alabama where he engages in interspecies communication, rock collecting, and frequent cloud watching. He is a regular contributor to the Canyon Country Zephyr, *an ex officio member of the notorious Kevorkian Skull Poets, and the translator of Zen poet JiBo, author of* When Thirsty, Drink Green Tea. *Some of Ludlow's best friends are raccoons.*

Canis rufus goes to town

the wolf was a ghost in a fur coat
a silhouette against the planets.
he slipped the time barrier
and walked upright
into downtown Atlanta.

on the third day sirens called
the faithful, lost souls, and madmen,
of which there were many.

human hair shackled the wind
lost inside a nocturnal incipience;
groupings - feral nature exposed
beneath sartorial plumage.

witnessing gravity's lunge
the wolf summoned atavistic totems
whistled an incantation
and opened the gates
of the asylum.

all that remained to do
was laugh -
his lungs expanding
filling the galaxy
with light.

Riddles

in the crack between worlds
wolves gather to chew the fat
old times not be forgot.

winter nights they howl
outside the parson's house
to remind him of his tenuous faith.

come summer they chase the moon
in its transitory glide, their footprints
leaving riddles in the loam.

CAPTIVITY & WHITE WOLF
STACI LYNN BELL

Staci Lynn Bell, a Chicago native, has lived in Western North Carolina for the past 5 years. Having moved many times as a child, her best friends were her imagination, books, and animals. Staci attended University of Wisconsin, Madison, majoring in Communications. She relocated to SW Florida, gaining popularity as a 25-year radio and television personality and animal advocate. In 1988 her environmental essay won statewide acclaim in Florida. After retiring from broadcasting, Bell worked for many years training dogs and rehabilitating rescues. Now retired, Ms. Bell is a member of the North Carolina Writer's Network and Ridgeline Literary Alliance. She has been published in Wild Goose Poetry Review, 234 Journal, *and numerous print and on-line journals. Staci shares her life with her German Shepherd and Black-Mouth Cur.*

Captivity

She once paced her steel den,
10 feet across, 10 feet back
measured steps her sole stimulation.

Her canines cracked long ago,
molars, gnawed down nubs,
witnesses of failed escapes,
her fangs no match for metal
or human hands that weave
wire together.

10 feet across, 10 feet back, 10 years now.
She no longer dreams about white tail deer,
conversing with the moon,
meadows of endless freedom.

She doesn't howl her mating call
weary of no answer.

Her dark sable coat is dull,
mirrors hollow yellow eyes,
a trace of the wolf she was born to be.

White Wolf

The chunk of ice breaks away, having held together just long enough for the arctic wolf to cross. Now ahead and all around him, gaps between the floating icebergs widen, forming smaller strands of frozen islands to choose from. The white wolf tries to keep his balance as he tentatively surveys his surroundings, his ice raft having drifted farther from the next tiny chain of frozen tundra. His piercing blue, color-of-sky eyes, squint in the brightness, almost blinded by the rays of the sun reflecting off the pristine sea water.

On all fours, the alpha male's nails scrape the ice, as his pitch black nose twitches seeking to sniff out where to go next. Adrift on the water, panic sets in, as he realizes the next jump may be his last. He has spent hours of precious time, searching for much larger land masses, in his quest to find food to feed himself, his life mate and their newly born pups. Now exhausted, he cautiously attempts to jump over the ever widening gap, trying to reach the seemingly elusive main berg, where he picked up the scent of meat…caribou, enough to meet the needs of his family for several weeks.

The white wolf's large paws struggle for even the slightest grip, tearing up bits of snow as he tries to get a firmer hold on his ice raft. Though anxious, he knows he must persevere. Three long sunsets have come and gone since he set out on his journey, with no food source to be found. Time is of the essence, the pups desperately need to eat…or they will die.

The arctic wolf senses that the time to leap is fast approaching or he will lose his chance, leaving him adrift at sea and his family to starve. Mustering all his ancestral courage, for he is a brave hunter and good provider, he takes one last long breath, commanding his powerful hind legs to launch him onto the last, almost miniscule piece of ice, hoping it will take him to his destination.

As the great wolf leans back on his haunches, he leaps over the blue abyss and time stands still. He appears to hang in mid-air, solitary, save for his black shadow which lies directly beneath him in the crystal water. His front paws just barely touch the next ice patch. At that moment, he digs knife-sharp nails into the frozen chunk. They hold slightly, for a few seconds. Then, try as he might, his body begins to slide slowly into the choppy waters of the Bering Sea. His outer coat begins to freeze, so cold it takes his breath away. His well-travelled hunting ground remains just out of reach.

Panting heavily, he tries to pull himself one last time, out of the water to climb aboard this ice vessel. The alpha male finally gets a small foothold, pulling himself to safety. But large waves propel the arctic raft further out to sea. He instinctively knows the next jump is impossible.

Resigned he lays his magnificent white freezing head on the patch of security he fought for, for so long, his heart heavy with thoughts of his mate and family, hiding back in their snow-covered den, far underground, awaiting his return, an arrival only he knows will never come.

His clear bright eyes, eyes that know a thousand tales, slowly close. He knows his own death is imminent. He can only wonder why this path, a path his ancestors took for millions of years…is no longer.

As the arctic white wolf drifts slowly away from land and out to sea, he turns his muzzle toward the sky and lets out a sorrowful howl, hoping his life mate will hear and move the pups to a more fertile, safe place. His body and mind are weakening, but he finally hears, way off in the distance a lone cry, that of his mate, saying more in her one call than a string of sentences.

CELEBRATION
AUTUMN BEVERLY

Autumn is a passionate artist whose preferred subjects are animals; wild domestic and even fantasy—particularly canids, her favorites being wolves.

She works mainly with colored pencil, and is now also making jewelry with nature themes.

She is just as interested in biology/ecology/ethology/mythology as she is with art; when she's not creating, she's got her nose in a book in educational articles or watching documentaries, learning about her favorite subjects. They go hand-in-hand at times as she aims to educate people with glimpses of these animals through her artwork. She hopes to inspire a love and understanding of nature, promoting coexistence.

Celebration. Colored pencil.

DISSIPATION & ST. FRANCIS AND THE WOLF

CHELSEA DUB

Chelsea Dub is an artist from Indiana and is currently pursuing a BFA in Painting and Animation at Ball State University. She enjoys working with various media, including sculpture, painting, drawing, printmaking, digital photography, and computer graphics. Being autistic and having learned to draw before she could speak, art was—and continues to be—both a mode of escapism and expression for her. Along with being a neurodiversity advocate, she is a feminist vegan, and her art often explores the interconnections between issues such as ableism, sexism, and speciesism. Through visual media, she hopes to effectively communicate these ideas and challenge society's marginalization of communities, including other animal species. Her art has been published in Wolf Warriors: The National Wolfwatcher Coalition Anthology, *featured in the Autism Unveiled Project and Art of Compassion Project, and exhibited in art fairs and galleries, including the Canon Tunnel in Washington, D.C. When not in Muncie, she lives in Noblesville with her family, including her two rescued cats.*

Dissipation. Woodcut print.

St. Francis and the Wolf   ¹/₁₀

St. Francis and the Wolf. Intaglio print.

DOG DAYS & ECHO
DANA SONNENSCHEIN

Dana Sonnenschein is a full professor at Southern Connecticut State University, where she teaches literature and creative writing. Her publications include Bear Country *(2009),* Natural Forms *(2006),* No Angels But These *(2005), and* Corvus *(2003). Her poems have appeared in numerous journals, including* Feminist Studies, Silk Road, Epoch, *and* The Northwest Review. *She howls regularly with the wolves at the Wolf Conservation Center in South Salem, NY.*

Dog Days

Softness of undercoat, guard hairs—
I stroke until I see the wolf's eyeholes,
and I wonder how many drawers of pelts

the museum has, what the bounty was,
how it feels to love or hate something
enough to want its skin, head to paws.

There's a stack at the banquet table's end,
black, silvered, tawny, sienna red.
I can't touch more, but the child at my side

plants her palms on fur and demands,
How could they kill them?
As a docent silently shakes his head,

her mother pulls the questioner past
dangling tails toward the coyote in a case
wheeled up for display in August.

Inside, a smoky yellow creature, slight
as the tricksters still circling out west,
beyond firing range and ember-light.

Then there's the eastern coyote
prowling the entry to the Hall of Mammals,
a one-that-didn't-get-away story

with a twist. New England farmers
hunted wolves down to the last snarl—
but not before canine rivals crossed

more than paths—so a hybrid of howl
and yip inherits the dark, and that blur I saw
last summer, trotting across the road, tail low,

turns and is coy-wolf, ears open wide,
eyes luminous yellow-green in a face
like something come back from the dead.

Echo

Here I am, where are you?
    Echo knew the sound of her howling
howling back to where she stood
    on the canyon's rim, how gold earth
underfoot purples with distance,
    how to run from winter to summer
by following the mountains south,
    the feel of snow, dirt, sand
between her toes, wind in her fur,
    the way thin ice rings when touched,
chiming a warning—a world
    sensible and sensed, beyond us—

Born in the dark and again, padding
    from the den's shadows into sun,
she licked and ate from her father's mouth,

stalked her mother's tail,
bared milk teeth and braved the world,
    showed belly to be spared,
and even then held her tail and head
    higher than the other pups,
feeling fell and alpha, playing look-out.
    Come winter she learned to scout elk
and moose, chase down the frail and faltering,
    leap for haunch or throat.

Like her mother's mother, Echo knew
    what the ravens' calling meant,
the scent of sickness in hoof-tracks,
    strength welling in a wolf's mark.
She knew the limits of her pack's land
    and who ran the nearby peaks,
how to follow the hieroglyphic scrabbling
    of voles beneath drifts,
the tingle and heaviness of coming snow
    and estrus thawing the senses,
shifting like spring before snowmelt,
    and she knew then to go off alone,

trotting all night, head low, like an arrow
    pointed toward the possible—
another wandering wolf, a silent slope,
    a valley where deer browsed saplings
down to roots. Solo, she knew to hunt
    mouse and marmot and snarl
to keep coyotes from her kill, to fade back
    into the trees at metallic click,
boot-fall, or breaking branch—to be
    just another gray streak
until she howled her kind's call and response,
    Here I am, where are you?

So for millennia the one
    and many have raised their heads

in ethereal counterpoint, near and far,
    celebrating the pack, dawn and dusk,
half-barking in alarm, wailing and keening
    when the death toll rises, chests
hollow, ears lifted for the missing howl,
    no two exactly the same. So
only Echo knew how to sound the O's
    of her resounding presence,
the notes we won't hear now, lost
    in the middle of a dark wood.

For Echo felt the noise of bullet knocking
    through flesh and bone,
the silence of heart stopping before
    muzzle-blast and sonic boom
brushed past the guard hairs
    at the base of her ears,
a crack that echoes, invisible yet
    wider than a crevasse
cutting through eons past and to come,
    filling my skull when I want
to howl and hear Echo howl back
    Here I am, where are you?

FLINT THE MEXICAN GRAY WOLF
KATT REINGRUBER

Katt Reingruber is an amateur photographer, currently residing in Albuquerque, New Mexico. Being a widow and retired, her time is now spent volunteering as a Zoo Docent at the Albuquerque BioPark Zoo. Working as a volunteer, there are great opportunities to advocate for one or many currently endangered animals. Katt enjoys advocating for several different animals, including the Giraffe, Asian Elephant, Nile Hippos, Polar Bears, and the Big Cats of all the continents, but the one that causes the most controversy, is the Mexican Gray Wolf. The BioPark over time has been a breeding facility, with about 50/plus pups, whelped here for possible release. Over the last several years five (5) brothers have been raised for their genetic diversity, than around the end of 2014 one wolf, "Flint" was sent to the Chicago Zoo, Brookfield, where he became the proud father of four (4) Mexican Gray Wolves. Volunteering has made Katt an advocate for the Mexican Gray Wolves, an animal that use to call New Mexico home before being eradicated by hunters and ranchers.

Flint the Mexican Gray Wolf. Photography.

FULL MOON & LONE WOLF, PACK WOLF
A.M. DUVALL

A.M. Duvall is the author of her own two novels, one was written with her mom. Her very first novel is called The Goddess' Words. *The second one is called,* For the Love of Ontario. *Both books have poetry and the first one also has short stories in it. The love of poetry was given to her by her Mom.*

A.M. Duvall has also been lucky enough to be in two other novels that were anthologies with other amazing authors. She is happy that the money from each novel goes toward an Animal Sanctuary in England and The National Wolfwatcher Coalition in the US. They are called Lupus Animus *and* Wolf Warriors, *respectfully, as well as this lovely novel.*

She lives with her two cats that drive her batty in a little town called Wiarton, in the province of Ontario, in Canada. Has loved writing since the age of twelve and is now just realizing her dream.

Full Moon

Where is the sound I always hear when the moon is full?
Why can't I hear it? Did they get hurt or worse?

No I refuse to believe that thought! They are too smart to get hurt by
the hunters around here. The hunters here are not like them.

Still where is their sound that soothes my soul? I need it more than
ever today! So much is going wrong in my life that my soul aches. My
nerves are shot.

I need their howls to calm me! Where are they? Should I go out to
look? If I do, won't they get scared of me? Who cares, I need them too
much right now.

Before I know what is happening I am outside of my house, heading to my own slip of forest. I stop suddenly to tilt my head and listen. There it is. The sound of a wolf's howl. More follow, and I stand perfectly still to have it wash over me.

My soul stops crying in pain. My nerves stop dancing in my body. I sigh. Then ever so slowly my mouth opens, and I let out my own howl.

They stop at the sound of my howl. Then start up again, accepting not judging. I stand there surrounded by howls and the full moon. Finally at peace, finally at home.

I howl again. They answer me. Their howls saying we are safe and at home. I smile and put my head back. Then I let out my biggest howl yet. Letting them know I am coming.

I shift into my wolf form. My clothes falling all around me. I made my choice today. Time to answer the full moon and play.

Lone Wolf, Pack Wolf

Suddenly there is the sound of howls.
Followed by a growl.
Then nothing is heard but silence.
The sound of other animals' defiance.
Hiding out in fear of being hunted.
They don't want to be the next animal blooded.
The silence helps the wolf search in the forest.
He is not looking for supper, only his pack which to him is cherished.
He is a lone wolf but one that has a pack.
They may not always be together, but they have a pact.
One of comfort for all involved.
He leaves from time to time when he becomes enthralled.
He always comes back when they call.

GOOD BYE
MICHIKO ENEI

Michiko Enei is a 25-year-old writer. She has Mexican and Japanese inheritance that greatly infuses her writings with folkloric scenarios and enriches them. Currently residing in Mexico City, she was born and raised in a small city in Guanajuato, Mexico, between dogs and books. She has an outstanding love for animals, especially canines. Her journalistic formation gives her writing perspective. Avid reader, activist for animal rights, interpreter for profession, passionate writer for conviction, Michiko has published a few short stories in Spanish with Editorial Endora *and* Grupo BENMA, *winner of the contest "Why do you love Mexico?" by* Gandhi Editorial *and finalist of contests "Venus de Noche" in Spain and "Young New Promises" by* BENMA *in Mexico.*

When Anna died, I instantly knew it. I didn't need to answer the phone or wait for the police to show at my doorstep.

I knew Anna had died because I felt it deep down in that place within me that only she occupied and it was not like a lightning of pain that had struck me; it was more like a sudden emptiness, like a big chunk of my soul had left my body because it actually had.

We had a beautiful service, exactly like her parents wanted. I stood there by her coffin with her quartz wolf necklace in my hand, the same one my grandparents had given her when we visited them at the Navajo preservation where they lived, saying the wolf was her animal. When I told Grandma we were getting married, she hugged me and said Anna was the one for me.

And indeed Anna was the one for me, the missing piece that completed the puzzles in my head and now she was gone forever. Two months I stared at my ceiling unable to sleep or do anything else but to think of her in the small apartment we had shared.

I don't know why it took me so long to go see my grandparents; maybe it was because everything there reminded me of her and my happiest times. When I got there, my grandmother was already waiting for me with stew served.

That night after dinner and crying, I dozed on the couch.

It was two in the morning when I heard it: the painful, fear striking yet beautiful howl of a wolf. I opened my eyes and felt the wind rushing through my pop's cabin and then I saw the silhouette of a big wolf, I felt it get closer and was paralyzed with fear until it stopped and stared at me with the same beautiful hazel eyes and that defying look Anna always saved for me. I reached out my hand, not even thinking about what I was doing and touched the soft white fur of her head.

Without even realizing I was changing, I saw my hands become paws and in just a blink, I was also a wolf like her.

She darted out the door, and I realized I was running behind her, the cool night air on my face and freedom gushing through my veins in an unexpected way. I don't know how much we ran playing, letting her guide me, until she laid on the grass and I laid besides her seeing her through my new eyes. I saw her breathe; we couldn't speak but I know she was Anna, for that emptiness inside me had been filled again. I felt her tongue licking my ears and eventually I fell asleep, feeling an unexplainable amount of love with that simple gesture. I opened my eyes and saw the white wolf walking slowly away from me. I wanted to ask her to stay but I couldn't get up and at the distance what I saw wasn't a wolf but Anna in her wedding dress smiling back at me and finally she was gone Then again, I heard the painful fear striking yet beautiful howl of a wolf, my howl, and woke up on the couch once again.

When I opened my eyes, the front door was open and two sets of muddy wolf paws trailed outside of the cabin; it was morning now, a beautiful sunny morning. I felt Anna's wolf quartz under my shirt. The pain was gone, and although some emptiness remained, she was at peace and so was I.

THE GRAY CASCADE
ROBERT BRADFORD

Robert Bradford is an American author born in Chattanooga, Tennessee on June 28th 1989. His parents are John Bradford, a banker, and Jimmie Bradford, a child and family specialist and case manager. Bradford has shown an interesting in writing since grade school, and by the time he was sixteen had found a part-time job working for a small town newspaper. In college, at Chattanooga State, he became a junior reporter during his first semester and went on to win multiple awards for his writing. After his transfer to Middle Tennessee State University, Bradford was published four times in two different issues of the university's artistic journal: Collage: A Journal of Creative Expression. *In April of 2015, Bradford's first novel,* Above the Pines, *a Young Adult novel about teens attempting to survive sexual abuse, was published by Thurston Howl Publications. Bradford is currently working hard on his sophomore novel, and hopes it is received as well as his first.*

There is no soil.
There is no green.
There is no moral.
This land's obscene.

There is no hunter.
Only hunted.
There is no runner.
They're all stunted.

The park is drying
And deer aplenty
The earth is dying
And doing so simply.

The final hour of this wasted land

They arrive, the graying pack.
And unlike man
They're taking it back.

The howling cries
The deer scatter
The pack is sly
What's the matter?

They act as rangers
To the Yellow land
There are no strangers
Where these wolves stand.

The river rises
The flowers bloom
The earth surprises
Thanks to a graying loom

Beneath a boiling sun
The pack parades
What it has undone
Like a gray cascade.

THE GREATEST GIFT OF ALL & IN WINTER
ALANNA KHUBIEH

The Greatest Gift of All. Color pencils and pen on Bristol paper.

In Winter. Acrylic painting.

GROWING GRAY
HANNAH E. CHRISTOPHER

She started seeing the wolves when she was nine years old. It was right after her father walked out the front door. He wouldn't come back again.

"Mom, there are doggies," she said, straddling her mother's knees with both hands. "Big doggies," she decided after some thought, because she had never seen anything so big or furry before. Her mother sighed and didn't look up from the kitchen sink. Her weathered hands plunged into the oily dish water and vanished in the grime there.

"Those are wolves, baby," she answered indifferently. "They're here to take your daddy away. Remember this, Georgie. Your daddy loves that pack more than anything."

She did remember, all through her teen years and well into her adult ones, but that never stopped her from filling in the holes in her heart with them. That never stopped her, the night of her thirteenth birthday, from clambering out of her second story bedroom window to come meet them in the hedges separating her forest home from the frighteningly dark woods. She left her window wide open. She shimmied onto the spindly branch brushing up against her window and climbed down backward, feeling out safe pathways with the edge of her tiny foot. I watched her from below: a pale smudge in my vision with a mane of fire, the view of her still childish body wrapped up in pastel pink nightclothes and coming to the edge of her mom's garden, heavy with wanting for something she had never known.

I wanted to speak, but I didn't then. It wasn't the right time. I knew, watching her watching the shadows between the trees, that she was thinking of the father she'd lost. The shape of his boxy face in the tiny unused shaving mirror propped up against her mother's dresser. The coarse rubbing of his kisses because of the perpetual stubble. The husky tenor of his voice. So I made myself comfortable in the small space her father's absence had provided me, with midnight glimpses of the burgeoning daughter he'd left behind. She fell into the leaf litter and drew stick figures in the mud. Over the rolling knolls, hopefully somewhere far away, the pack began to howl. Georgie Marland cupped her hands around her pretty pink mouth, threw back her rusty head, and cried a painful chorus to the moon. Her mother burst from the front door then and dragged her back inside by the elbow. Later, Georgie cried softly in her bed. Her window was still open, a smattering of her birthday cake icing smearing the sill because she hadn't washed her hands after being sent prematurely to bed for smashing it.

At fifteen, Georgie was making more and more late excursions into the woods. She was getting recklessly good at them. Her mother hadn't caught her in many months, and that last time was only because I'd accidentally brushed the potted plant on the front stoop and caused it to crash and break against the brick. When Georgie found little gray hairs flecking the ruined chrysanthemums littered through her now gated and overgrown lawn it only served to propel her curiosity. She rode to the market ten miles north and bought a new pot of painfully pink chrysanthemums and a pound of bloody buffalo steak with her chores money. She gave the chrysanthemums to her mother. She dropped the steak out of her bedroom window. It landed with a wet plop at the base of the knobby green ash tree. By doing this, Georgie Marland acknowledged what I had done. She knew I had knocked over her mother's favorite flower. And, in return, she gave me the steak.

The pack was elusive, their summer bodies making ghosts of the woods. That never stopped Georgie from pursuing them. Fruitlessly, she would sneak from the second story every night after her mother's labored breathing had sidled into gentle snores, and she would run off through the thick woods enveloping her hidden house in the forest. She had never questioned why it was hidden, or why she could not attend public school, or why, at age sixteen, her mother started looking at her funny, as if she was one of the advertisements between her mother's soap operas advertising the kinds of pills only men should buy. She understood only her pull to the woods, to the pack. It drew her forth from her room every night like clockwork. Her one solace, her one escape.

As she grew ever more adventurous and her treks took her farther and farther from her house, I trailed her scent and made certain she got back without injury. Once, I killed a mountain lion. Blood licked at the tendrils of a fern that grew monstrously over the roots of a ponderosa pine. It was mine. The cougar floated peacefully in an ugly green lake not too far away. Georgie never saw this. She never saw me slowly repairing myself in the forest with pine needles and dental floss I'd stashed underneath a rock with an old satchel full of clothes and a pair of ruddy running shoes. I sometimes wonder if she noticed my absence in those times I was too injured to return each night to the spot below her window. I wonder if she missed me as much as I missed her. But I think she probably loved my absence more than my presence. When the pack caught wind of the reek of my blood spilling onto the shriveling autumn floor, they howled all the louder. That was how we celebrated Georgie Marland's seventeenth birthday: with our blood.

It was her nineteenth birthday. Her mother made her a little lemon cake with cream cheese frosting. Her boney fingers worked meticulously around the edges, creating trilling curls and artful shapes out of green and blue icing tubes. Begrudgingly, she also included a wolf on the top. Georgie had requested this in advance. It was a little gray wolf, standing silently in dollops of thick, sweet paste. His eyes were two pinpricks of yellow, carefully applied with a toothpick. Georgie sat at the kitchen table as her mother set out the cake, taking it in with awestricken brown eyes.

"Thank you," she said, the wonder in her gaze infiltrating her voice. "Thank you, mom. It's beautiful. You should open a bakery."

Her mother rubbed her bare elbows and glared down at the cake with venom in her thinly penciled features. When she spoke, something stiff and hated moved in on her throat and constricted her syllables. I'd never heard Georgie's mother crying. She always closed her windows. Her cheeks were splotchy red where they used to be divinely pale, just like her beautiful daughter's. "Maybe one day. When you're all moved out and grown up. Then I'll open a bakery. I'll sell cupcakes with wolves on them. Maybe they'll taste like buffalo steak."

Georgie laughed. "Nobody would eat them," she said.

Her mother gave up a wry, practiced smile. "A few people might. You never know. You want candles, or do you just want to eat?"

"Skip the candles," Georgie decided, her hands itching already for the serving knife her mother had put out next to the cake on its engraved silver platter. "I'm old enough now that it doesn't matter. I reckon I'll be growing gray hairs any day now. Shame. I love my hair, I might dye it red again after I go gray." She cut herself a sizeable serving of cake, laying it carefully sideways on one of the paper party plates her mother had borrowed her bike to purchase a month before. They were purple and had cost her a dollar, plus tax. Twenty plates to a cellophane wrapped package. From Georgie's chosen plate, the perfectly preserved eyes of the icing wolf stared up at her, unblinking. She broke the contact and looked at her mother instead. Brandishing the icing-crusted serving knife, she offered, "Do you want a slice, too? Or are you still on that sugar-free thing?"

Her mother sat next to her at the table and accepted a miniature purple plate from the stack of eighteen untouched others. "I would like a piece, yes," she answered quietly. "Just this once, I think I can break that *sugar-free thing*. You only turn nineteen once, Georgie. I feel like I've turned fifty ten times over."

"Oh, shut up, mom," Georgie insisted, sliding her mother's thick slice of white cake onto her plate. "You don't look a day past twenty. Now eat this cake and get fat with me."

When they were done, Missus Marland tupperwared the other half of the cake and went to work over the stove, preparing a dinner so fragrant I thought for sure I'd flood their garden with my salivating. "I'm making your favorite, Georgie," she called into the living room, where her daughter spread out on the ugly paisley couch and read a book with words that mystified me, as she was often prone to do. "Venison stew and mash for my growing girl on her nineteenth birthday."

"Thanks, mom!" Georgie shouted back, her thumb on the last line she'd read. She turned the page and dog-eared the top cover between her thumb and forefinger, working her prints into the ink. She smiled.

Clanking pots and pans in the small, cluttered kitchen. Silverware being set on the chapped oak table, napkins being torn from a roll and folded into uniform shapes. Soapy dish water over used pottery. Glasses sloshing full of water and small ice cubes with air bubbles infinitely suspended inside of them. The sights and sounds of a world I had never been a part of. I took a step forward and stopped when my foot mashed into the loamy ground surrounding the garden. This was Georgie's day. I wouldn't be the one to ruin it for her. Not yet.

"Georgie, soup's on!" her mother announced.

Georgie flattened her book on the side table and bounced fluidly to her feet. She wore a tattered pair of wool socks, so frightfully blue they stung my eyes to look at. Intoxicated by the fumes of her mother's cooking, she stumbled into the kitchen and sat down to a hearty deer stew with her mother. She ate her mother's bowl, too. Her mother hadn't touched a spoonful, but stared mournfully at her daughter over her full glass of water. She traced the moist rim with her pointer finger in much the same way Georgie had caressed her book earlier.

Aware of the change in the air, Georgie stopped slurping the remains of her soup and glanced up from her spoon. She blinked twice. "Mom?" she asked, suddenly childish as the day I'd first seen her. "Is something wrong? You look upset."

"You're all grown up now."

"But I'm still your little girl. I'm still Georgie."

"Will you go outside tonight?" her mother asked. Georgie froze. She dropped her spoon, and it clattered loudly at the bottom of her glass bowl. Her mother sighed, features gradually softening like butter in the sun. I was reminded of the game children often played with their crushes. Take a buttercup and rub it underneath your chin to find out if you're really in love. Georgie's mother had a smile as sad and solemn as a buttercup. She stood, ran her fingers through her daughter's downy ginger hair, and sighed. She took Georgie's hand gently and stood her up as well. "Come with me," she said, a request and not a demand. "I invited someone else to celebrate with you. I think he wants to take you out to the town. You want ice cream? I'll give you money for ice cream."

"What? Who are you talking about? I don't have any friends, mom." She laughed. "We're not...well, I never made any. Who is he?"

Her mother didn't answer. At the time, I find it hard to believe that Georgie did not know who her mother was walking her to. Through the entry, out the door, over the brick porch and past the dormant chrysanthemum in its big plastic pot, down the two brick steps, out into the garden. I stiffened. I hadn't expected it, really. Missus Marland, Georgie, and me. Missus Marland regarded me with somber, sunken eyes. She was a pretty woman, with hair like her daughter's would be in fifty years' time: softly dampened by gray and cut short because she could no longer find the time to care for it. Slender and avian in her pale green shawl, she stood over her daughter like a silent threat. I understood her eyes clearly. Her pensive stare. She patted her daughter once on the shoulder, her fingers lingering for a few moments over her thin neckline, and then disappeared into her open front door. The screen fell shut against the frame with a dull rattle of plastic and wire.

I fidgeted on my unfamiliar feet while Georgie Marland glassed me with marble eyes. For all my fear, I couldn't stop looking at her, hoping beyond hope that she would not run away, would not leave. I kept imagining her as a lithe child, climbing backward down the tree in her backyard and running headlong into the woods in search of the father she never knew.

What did she see that she suddenly spoke? I never knew. She never told me. She said, "Who are you, and why do you feel so familiar? I swear I know you. But I don't know anyone."

"My name is Wolf," I replied briskly, without thinking of the consequences, "and I've known you since you were very little, Georgie. I think I love you."

She smiled then. A wry, resisting smile. "Whoa there, tiger."

"Wolf." I corrected subtly, under my breath, "Gray."

"It's an expression. What I mean is that this is all happening a little fast. My mom gave me money for ice cream. I'd like to hear what you have to say, but do you think it could wait until we get into town? Let's talk this through over a quart of blue moon."

It was all so easy, as if I'd been around her my entire life, breathing her in and moving next to her. Of course, I had done all those things. But never so close before. The proximity made me drunk. As she pedaled furiously up and down the empty lanes of the only road leading in and out of town, I found myself struggling to hold on to her waist. My hands kept loosening when her hair tickled my nose. She laughed aloud when I sneezed on her neck. I tried to grow accustomed to my strange human limbs. The way they bent and folded and covered her up with unfamiliar skin. A little brown satchel bumped at my waist, catching finally on my tightened leather belt as Georgie turned the last corner and the tiny tinkering town came into full view from the hilltop.

I'd never been to the town before. I didn't know what it was called. It looked like Georgie's Christmas tree from so high up. Every year right after Thanksgiving dinner, Missus Marland would take Georgie into the cramped living room—eventually it would be the other way around—and they would put up red and green and silver and gold Christmas decorations. Deft hands aligning glorious twinkling strings of lights up with brittle green branches. Sappy fingers that wouldn't come clean no matter how much Georgie sucked on them or held them under the warm tap in the bathroom she shared with her mother.

This is what the town felt like, riding into it for the first time on the back spurs of Georgie's battered Schwinn bicycle. Like the holidays in full bloom, the rich reek of hot chocolate and whipping cream in porcelain collared mugs, a glazed ham on a perfect white table clothe with seats enough for four, plates enough for two.

"Do you like ice cream?" Georgie shouted over the biting wind.

I struggled to shape the words in my mouth. Cold flooded my fingers and cheeks and made my thin, unguarded skin numb. "I don't know. I've never had any."

"Never had ice cream?!" she practically screamed. "I'm ashamed of you! This is a blemish on our new friendship that must be removed, post-haste! To the Dairy!"

"To the Dairy?" I tried it out on my throat, eventually turning it into a sort of war cry for the desperately uncertain, a wobbly thunder in the mountains of Montana. "To the Dairy!" I howled. "To the Dairy!"

Georgie laughed again and joined in without hesitation. Her feet made quick blurs of the faded yellow road markers beneath the bike tires beneath us. "To the Dairy!" Our mingling voices echoed down through the treetops. We startled birds and late, lost hikers and did not care.

She backpedaled, and we jerked to a hasty five mile simmer at the edge of town. Buildings like pastel boxes with carved windows loomed up on every side. Some had cute white porches and old lawn furniture, moldy from the rain and dew. Others lacked both. Still more were glowing with vibrant life. Shoppers coming and going from open storefronts and families of three loitering on the warmly lit sidewalks that ran alongside the road. A few looked our way strangely. But most did not look at us at all. We coasted into the parking lot of a small shack the color of birch bark, and Georgie instructed me on how to properly dismount a stopped bicycle. She pulled a slender bike lock from her coat pocket and used it to lash our ride to one of the decorative trees sparsely coloring the barren concrete landscape around us.

"This is the Dairy," she explained, jerking her chin toward the shack. A hand-painted sign with the same name in scrawling script not so dissimilar from her mother's cake curls agreed with her. Below that, there was a menu with ten or so different flavors listed on it in different fonts. The flavor of the day was lobster bisque. "Best ice cream anywhere. Only ice cream anywhere, really, if you live here. You okay?"

I itched the back of my ear absentmindedly. I was having a hard time focusing in on all the lights and sounds in this town. Growling car engines, shimmering windows, the brilliant red behind the greengrocer's as the sun sank into the horizon, hitting every pane of glass on its way.

Georgie leaned closer to my nose than I would have liked her to. She scrunched up her chocolate eyes. Her mouth screwed into a tight, humorous smile.

"You don't live here," she said, "do you?"

"No, I live in the woods by your house. I don't go out."

"Who are you?"

"I told you, I'm Wolf."

"Are you really? You're not joking? You're a legitimate wolf, with the tail and the ears and the nose and the whole shebang?"

"Well," I uncomfortably replied, "not right now. Listen, Georgie…" I paused. Her name felt foreign and wonderful on my tongue, like swallowing a live wire. "I can only be like this for twenty-four hours each year. I'm almost out of time, but I'd like to ask you a few things first, if you don't mind."

"What time do your paws grow back?" she asked without skipping a beat.

I blinked, stunned for a moment into silence. "Midnight. I always change at midnight, the night of your birthday, and then I spend my twenty-four hours, and then I change back."

"Why?"

"Because that's the night I choose." I left out the part about the mountain lion. To my undying relief, she didn't press any further about the conflict that momentarily marred my features then.

She examined my face as if the words I'd spoken hung in the air around my mouth like the bubbles in her mother's ice cube trays. After a long moment, she leaned back comfortably again. I breathed a deep breath I hadn't realized I'd been holding. Georgie Marland laughed. A man holding a lumpy cone in one hand and a toy poodle in the other glanced over from a pan-sized picnic table and threw us a funny look. His dog wore a sweater with "MAMA'S SWEETEST" stitched lovingly into the collar. It bared its push-pin teeth and yipped at me.

"Well, Wolf," Georgie instructed lightheartedly, "if all this is true, I would recommend going without any chocolate in your ice cream. I'm getting blue moon. You have a preference?"

"Er," I fumbled with saying, "no, I'll get whatever you're getting."

"Even if it's laced with coke?"

I beamed uncertainly. "Sure, sounds great."

I didn't understand why this time, but she laughed again. Mama's Sweetest toy poodle yipped louder, squirming futilely in the crook of her owner's thick arm. He shot us an apologetic shrug as we passed his bench on the way to the Dairy's ordering counter. I hung back while Georgie ordered. "Two waffle cones please," she said, and, "blue moon flavor, no toppings, thank you very much." Georgie handed the vivid blonde spit of a cashier a crumpled up twenty and shoved the change deep into the left pocket of her blossom-bottomed jean shorts. She propped her elbow up on the white plastic countertop jutting out from the sliding glass separating us from the fluorescent organs of the Dairy itself. I adjusted the napkin dispenser to match the edge of the counter.

"So," Georgie started. I could feel the curiosity buzzing from her skin, like flies around the sticky garbage can directly behind me, like sparks flying from a flame. "What's the relationship like between you and my old woman?"

"Huh?" I asked, picturing Georgie squatting to mark her territory over a shuddering lady with wrinkles for a face.

The little cashier's window reopened, and the cashier handed out two spindly waffle cones filled beyond their rims with cold domes of cream as blue and fragrant as Georgie's socks. Georgie took one and handed it to me. She started eagerly on the other one as soon as it was in her hands. "I mean," she rephrased between licks, "how do you know my mom?"

"Oh," I said, regretting my earlier vision, "I don't, actually."

"What do you mean?"

"I never really talked to your mom much. I knew your dad."

She froze. In the brief lull between rapid questions, I nipped a small bite from the treat she'd entrusted me. The flavor burst over my tongue like her name did. All fiery hot and intensely satisfying in a way I could not name. All successive bites were taken with great care. The smaller the bite, the longer I'd have to savor it all; to take in the two scoops of blue moon and a twilit evening in a stranger's town with Georgie Marland.

She fixed me with her deep brown eyes, her mouth set at an

awkward angle. "You knew my father," she said. "You knew him."

I shrugged absently. My tongue had gone numb from the ice cream. Like eating snow when I couldn't find any running water. "I knew him, yes. He was a strong leader, stronger still for leaving to start a life with your mother and with you. But I knew he would eventually be drawn back again. We talked sometimes, he and I, after you were born. After I had been thrown out of the pack."

"You said you knew him," Georgie insisted. A small drip of pearly blue ice cream glistened over her fingers as her warm hands melted the insides of her cone. I honed in on my unfamiliar expression, warped and reflected within the drip, while I took another bite of my own. "You keep using past tense. Is he alright?"

"As far as I know," I replied truthfully, gauging her wide-eyed reaction, "he's doing well. I hear his voice in the woods sometimes. His howl. You hear it, too. I'm not a part of the pack still. I'm never allowed back. But he said some things to me before he left your house."

"What'd he say?"

"Mostly things about you."

"What did he say?" she urged again.

I swallowed. "Your ice cream is melting, Georgie."

She scrambled her thoughts and her mouth to catch the blue rivers dripping freely over her fingers and the backs of her hands. She'd been clutching her cone so tightly, it'd cracked straight up the center. She slurped the rest of her dessert from the bottom of the cone and we headed back to her bike in silence.

On the way back to her house, we walked the bike up the hill. Change from Missus Marland's ice cream money clanged loosely in Georgie's pocket. She braced her hands forcefully on the curved handlebars of her bike, gently guiding it up the steep slope while I, lamenting over the errors of the speeches I had for so long prepared in my head while I watched her grow older, walked on the other side of the bike, not making even a footstep's worth of noise.

Georgie huffed an angry sigh. I kicked a pebble, and it skittered across the black tarmac and into the dark forest beyond.

"So," Georgie finally said. I tried to count how many times she had said that word so far tonight. So. So, what? "My father," she tried again, "he was a wolf."

"He is a wolf," I corrected her flatly.

"Yeah, yeah, whatever. But he was a wolf. What does that make me?" She said this sternly, punched out each syllable like expelling cherry seeds from her rolling tongue. I chanced a look at her face. It was carved from stone. Marble, in the moonlight. "Am I Georgie Marland, human, or am I Georgie Marland, wolf?"

I forced a wry grin. It felt crooked and wrong already on my too small mouth, like trying to force cereal down a child's throat. Bare spots between the bangs gracing my forehead suddenly felt chilly, exposed. Even my patchy, thinly grizzled chin felt sparse. I had only developed the beard this year. Last year, it hadn't come up when I'd changed. It was a nice look, I thought.

"I don't know," I answered. "Quite honestly, I've never been able to tell the difference between the two. Wolves and humans, I mean. You're Marland, Georgie. I'm Wolf, Gray. We both have four limbs and some hair and eyes that see the world differently. We both eat and sleep and survive. Some more than others. Sometimes, when the moon hits the sky just right..." I framed the half full moon overhead with my thumbs and pointer fingers, whistling. Georgie followed my gaze curiously. "We all howl."

She asked in a dull whisper, "Why are you here?"

We stopped in the middle of the road. Behind us, the twinkling, starlit city began to shut out its lights. Individual storefronts blipped out of existence gradually. Fluorescent bars of light buzzed in and out of sight. Ahead, the road sloped upward into a dark and looming wood, the wood where Georgie's house lay nestled as if placed by the very hand of God. The hand of her mother, really, who had so carefully constructed her childhood so that Georgie would not know. So she would not know the differences between wolf and man.

It was a lost precaution. Most precautions are.

I gazed up at the moon again, now almost at its halfway mark in the sky, and crooned softly. Georgie let her bike drop to the pavement. Little yellow lines dashed underneath it like ants late to a picnic party.

"Why are you here?" she repeated. "Really, why are you here?"

"I'm here because your father wanted you to have this choice. I can't live as a lone wolf forever, I'll die. That's just the way the wild works. But we have a chance, you and I. I'm not going to make you do anything," I said. "You can go home if you want, and I'll leave and stop watching over you. You can live a wolf's life in the city. You can watch your mother grow old and die and then you can take care of her house and buy lots of chrysanthemums and cook venison all the time."

"Gray," she snapped, "stop."

I stopped and glanced across the carcass of the bike and into her eyes. Like the city, they reminded me of hot chocolate on her mother's kitchen counter on an early Christmas morning. A chill in the air told me that those days weren't far away now. I would have to find my way in the cold to a territory suited for a lone wolf. Or two wolves. It all hinged on the choice her father had left her with when he ran all those years ago.

When I looked in her eyes, I knew her decision had already been made. Perhaps she had made up her mind the day her father walked out. Perhaps she made it only because I asked her, only when I asked her. I blinked to break the contact. The intensity of her stare frightened me in that moment. I saw a predator, not for the first time, slinking through her gaze.

Oftentimes, I wonder what Missus Marland is doing. She must have expected what came next. No one from town would recognize her daughter, she had made sure of that, but would they recognize the bike in the middle of the main road? Even after it had been sped over by three different SUVs and almost flipped a moped. Missus Marland recognized it.

I have a dream sometimes about her mother. She's sitting on the front stoop by the sunset pink chrysanthemum Georgie bought to replace what I broke, picking petals off a bloom plucked by her hand. Her husband is sitting next to her, all four legs firmly planted on the hard brick step leading up to his old house. A house he'd built for hiding. His tongue lolls out happily. She scratches him between the ears and bites her lip.

"I should have known not to love or trust a wolf," she says. "They've never stayed long. That's the only difference, I think, between you and I. You can't keep a wolf like you can keep a man or a woman."

She grimaces then, a scowl that morphs her beautiful thin features, turns her eyes the texture of gravel at the bottom of a crystal clear pond. "Loving the pack more than anything," she repeats, often until the sound of my own breathing and the breathing of countless others wakes me. "Loving the pack more than anything."

HIS PAST CAUGHT UP WITH HIM
JITKA SANIOVA AND RICHARD BROOKES

Jitka Saniova and Richard Brookes met on the Internet several years ago. In the course of becoming friends, they found they have many common interests, including a love of reading and writing.

Jitka is a Czech writer and photographer with seventeen books to her credit. She also is a prolific writer of articles and a digital artist creating photomontages and enhanced photos.

Richard Brookes is a retired insurance executive who has been writing for about eight years. His stories have been published in several magazines. He lives in California.

*For approximately four years, they have been co-operating on a number of writing projects. Together, they have published stories in several American magazines (*Xoddity, Cabaret Magazine, Dragon Laugh, *etc.), and they have written two screenplays – the first one, a fantasy called* The Wolf Queen, *has been accepted by a producer in Australia who is currently arranging financing. The second,* Anabar, *also a fantasy, is with an agency in Ohio.*

Among their common interests is a love for animals and nature, reading books, photographing, and good TV series and movies.

His Past Caught Up with Him
(The Rain Always Comes *After* the Puddles)

Josie lived in an ordinary town, had ordinary friends and lived in an ordinary house. Her life was so *ordinary* that she was feeling quite bored. When Josie became bored, that could be dangerous.

Josie's friends thought of her as an idea person. Whenever one needed a new, fresh idea, Josie was the lady who could supply it. Like now – she blew dust from her ancient telephone, swept away the cobwebs around the phone directory – even the white pages were yellowed - and found the number she wanted. She dialed the number carefully. Soon a male voice answered. It was a question of three or four minutes, and she had convinced her nephew Martin from New York to come visit her. Persuasion was another of Josie's talents.

Hanging up the telephone, she approached the clump of fur in the corner beside her bed. It seemed to be breathing deeply and regularly, mingled with what sounded like snores.

"Zephyr, get up, we must prepare for a visitor."

She swept away the webs from around the gray wolf. The animal was yawning now and creakily stretching his body.

"No, Zephyr, you mustn't call Martin a half-witted stockbroker! That's really not at all polite. And he is, after all, my only nephew." Of course, Zephyr could not talk, but Josie clearly heard his comments nonetheless.

There was a knock at the door. When Josie opened it, her neighbor Ursula displayed her marvelous new dentures in a broad smile. Josie's welcome was cool. "Ursula, I'm very busy now. Martin is coming for a visit. I must do my shopping. Will Mr. Grek's grocery be open? I always forget his hours. Are they 2 AM to Noon except Labor Day and Thursdays?"

"Oh, Josie, haven't you heard?"

Josie tilted her head to one side to favor her good ear. "Mr. Grek died almost a week ago," declared Ursula.

"Oh, that's sad. And inconvenient to say the least," Josie sighed, "but this doesn't mean he can't continue to operate his store does it?"

Ursula frowned, thoughtfully. "Hmmm! Of course, you are right. May I accompany you?"

Josie knew she would lose time trying to discourage Ursula from this wish. Ursula's mind wasn't as malleable as Martin's. So she nodded her assent, "O.K.! Let's do some serious shopping."

Ursula pulled a small mirror compact from her purse, touched up her ultra-violet lipstick and eye shadow and reported, "I'm ready."

Josie grabbed her old carpet bag. "Zephyr, get moving; you're a wolf, not a sloth!"

The wolf stretched yet again and lazily looked around.

"No, Zephyr. Nothing has changed while you slept. No need to waste time gawking."

The wolf snuffled and followed the two women who were already headed toward Mr. Grek's store.

Martin, driving his white Mercedes, muttered to himself, "Damn,

damn, damn. What am I doing? Why can't I simply tell her, I don't want to come to your dull little town. I could be flying to Rio, Paris, Prague, Rome..."

If the truth were known, and he would quit fooling himself, Martin was not adventuresome enough to go to any of these places, even if he could have afforded it. Martin's Mercedes was mortgaged to the max, and he was a month in arrears on his apartment rent. It was very expensive to live in New York, and Martin was not the flushest nor most capable of Wall Street brokers. The Mercedes approached the big "WELCOME to...." sign at the outskirts of Aunt Josie's town. The bottom of the sign had been broken off years before.

"And to what do I agree?" Martin deplored aloud, "Instead of strolling on the Champs d'Elysee, I will chat with Aunt Josie and her friends about their uneventful lives in her tiresome little village!"

Martin passed the sign. The land behind him closed itself as a zipper might close open jeans. His Mercury became dark blue.

"Damn, where do I go now?" Martin scratched his head in puzzlement. The town was so small, how could he possibly be lost? But somehow the town looked different every time he was there. He stopped the car and got out in front of Mr. Grek's grocery to ask directions.

"My dear Martin, you're here already?"

Martin turned toward the voice. He didn't know if he should be more amazed about just alighting from a car he didn't recognize or the sight of the very peculiar pair of women that greeted him. Ursula could be called Violet Incarnate – with the exception of her teeth, everything about her was a shade of violet. Josie, on the other hand, had a look that reminded him a little of a furious Elizabeth Taylor in *Who's Afraid of Virginia Woolf?* And yet her manner was that of a kindly, even doting, grandmother. Her white hair was done in a style perhaps reminiscent of a Fauvist painting. Martin could not quite decide if her blue dress was next year's style or simply a tawdry frazzle. The wolf beside Josie looked at Martin with rheumy eyes and licked its wet nose.

"Martin, what's the matter?" asked Josie. Martin could not seem to get his mouth to return to a closed position. Martin, at that moment defined the word, "nonplussed."

"My car...I have a white Mercedes," he responded, staring forlornly at the Mercury parked at the curb.

Josie and Ursula both looked at Martin in puzzlement. "Martin, I don´t want to be impolite," Josie said, "but your car does seem to be blue."

"But that´s the point. It was white! A white Mercedes! White as your hair, Aunt Josie," Martin exclaimed somewhat ungraciously.

"I see that Wall Street has taken a lot out of you, Martin. I am glad that you´ll be able to relax for a time in our peaceful town," Josie said with genuine concern.

"Wall Street has nothing to do with this!"

"In my experience, Martin, it is just highly stressed people that are so distraught."

"My car was white!" Martin exclaimed.

Josie looked at Ursula. Ursula smiled, with white teeth slightly besmirched by fresh violet lipstick, and said, "O.K. Perhaps it was white, but *now* it is certainly blue."

"Do you think it is normal for a car to change color during a trip of a few hundred miles?" Martin replied a shade testily.

Ursula thought as hard as Ursula could think. She said hesitatingly, "I really don´t see that it is all that strange." Smiling nervously she added, "But I have never had much use for cars, or trips for that matter."

Josie gave Ursula the angry Virginia Woolf look. "Martin is exhausted, and he needs a rest. You know stockbrokers!"

Martin wanted to protest, but he decided that changing the subject was the best course of action. "I need to buy some aspirin," he announced, rubbing his temples with the tips of his fingers.

Josie´s face lit up like a thousand watt bulb. "You can buy aspirin from Mr. Grek at his shop."

"Perfect."

"Just, ummm..." Josie hesitated and then motioned Martin closer and whispered, "Mr. Grek died last week, and he isn't completely accustomed to it yet. You must be patient with him, he gets a little confused about time."

Martin opened his mouth to say something, but Josie was quicker. "Don't be afraid, he is always courteous. He isn´t distressed at all. He just must learn not to get his tenses confused."

Josie put her packages in Martin´s blue Mercury while Martin tried to comprehend what he had heard. Then, both women and the wolf walked into the shop.

Mr. Grek's shop was clean and well-organized with a wide choice of goods. Mr. Grek seemed benign if not totally congenial. He was dressed in a black suit and a white shirt. On his round, almost bald head, perched a black hat. His ashy white face beamed with his best "greet the new customer" smile. "You were welcome to my shop," he said with a small bow.

"Mr. Grek, my nephew Martin needs some aspirin," said Josie. And then she was struck with another of her bright ideas. "And I would like to show him your shop. You know, he could find souvenirs for his New York friends."

Josie nudged Martin with her elbow. Martin tried to smile and nodded.

Mr. Grek bowed again and said: "He has surely found something interesting."

Josie whispered to Martin, "He means, you will find something interesting. As I explained, he is confused with time since he died."

Martin allowed Josie to push him around the shop. Ursula waved to them and headed – as was usual – to the cosmetic section. It was impossible for her to resist buying lavender eyeshadow or violet lipstick. Zephyr yawned and looked around for a place to nap.

Martin and Josie walked among the shelves of merchandise. Everything looked normal and yet not quite right. Martin picked up a large grapefruit and thought, *I could make fresh grapefruit juice*. At that moment the grapefruit in his hand changed into a glass of cold, no doubt refreshing, grapefruit juice. Martin screamed and almost jumped out of his skin.

Josie, Ursula and even Zephyr ran to him. "What happened, Martin?" asked Josie.

He pointed to the glass with grapefruit juice. Josie and Ursula looked at each other. Mr. Grek appeared and asked, "Why will this elegant young man scream here?"

Josie turned to Mr. Grek. "I don´t know yet." Then she looked at Martin and added, "Martin, if I recall well, you do like grapefruit juice."

"Aunt Josie, don´t you understand?" cried Martin desperately, "In New York, I buy a grapefruit, take it home, cut it, put it in the juicer and...I have a glass of juice to enjoy. Here..."

Josie laughed and waved in a broad gesture, "Martin, I always think that, in New York, you people simply make a lot of fuss with everything."

Mr. Grek nodded, "I will hope that you had enjoyed the juice," and walked away.

Zephyr looked at Martin and licked his chops.

"No sausage, Zephyr. Not now."

"What?" Martin asked, now totally puzzled.

Josie sighed, "When Zephyr looks at you, he always envisions a sausage in his mind."

Ursula grinned, observing Martin's long, slim body. Then she looked at his jeans and uttered dreamily: "And I as well..."

"Ursula! This is my nephew!"

"Well, I wouldn't have a problem with it, but if you think...O.K., I understand. Hands off." Ursula sighed and went back to shopping for violet nail polish.

Martin resignedly drank from his glass of grapefruit juice as he followed Josie through the store. Zephyr searched each face and decided to follow Mr. Grek.

"Ah, Zephyr, will you have wanted a sausage?" Zephyr was salivating. "Just a moment, I was giving it to you immediately. I will have had one here," Mr. Grek promised.

Martin wiped perspiration from his forehead and thought: Anyone who thinks that the stock exchange is a madhouse should experience this.

"Look, Martin, don´t you like this spoon that changes its size according to the proportions of your mouth?"

Martin didn´t answer. He just stared, wide-eyed.

"You don´t like it, I can tell. And what about this frame that becomes as beautiful as the picture you put into it..." Josie inspected the item. "Now I understand why Ursula put this back, it really isn't a good idea...Martin?"

No response.

"Martin?"

"I need an aspirin," he said weakly.

Josie sighed. "Hmph, you people from New York can't think of anything but aspirin! You will overmedicate yourselves, you know."

Josie turned to Martin. Seeing him pale and speechless, staring out the window, she blinked in surprise and went to the window to discover what Martin could possibly be staring at so intently. In front of the shop was parked a white Mercedes and beside it was Martin looking at the shop and smiling.

"Why is it that you need aspirin, Martin?" asked Josie with a frown.

"I see myself outside," whispered Martin, in deep shock.

"That's certainly not at all strange," laughed Josie. But then she advised earnestly, "Martin, if I were you, I wouldn't take any medication; you will need all your faculties."

The Martin outside smiled at the shop window and walked to the entrance. A moment later, a green Mazda, somewhat the worse for wear, pulled up in front of the shop. Martin got out and proceeded to the door.

The Martin inside looked accusingly at his aunt. Josie tried to look innocent. She shrugged and said with a forced laugh, "I believe they have found you."

Seeing these happenings, Ursula came to the conclusion that it would be more interesting to join Josie and her nephew than to look at cosmetics.

"There are three Martins," she said with sincere joy and admiration. Josie and Ursula eyed three completely identical Martins dressed exactly the same. Well, almost identical.

"Would someone explain to me what is going on here?" asked Martin.

"You are the original?" asked Josie.

"Of course," Martin shouted, then he looked at the two Martins standing beside him, "I don´t know who they are, but..."

"Don´t think you are in some way superior," sneered one of the other Martins.

"How can we tell them apart?" asked Ursula nervously.

"Hmmm. How can they tell themselves apart? That is even more important!" Josie said.

"I know," Ursula said, excitedly, "That one has two fewer wrinkles on his forehead than the one in the middle, and on the contrary, the third one has three wrinkles more."

"Ursula, they won't have time to count wrinkles."

Ursula bit her lip. "This is true, Josie. O.K., now it is your turn. I have used up my ideas."

"I´ve got it!" Josie´s eyes shone with success. She looked around and found three cans of paint and brushes. She went to Martin #1 and asked, "What street did you use to drive here?"

"25th Avenue, you old bag," he said scornfully.

Josie gave him a look that would frost the windows of Hell. She pondered the problem briefly, then smiled and said "O.K. so we will give you a pink jacket. Pink because of "P" as in 'past'."

Ursula took a brush and drew pink stripes on the back of his jacket.

Then Josie faced the other Martin and asked him the same question. "I came by way of 32nd Avenue," smiled Martin #2.

"So you will be blue, like the future."

Ursula looked at Josie questioningly. "Josie, I am not as clever as you, but 'future' starts with 'F', doesn´t it?"

"Makes no difference. I am fond of blue so the future will be blue."

Ursula didn´t protest and she proceeded to make blue stripes on the back side of Martin #2's jacket.

"So you are the one that just came to visit from New York," said Josie to the third one.

"Of course, and who are these two lunatics?"

"One thing at a time, please," pled Josie. "So you will have a big black 'Z' like the 'present'."

"But there is no "Z" in the word 'present'," wondered Martin.

"But can I hear it in there," said Josie, firmly.

Ursula nodded, opening a black paint can. "I hear it as well." Then she made a big black "Z" on Martin's jacket.

"So, it's done," she said, satisfied.

"Aunt Josie, can you explain me what is going on here?" said the Martin with 'Z' on his jacket.

"You have to go away now," she ordered the two other Martins. The Martin with the pink sign, grinned evilly and said to the Martin whose jacket bore the blue mark, "I'll be seeing you, buddy!"

The blue Martin nodded and replied, "You can be sure, you creep!" They left the shop, got in their respective cars and drove away.

Martin didn´t know whether to simply remain puzzled or to try to ask questions. Fortunately Josie decided to be communicative, saving him the effort of making a decision. "Nephew, you must prepare yourself for a battle."

Ursula put her hand on his shoulder and sighed: "If you could only imagine who those two are..."

Martin said, "I can guess that the pink guy is my past, and the blue is my future. But..."

"Wow," yelled Ursula and looked at Martin in disbelief, "how did you guess that?"

Martin smiled ironically, "Like any stockbroker, I have attained a certain level of education."

"Wow!" Again, Ursula's face brightened with admiration.

"What my education is not up to is comprehending why they could want to kill me."

"Correction, my dear," Josie put up her forefinger, "there is just one who wants to kill you, well, he wants to kill both of you. The pink Martin is a threat to both you and the Blue Martin."

"But why?"

Josie coughed. "Well, we won't go into your past. Let's just say that you weren't an angel in the past and now you have changed for the better, but as you know..."

"It isn't so easy to eradicate your past errors."

Josie nodded. Ursula grinned and clipped Martin playfully on his jaw.

"He will definitely want to kill the blue Martin," thought Josie aloud.

"And me?"

"That depends," Josie looked at him, frowning thoughtfully, "He can be stronger retaining you, perhaps, but he can also live without you, of course, if it comes to that."

Martin had no taste to return to his past way of life. "But why didn't he just kill us both while he was here?" frowned Martin.

Josie rolled her eyes. "Try to rise to your level of education, Mr. Stockbroker."

Ursula laughed. "You'll think of the solution, I'm certain."

It was Ursula who finally broke the embarrassed silence. "Why do you think Josie and I pay so little rent for our houses here?"

Martin shrugged.

Ursula looked disappointed. "My, what do they teach you in New York? It is clear we live in an area where one is in the future and yet also in the present. So Josie and I live in the future. We are older and, well...who would want to be older? So we pay low rent. But the present Josie and I are still part of us. We can't be separate, and yet we seem to be older although we aren't. Do you understand?"

"No."

"Martin, my small brain understands this! You are a stockbroker on Wall Street."

Josie giggled. Martin looked at her sharply.

"I know, my dear Martin," explained Josie, "it isn't customary, but it is really very clear. Consider Mr. Grek. He died. So now he must be dead."

"This is usually the way," said Martin.

"But in the present Mr. Grek is alive though he is dead in the future. This would happen to you if the past Martin would try to kill you here. Do you understand?"

"I am trying my best," answered Martin, thoughtfully. "And so where will he try to kill me?"

"It must be out of this area," Josie said. "Where the past, present, and future are completely separate. The risk is too great otherwise."

"And why did the blue Martin leave me when he isn't in any danger here?"

Josie muttered, "These New Yorkers," then she smiled and answered, trying to be patient, "He can't stay here for long when he isn't invited. He would have to have a visa because he isn't a 'resident'. Another question?"

"Ah, some other time, perhaps," Martin said quickly.

Ursula beamed her admiration, "You have it! I knew you were clever!"

Martin smiled, but Josie's face was concerned, "You should have a guide with you."

"And what about you?"

Josie gave him an exasperated look. "Martin, I have no visa for other parts."

Suddenly, Mr. Grek appeared. "Josie, I will give two hot dogs to Zephyr."

"What?" said Josie.

Mr. Grek frowned. "I would say that I will gave him hot dogs."

"Aha," Josie understood and called, "Zephyr!"

The wolf arrived vigorously licking his chops. Josie closed her eyes and pondered. Ursula put her forefinger to her violet lips.

"Shhh!" ordered Josie with her eyes still closed.

Martin's eyes widened. "I said nothing."

Josie opened one eye and said to Martin, "Not you. Zephyr. He's one huge chatterbox, and I need to concentrate."

Martin glanced at the silent wolf. Zephyr laid his head on his paws and sighed.

Finally Josie opened her eyes and said, "Done."

"What?" Martin asked, and he was immediately sorry.

"You don't know about wolves?" asked Ursula, disappointed.

Martin's self-confidence suffered another hit. Ursula sighed and she explained. "Wolves don't need any visa. They can wander all over, free as birds."

"Well, that's nice to know, but I was asking what is 'done'."

Ursula looked at Josie with obvious desperation. "You know, he begins to remind me of my nephew Matthew who works for NASA. He has studied the stars for years, yet he also knows nothing when he comes here."

Josie nodded. "It is a rarity that I could so easily agree, Ursula, but in this case I must." Josie looked at Martin with this expression: *My nephew is an ignoramus, but I love him anyway!*

Then, Josie proceeded to explain. "I had to strengthen Zephyr's psyche. Now, he can recall his past as well as his future selves. Perhaps you would now ask why he couldn't ordinarily recall them?"

Martin smiled wanly. "That would have been my next question."

"Think, Martin," Josie knocked on his forehead. "If Zephyr and his other selves could find each other at any time, I would never know if I have in front of me a Zephyr from the past or a Zephyr from the future or my own Zephyr. Zephyr also lives in the future and is joined with his present self. That makes it even more difficult to determine to which Zephyr I speak. You can imagine what that could mean!"

Josie rolled her eyes. Martin did the same and tried to be convincing when he said, "Yes, I can imagine it. Oh my God!"

Zephyr stood, lifted his head and howled. In a short while, two wolves ran to Mr. Grek's shop. Martin blinked once and the wolves were inside. One after the other, they merged with the Zephyr already there and he was transformed into a huge, powerful and gorgeous gray wolf.

Martin's mouth dropped open. "But he was scraggy. Just skin and bones. Like a broomstick..."

"Never call my Zephyr a broomstick," thundered Josie so loudly that a picture fell off the wall.

"No, no. What I wanted to say was that he was... he is now so beautiful."

Josie leaned to Zephyr and petted him. The wolf sat attentively. She turned to Martin. "Wolves can sense the boundaries of time and dimensions; you can trust him. Zephyr is now what we call 'achronal': he lives in the past, present, and future with equal facility. Now, Martin, recall that the pink Martin wants to kill the blue one. He may take no action against you until he is sure that you won't join him."

"You must not kill the blue Martin by accident. If you do, you are a dead man, nephew. Or I should say that you will soon cease to exist. You must kill only the pink Martin and you can't allow yourself or the blue Martin to be killed!"

Martin nodded agreement. For the first time since he had arrived in Josie's town, he began to feel fear.

Josie patted Martin's arm. "Perhaps you aren't the most clever, but I believe that you can manage this."

"Thanks for your confidence." Martin had to smile. Two post-graduate degrees, a broker on Wall Street and Josie's evaluation: *you aren't the most clever.*

Martin and Zephyr started to walk away. Ursula looked at them and began to cry. "I will describe this wonderful, romantic scene in my next novel. Possibly Harlequin will finally accept it."

Josie put her arm around Ursula's shoulder. "Don't give up, Ursula, I am certain they will recognize your exceptional talent."

"I agree," said Ursula and cried still more.

Zephyr ran a short distance in front of Martin. It looked like they were in New York. They passed across 10th Avenue, 9th, 8th, and finally, they turned on Broadway, and that led them to Times Square. Zephyr stopped just short of entering the square. Martin looked around; where was everybody?

"Why did you stop?" Martin asked Zephyr as if the wolf could answer. The wolf refused to go on.

"There is nothing in front of us," Martin indicated with an outstretched hand. "What a guide! Now I must lead you," muttered Martin and stepped forward. He crashed against something completely unyielding and fell to his knees. Totally puzzled, Martin got up and approached the "hard nothing" and carefully felt it. Immediately, the upper half of his body was sucked into the space beyond, which was not Times Square by any stretch of imagination.

Martin saw a red sandy desert scattered with white clocks of various sizes, bleached bones, and lots of currency of various denominations. He reached for a bill, as stockbrokers could be expected to do, and it began to meld with his fingers.

"Zephyr, help him!" Josie's voice came from the blue above, although there was no sign of her.

The wolf stood and braced himself, grabbed Martin's jacket in his teeth and began to pull him back.

Martin's hand had already been replaced by a two-dollar bill when he felt himself being pulled back, but the money was pulling him inexorably into the desert wasteland. Zephyr was drawing him in the opposite direction. Martin felt that it was inevitable that he would break in two. He took a deep breath and tried, with some effort, to help Zephyr. And, with a popping sound, he fell back into Zephyr's paws.

The wolf howled a complaint directly in Martin's ear.

"O.K. O.K. I should have trusted you. I'm sorry. Does that suffice?"

The wolf nodded. Martin got up and followed the wolf who walked carefully around the transparent barrier.

When they came to a white bench next to a patch of green grass, Martin felt relieved. The wolf stood beside the bench, his sensitive nose testing the air. Martin sat on the bench. The wolf was, as always, alert. Martin leaned back to relax...and felt a falling sensation.

Zephyr jumped on Martin to hold him.

Martin had a sensation of whirling greenness and a huge knife pointed at his neck. Zephyr pulled at his shirt, and Martin returned to the right dimension. Shocked, he gingerly felt his neck and looked wide-eyed at Zephyr. He was going to say something, but there was no time. The air opened, and a Martin brandishing a big knife jumped outside, or was it inside? Martin leaped from the bench.

"Which are you?" asked Martin.

"First, you show me, who you are," said the Martin with the knife.

"I haven't the taste to turn my back to you," the present Martin assured him.

"My feeling exactly," grinned the other Martin.

They watched each other, looking carefully in each other's eyes, following each other's movements. Martin stepped to one side. The other Martin did the same. Zephyr yawned and lay down with his head on his paws.

One of the Martins jumped forward. The other turned quickly, but it was enough for the real Martin to see the blue color on his back. Martin sat on the ground and laughed. "It's O.K., friend, I am the real one." Martin got up, turned and showed the "Z" on his back. They were both relieved. But not for long.

It was as if the scene were a painting and the canvas tore. For a split second, a hole appeared in the "air," and the third Martin jumped through. He gave Martin a big shove causing him to lose his balance. It was just that he didn't fall on the ground at the place where he was. He fell into a transparent door that had opened and...

Zephyr opened one of his eyes, sighed, and got to his feet.

...Martin dropped into a green landscape with many glass doors distributed about with no apparent rhyme or reason. He walked to one isolated door and opened it slightly to look behind it. Experience taught him that what he saw through the glass might not be what was actually behind the door. Zephyr stretched his legs and licked his muzzle recalling the delicious taste of sausage...oh yes, it was time to find the Martin for whom he was the guide.

Martin was shoved again, only God knows by what, and beyond the door he saw a blue landscape. There was cerulean blue and cobalt one. Azure, aquamarine, and Prussian. Martin stepped into the magical landscape, the "Z" on his back turned blue, the terra firma changed to water and he fell into a very, very deep sea.

He fell, fell, and fell. And descended some more.

Although he was falling through water, he found he could breathe. The water felt like velvet caressing his cheeks. He smiled contentedly, but was shocked from his reverie when he saw another Martin swimming toward him. Martin panicked and tried to swim away. The other Martin gained rapidly. Martin saw a door in front of him. When he reached it, the other yelled, "Hey, I can see the "Z" on your back, no need to be worried!"

Martin looked in the other's eyes. He recalled clearly there was a period in the past when he couldn't be trusted to tell the truth. Martin grabbed the handle and quickly opened the door.

Zephyr stood quietly in the green land. Like all wolves, Zephyr was smart enough to be able to compute that Martin would reappear at that spot after ten wolfish minutes. Zephyr considered how to utilize these ten lupine minutes. His first thought was to lay down, but then he spotted the blue Moon and, as wolves are wont to do, he gave chase.

A knife whizzed close by Martin's head. "Oh, damn..." Martin yelled and ducked. He had stepped into a land where there was nothing but sand in all directions. Just sand and...Martin tried to focus his eyes on an object far away. It looked like a...yes, it was a castle with golden towers. Martin laughed and started to run toward it. He felt joy and elation looking at the gorgeous building. He ran toward it. He was sweaty and thirsty, but happy. He ran until he was exhausted and then ran some more.

Zephyr howled at the blue Moon. The sight of his gorgeous chest and profile made the Moon smile. Zephyr stared at it, and in a short while his spirit separated form his body and leaped to the Moon.

Martin was within 200 feet of the entrance to the majestic castle. Each step was now agonizing. He had no idea what he would find there, but he knew it would be something splendid.

A shot from a gun kicked up sand near his feet. Martin fell to the ground and turned to look back. There was no one. He looked toward the castle. There was a Martin. But which one?

Martin looked at the Martin in front of him brandishing a gun.

"I don't want to hurt you," said Martin and, getting up, put his hands in the air.

The other pointed the gun at him. "I don't want to hurt you either. If you are on my side, of course." Then the other gestured toward Martin's back. "But he has a gun too."

Martin stood between the two Martins. One, the Martin of his past and the other his future self. He was afraid to turn his head but he heard approaching steps. The Martin in front of him pointed the gun at the man behind him.

"Don't do it," yelled Martin.

"I must save our future," said the one in front of him.

"The future according to your imagination?" asked the Martin in back, ironically.

"Exactly," said the one near the castle and pulled the trigger.

Martin jumped back and knocked the Martin behind him to the ground. Martin quickly looked at the back of the Martin pinned under him. Blue stripes.

The gun fired again, but both Martins were able to jump away. The castle began to darken and changed to a shadow. The shadow grew and absorbed the Martin standing in front. The three were separated again. The Martin with the pink stripes had melted into the shadow, and the blue Martin became transparent and had soon vanished as well. Martin panicked. He started to run aimlessly to escape the confusion he felt. He ran across the endless sandy landscape. He ran for his life. Suddenly the sand under his feet vanished, and Martin once again was falling...

Zephyr loved the Moon caressing his spirit. However, something disturbed him. Ten wolfish minutes still hadn't expired, but he knew he had to return. Zephyr jumped into his body and alerted his brain.

...smack into the center of the trading floor of the New York Stock Exchange. It was empty and silent. Martin looked around as if he had never been there before. What a strange feeling when the desks, computers and the big board are dark and deserted. But Martin had no time to wonder. A huge bear appeared at the door and loped toward him. Martin started to run. He opened the door to a restroom and...

The wolf loped to the door in the center of the land. There was something strange, his instinct warned him, but he couldn't divine the concrete reason. Zephyr stood in front of the door, not fearful, but alert.

...Martin was sucked inside and confronted with a strange stony landscape.

The wolf pawed the door, and it opened. Zephyr immediately spotted Martin lying in on ground with his head bloodied. Zephyr went to him and began to lick his face. In a few moments, Martin opened his eyes and smiled at the wolf. Zephyr joyously wagged his tail while Martin tried to clean his head with a handkerchief. The Martin displaying the pink stripes on his jacket got up and looked around. Zephyr ran forward, then paused and turned to this Martin and looked at him expectantly.

"I'm coming," he said and followed the happy wolf.

The Martin of the stony landscape was furious. He couldn't find any way to escape this terrible place. His hands were covered with blood. He knew he couldn't last long in this land of sharp stones. He was frightened. One boulder reminded him of a human figure. He could imagine himself looking like that if he had to remain there much longer. Martin picked up a rock and threw it against a boulder. "Damn, how I can get out of this place!"

An echo repeated his words, and the rock ricocheted from the boulder and struck Martin and brought him to his knees. He closed his eyes in pain and held his bruised shoulder. When he opened his eyes, he saw brown shoes in front of him. He looked up and saw a Martin.

"No worry, I am the blue one," said Martin, smiling. "I saw your Z, so I felt safe approaching you!"

Martin got up and looked at the back of the other Martin relieved to see the blue stripes. They smiled at each other.

"Man, it's a relief to see you," said Martin. "How did you find me?"

"I didn't," said the Martin with the blue stripes. "I fought with the pink Martin, your past. I hit him quite hard and he fell."

"So is he dead?" cried Martin hopefully.

"Unfortunately, I can't be sure," sighed the blue Martin, "I wanted to check to see, but suddenly I was sucked into this godforsaken place."

"I hope he is dead!"

"Are you finished with your past, and you are definitely on my side?"

Martin reflected. "Yes," he hesitated, looking down at his shoes, but then he was able to say, "I guess it is hard to kill a part of oneself, but in this case...my past must die so that my future can live."

The blue Martin hugs Martin. "It won't be easy, but we will accomplish it."

Zephyr stopped in front of an invisible wall. He howled, and immediately there was a disturbance in the air before him...

Both the present Martin and the blue Martin saw the air begin to swirl.

"This must be the pink Martin," yelled blue.

Martin nodded, "Do you still have the gun?"

The blue Martin took it from his pocket and looked at Martin eagerly. "You should do it! I could, but... "

Martin hesitated, but then he realized that the other spoke the truth. "You're right, my future must be without any blemish. I am the present and responsible for finishing the past."

Martin took the gun and waited. Zephyr, his tail wagging, appeared first. Zephyr enjoyed traveling in the whirlwind. It refreshed him. Then, the pink Martin was deposited not so gently in a sitting position on the ground.

The pink Martin stood up and brushed himself off. He and the blue Martin stood some distance from each other, while the Martin of the present stood opposite them both, making up the third point on an unmarked triangle.

Martin pointed the gun at the pink Martin. "I'm sorry, but I must..."

"Wait," screamed pink Martin, "don't do it!"

"I have no choice!" said Martin, with deep regret.

"Wait a moment, Martin, I must explain something...!"

"No explanation, no further wasting time!"

It was difficult to shoot at oneself, but Martin knew that it must be done. He pulled the trigger.

There was an evil laugh.

Zephyr quickly sprang at the Martin in the pink jacket and knocked him down. The bullet, missing the pink Martin, ricocheted from the hard stone and struck the blue Martin in the chest. He fell, a bullet in his heart.

Martin of the present was aghast. He looked at the blue Martin, his future, dead on the ground and screamed, "Oh, my God!" With the wide-eyed expression of a madman he turned to Zephyr and screamed, "You miserable beast. Are you insane? Look what you have done! The fairy tales are true – you are an evil, hateful animal!"

In the meantime the other Martin kneeled by Zephyr and petted him. "I´d like to thank you before I take my jacket back."

"What?" cried Martin of the present, now tearing his hair despondently.

The other Martin went to the body and took off the jacket. "I was unconscious, I had no idea he exchanged jackets with me," he explained while putting on the jacket with blue stripes.

Martin pondered the puzzle for a few moments. Then he looked at the live Martin before him. Their eyes met and Martin of the present sighed in relief. How he could have been so blind? This guy is clearly his future – he can look into eyes of this man without fear, hesitancy or even an uneasy feeling. The other was as false as he had been in his past. Then Zephyr must have...

Martin approached the wolf. "I´m sorry, Zephyr. I regret my words."

The wolf turned his back to Martin. He tried to apologize further to Zephyr, but the wolf growled menacingly. A whirlwind approached.

Both Martins and a very aloof wolf found themselves smack in the middle of Mr. Grek's store.

"Shoo, shoo, you must go away," Josie directed the future Martin from the shop.

"Why?" asked Martin, but Josie's cold look nipped his query in the bud. "O.K., but please, just a moment," pleaded Martin.

He went to blue Martin and hugged him.

"You must be better. I want to be...I must be better than he was," said the future Martin, and the other nodded his agreement.

"Thanks for everything," said Martin.

"Oh, I love sentimental scenes." As Ursula wept, violet mascara ran down her cheeks. Josie sighed, clutched blue Martin's jacket and steered him toward the door. As blue Martin left the store he yelled, "Martin, buy Bitesoft shares."

"Do you think this is a good time to be buying?"

Blue Martin shouted, "Didn't you notice that the bear was running away?" And he was gone.

Oh, I was thinking that he was running after me, thought Martin. He smiled to himself. Who could know better than his future self? With a screech of tires, the blue Mercury drove away.

"What is Bitesoft?" asked Ursula of Martin.

"Biological testing software."

"That sounds great, I must use it in one of my novels, but I must make a note of it. My brain wouldn't recall this." Ursula fluttered her violet eyelids.

Martin looked at the wolf whose back was still turned. "How I can make peace with him?" he asked his aunt.

"When Zephyr is offended, he doesn't make up easily. Yes, I can tell Zephyr is deeply hurt."

Martin went to the wolf and pled with a sincere voice, "I'm sorry I called you stupid and said that the cruel tales about wolves are true! Please accept my apology."

No reaction.

"He was O.K. with the blue Martin," Martin complained to Josie.

"Really? That means in the future you and Zephyr will be friends."

"I can see it clearly", Ursula beamed with excitement. "Martin and Zephyr, friends forever. I will write a screenplay about how Zephyr is lost as Martin moves across the country and Zephyr makes a long, dangerous journey even though he is injured, yet he finds Martin, and there is a glorious reunion. I am sure it will be a big hit!"

"I don't want to spoil your enthusiasm, but that movie has already been made," said Martin.

Ursula sighed. "This is the fate of all of us who live in future." Josie laughed. Ursula frowned and began to cry. "How you can laugh at my tragedy?"

"I'm not laughing at you."

"Ah, you have been conversing with Zephyr," Ursula said and dried her tears.

Josie nodded and turned to Martin. "Zephyr could make peace

with you - you know wolves are very proud creatures - but right now Zephyr is three wolves in one. Do you understand? He must be very concrete, material, at this moment."

Martin laughed. He turned to Mr. Grek, "The biggest hot dog you have." Zephyr turned to face them and his tongue ran over his lips. Ursula tugged on Martin's sleeve and proclaimed, "I have an idea. I will write a novel about Wall Street. Martin, will you be my consultant?" Ursula didn't wait for an answer to pose her first question. "I have heard that there is a bear there. What other animals do you have in the stock market?"

"There is a bull. A bull and a bear," answered Martin while feeding Zephyr the hot dog. To Zephyr, "I apologize for my rash words, your wolf majesty."

"Only two animals?" Ursula looked disappointed. "Such a very poor place."

Martin thought for a moment and said jokingly, "Well, not just two. My girl-friend Teresa says that her boss is a rat."

"You have a rat for a boss?" Ursula thought about this, "But that means that you must be very careful where you step."

Martin took a deep breath to explain to Ursula, but she was quicker. "The Chief of Wall Street in my romance will be a stallion or perhaps a lion," said Ursula dreamily.

"Ten dollars," smiled Mr. Grek, his hand out to receive the payment.

"What?! Ten dollars for a hot dog?" asked Martin in disbelief.

"This is the usual price for out-of-towners. You must take into account that you buy your hot dog in a store where the present and future are joined – it means you pay the present price, plus the future one. And of course the sales tax at the present and future rate plus interest..."

"O.K. I understand," interjected Martin quickly to forestall another incomprehensible explanation.

Josie smiled, "Zephyr says that it would be very nice of you to buy him a subscription. A subscription like yours to the Wall Street Journal."

"Annual subscription? Wall Street Journal? He is able to read?" Martin was again astounded.

Josie rolled her eyes. "Who is speaking about reading, Martin? Zephyr wants an annual subscription of hot dogs. So every morning he can come here and eat his hot dog."

Martin shook his head. "Very smart."

"Of course, wolves *are* smart," Josie smiled sweetly at Zephyr. "He says then he will be happy that he saved your future, and he will forgive your terrible words."

Martin looked at the jolly wolf. It was extortion, but he had to smile. Martin pulled out his credit card.

"Martin," Josie asked sweetly, "seeing that you are in such a generous mood, wouldn't you like to give me a subscription to the cooking magazine, *Recipes from Martha Stewart's Kitchen*?" Martin heard a you-had-better-not-refuse tone to her voice.

Ursula touched Martin´s shoulder. "And to me a subscription to *How to Become A Professional Writer*? I will make you famous, Martin."

Martin nodded and smiled until Mr. Grek presented him with the credit card voucher for his signature.

"You were to sign here," Mr. Grek said.

Martin's smile froze when he saw the amount but he dared not question it (past and future sales tax, he supposed were involved). Then, he saw the beaming faces of Zephyr, Josie, and Ursula. He signed.

The black "Z" on his jacket turned to blue.

Martin looked out and saw his blue Mercury. He had been keen to have a blue Mercury... or was it a white Mercedes? Then he realized something else was strange.

"We must hurry home: the streets are wet, and it will soon rain," warned Josie.

"A big rain. Look at those huge puddles," said Ursula.

Martin said without thinking, "But puddles come after a rain, not before."

Josie just smiled. Ursula looked nervously at Martin. "I know I'm not meteorologically inclined, but even my brain understands that first water must evaporate from the puddles to create clouds and then the rain can come down. Isn't that the usual way?"

Josie hugged Ursula. "Of course, my dear, it is totally normal. You are aware, though, that New York is quite a strange place, and things happen differently there."

Ursula sighed in relief. "I'm really happy to live in our completely normal town. Oh, it can be boring sometimes, but at least we can be sure that the rain always comes *after* the puddles."

HOW WOLF LEARNED TO HOWL
MARGE FISHER

Marge Fisher was born October 21, 1938, in St. Louis, MO. She attended Lindenwood University as an older student while she was employed at the Federal Reserve Bank in St. Louis as a Senior Analyst and graduated with a BS in Business and a BA in Communication in 1989. Marge became a Volunteer Storyteller and Docent at the Wolf Sanctuary in St. Louis where she heard her first wolf howl and was never the same after that.

There is a very old legend of how Wolf learned to howl. As with all Legends, there is no way to prove, or to disprove, what really happened. The story is very old and has been passed down from one generation to another for a very long time.

It begins with Wolf sitting on a small rise of land under giant trees whose sprawling branches hid him very well. He was watching a group of Humans, and he thought Humans did very strange things. These Humans were sitting around a large fire. Wolf knew fire was a terrible enemy and he couldn't understand why anyone would get so close. Didn't they know that at any moment fire could jump up and kill them?

Wolf had been drawn to this spot by the strange sounds floating in the air, sounds that had drifted many miles on the night air and whispered and teased around his ears; sounds that deeply disturbed him and his mate as they lay at the mouth of their cave. Wolf *had* to follow the sound. He had left the cave in a ground-eating lope.

It was the darkest time of the month, the time between the end of the old moon and the beginning of the new; an uneasy time when strange things could happen. Now, hidden safely hidden in the trees, he watched the scene below him, watched the Humans and the fire. It almost looked as though they had caught his powerful enemy in the middle of their circle and would destroy it, but *no*, they were throwing branches at the fire and it was growing even larger! Wolf watched in amazement, almost forgetting the strange sounds that had pulled him there on strange invisible strings.

The flames leapt higher and Wolf shrunk back further into the trees. *Suddenly*, the strange noise began again, and Wolf began to tremble! The sounds gave him a shivery feeling that made his skin quiver and lifted the hair along his back; his fangs gleamed in the darkness and he began to pant. Something was happening to him that he didn't understand and couldn't control. He had to get closer! Ever so quietly Wolf crept down the hill towards the sounds.

The Humans could not see beyond the bright ring of the fire into the blackness beyond. As time went by some of them learned to sit far back from the fire and never stare directly into the flames. Death could creep quickly and quietly upon the foolish ones who could not see beyond the ring of fire into the blackness or to what stood on the other side watching and waiting for them to fall asleep, but that was not to be feared this dark uneasy night.

Wolf crept closer and closer until the strange sounds shivered through him. It wasn't enough! He *had* to get even closer to the sound. A strange little breeze tickled Wolf's ears. The breeze whispered closely guarded secrets into Wolf's willing brain and in that dark strange night unusual things began to happen.

Slowly, carefully, Wolf stretched his long frame forward, stretching with all his might. He measured almost six feet long from the tip his nose to the tip of his tail. Wolf leapt upward against the rough bark of the tree trunk, dug his sharp claws into the wood as far as he could and began to pull his long body erect! Wolf *stood!* Shaking, he braced his body against the tree. That strange little breeze whispered encouragement in Wolf's ears and the dark night became even darker.

Gray brown needles from the sheltering pine tree showered down on Wolf from above, mixed into his gray fur and made a rough looking cape that covered Wolf's body from head to toe. Slowly, awkwardly at first, Wolf began to take shaky steps forward. The night wrapped him in its magic and he began to take on the appearance of a tall, narrow shouldered, slender Human wrapped in a fuzzy gray brown blanket. Wolf began to look very much like the other Humans sitting around the leaping, dancing fire.

Ever so softly Wolf moved until he stood at the very outside of the circle, just behind a female Human with a baby strapped to her back. A few eyes *might* have glanced his way momentarily, but the fire cast flickering shadows and the blaze burned brightly into their night blinded eyes. Wolf listened, the sound rippled through him. He tingled and shivered and then, the noise *stopped!* He whined softly deep in his throat, wanting the sound to continue, *and then it began again!* His soul stirred. He listened and listened and when he could stand it no longer, he turned and ran back toward the protection of the trees.

Wolf wasn't as careful this time. A small Human who had been asleep opened her eyes and saw a tall Human in a soft grey brown blanket, drop to all fours and lope away. "WOLF! WOLF!" she screamed, but no one heard her above the noise. She stared into the darkness, but Wolf was gone never to join a campfire again.

Far up on the ridge, Wolf rested, he was panting heavily. He shook himself vigorously and grey brown needles flew everywhere, but the taunting, teasing noise that had followed him in his headlong race up the hill continued to torment him with its presence.

Gradually, the tension became so unbearable that Wolf lifted his face to the sky and sent note after note of glorious sound flying towards the stars. The Humans, *singing* around their campfire below stopped in hushed silence to listen. What is that sound they asked one another? The little female Human toddled into the circle and cried, "WOLF! WOLF!" but her mother snatched her quickly away from the flames thinking she could be burned. No one heard her voice.

Far up on the hill, Wolf sang and sang. He couldn't help himself, it felt so good. A few miles away his mate heard his howls and lifted her face to the sky to join him in the first Wolf song ever heard. She too felt the joyful pull of the music and she sang her song to the stars and to her mate.

From that day to this Wolf loves to howl and Humans still love to sing around a campfire. They should however, remember to *never, ever* stare into the flames. There is no way to tell what may be out there watching them!

THE HUNTER
JENNY H. THORNTON WOODLEY

The Hunter. Photography.

IDENTITY CRISIS:
FROM THE FILES OF DEPARTMENT 118
LAYSON A. WILLIAMS

Based in Sacramento, California, Layson Williams writes science-fiction, non-fiction, and fantasy stories, as well as fictional tales based on religious beliefs. He published in the final issue of the now-defunct magazine Fang, Claw and Steel. *Rough drafts of other stories can be found online through* The Werewolf Cafe, *and he is looking for "more opportunities to introduce the World to the world in his head." When not working full time, Layson enjoys watching the comic book world unfold on the silver screen and checking Facebook.*

1

The familiarity of her desk gave little comfort. Kate knew this day would come. She was fully aware of the stipulation: three or more reports of the same subject matter, within a six month period, required mandatory investigation by an appropriate department of the American Empire.

It couldn't be Department 41, who dealt with wild animal reports. No, it was Department 118. They already came to town regularly to manage the scooper population. It was Dep:118 who recommended Kate come to Loughlin to discuss her dreams, rehabilitate. Now they would learn of the change in her dreams, the tracks in her back yard. They would learn what she had become. But what were their intentions? Kate abhorred the thought of being gunned down, or put in a cell for study, or sliced open on a cold metal slab. Her stomach clenched with the thought.

She studied the agents as they made their way through reception. They were different from the usual pair. This man was young with brown hair, a straight nose and strong eyebrows. He acted timid, but his eyes took notice of everything. Not good. The woman wore shoulder-length straight hair, raven-black, and had high cheekbones along with other Native American features. She stood with confidence and authority, a military posture. Even worse.

What did Uncle Ollie say that one time? 'Keep your friends close and your enemies closer?' She wasn't sure these agents were enemies, but the more she knew about their intentions the better.

With a scoot back from her desk, Kate stood and straightened her pony tail keeping a full head of chestnut hair out of her face. She looked at the paper mache dinosaurs on her desk, each a gift from Ollie's son Tristan. Kate patted the triceratops on the head with her finger and asked it to wish her luck, then made for Ollie's office. Soon she heard the elevated tones within.

"Three reports submitted of the same subject in six months, Sheriff. That's a mandatory investigation."

"Wrong. There were only two reports."

"You sent the missing one to Dep:41, knowing fully well Mr. Riley Banks claimed it was a werewolf in both reports, not a wild animal."

It sounded like the woman agent had Ollie cornered. Odd, Uncle Ollie didn't make mistakes like that – not intentionally, anyway.

"Oh, he claimed werewolf on both? Oops, missed that." His sarcasm betrayed his intention.

"Enough, Sheriff. You knew what you were doing. That alone constitutes misdirection. This investigation starts now, and you are required to give us full cooperation. If I get the slightest inkling you're misdirecting or neglecting, in any way, I'll throw the whole Empire at you. Do I make myself clear?"

Kate stood behind the agents. Ollie's hazel eyes burned fiercely. The female agent leaned over Ollie's desk, her fists planted almost into the wood. Her cold stare glared all manner of intimidation at him. Ollie was stubborn as a mule sometimes. But the agent's stare along with the threat hanging in the air whittled away at his resolve. "Crystal."

"Good." The woman stood up. "Now, we require an escort as we interview Mr. Tippowitz and Mr. Banks."

"Well, that's a problem, because one of my deputies is out sick and the other is dealing with crap since before you got here. You'll have to wait."

"Then you can take us."

"Sorry, Town council meeting today. No way out of it."

"Didn't I just tell you how important it is you to cooperate with me?!"

"Rachel?" The male agent's voice came across firm, but discreet.

"Not now, Chris."

"Mind if I step in?"

"Yes!" She looked around at the male agent, and then sighed annoyingly. "Fine, whatever." She stood back, surrendering the discussion to her partner.

"Sheriff Taylor, I'm new in Loughlin. I don't know about the situations here. I'm told Dep:118 comes to your town frequently without trouble, but now you're set on avoiding this case. The only difference I see is the subject of investigation. Why are you so concerned this time?"

Ollie leaned back in his chair and sighed, visibly calming down. "Loughlin is different than any other isolation colony. Others have to be completely self-sustaining, as little contact with the Empire as possible." He shook his head. "Not us. We're the Empire's little 'satellite.' Our population is made of all those who feel ridiculed by Imperial society – alien abduction victims, faulty genetic mutations, apocalypse heralds, you name it. They come here to get away from the mockery of everyone else. More show up every year. The Empire follows their numbers and progress regularly. I got no problem with that."

"Then what is the problem?"

"The problem is you two and why you came. People here are very susceptible to conspiracy theories and paranoia. If you guys come prancing around interrogating people about werewolf sightings, you'll start a riot." Ollie flamboyantly waved his hand toward the front of the building. "And then you'll just waltz right on out. We don't need you stirring up the sewage and leaving my guys to clean up the mess."

"I see your point, Sheriff. But if there really is some creature out there, you're sure to have more sightings. And if that creature attacks, you won't be able to stop a riot from happening no matter how hard you try. Wouldn't it be better to investigate the issue now, discreetly, and maybe resolve it before it goes too far?"

Huh. The male agent considered Ollie's concerns seriously, and agreed with them. Kate was a little surprised. Of course it could all be a 'good cop, bad cop' performance; it certainly felt that way.

Ollie stared at the male agent for a few seconds. A smile almost manifested, but not quite. "Discreetly?" He pointed at the male agent. "Okay, you I like. But it still doesn't change the fact that I have no escort."

"I can take them." The words were out before Kate even realized it. All eyes turned to her, but she focused on Ollie's.

"Kate, you're not a deputy."

"Well, n-no, but it's just taking them over to visit Earl and Riley, right? I know where they both live."

"Katie, I can't use you in the field in official capacity. You're not qualified."

"If I may, Sheriff." Wow. He actually raised his hand. "If Kate stays in the car and only Miss Blackwood and I go to their doors, we'd merely be using her as a guide. Would that still qualify as official capacity?"

Ollie took a deep breath and exhaled slowly, staring at his desk for a moment. He clamped his forehead with his right hand, his salt-and-pepper hair cascading over the thenar space. "I suppose, but I still don't like it." He looked at Kate. "Are you absolutely *sure* about this?"

Kate shrugged. It wasn't like she could get out of it now. "Yeah, I'm sure."

"Be careful. And don't give Riley any cause for panic, you hear me?"

"I'll be okay."

Ollie raised his eyebrows and gestured to Kate. "Alright, well, there's your guide. Kate Crenshaw, meet Rachel Blackwood and Christopher Hansen from Dep:118."

Kate greeted them as she shook their hands. The man had a steady and firm handshake, but the woman squeezed too hard.

"You ready to go now?" Agent Blackwood asked.

"I guess so."

"Good." She bade farewell to the Sheriff with a nod and walked out of the office.

Agent Hansen stayed behind and shook Ollie's hand, thanking him once again. He offered to follow Kate out of the office, something of a gentleman. "By the way, Miss Crenshaw, you can call me Chris."

"Thanks, and it's Kate."

As they left the building, Kate hoped she wouldn't regret entering a first name basis.

2

The agents led her to an old fashioned ground-bound vehicle, a four-door car with a small open cargo area in the back. It looked like a cross between a car and a truck. Kate expected imperial agents to be flying a craft, not driving a car, but she was not in a position to complain; she didn't own any type of transport.

Chris opened the back door and Kate climbed in. The two agents took the front seats, with agent Blackwood piloting the vehicle. As they continued, Chris started a conversation by asking Kate what she knew about Earl Tippowitz.

"Not much. He's a scooper like me, one of the more stable ones. He only stays here in the hope of getting some answers, but he makes regular visits to his family up north as long as the Empire allows it. That's where he was heading when he saw whatever he saw." Well, might as well put out some feelers now. "So do you guys really think it was a werewolf?"

Chris shrugged. "Stranger things have happened, believe us. Forgive me for prying, Kate, but you said Mr. Tippowitz was a 'scooper' like you. What's a scooper?"

Kate resisted rolling her eyes. This guy works for Dep:118 and he doesn't know what a scooper is? He must be *really* new.

"Slang for an alien abductee," Agent Blackwood explained.

"I see. May I ask when you were abducted?"

"Sometime after I left Serendipity."

"The isolation colony?"

"Yeah. Mom moved there after the Empire finished some mutation project. I hated it. Even before I turned nineteen I kept saying my destiny wasn't going to be in Serendipity."

Chris huffed.

Kate stared out the window, watching the scenery pass by. "Anyway, I ended up in Aisleton and started having nightmares. An imperial counselor put me in touch with your Department. Two of your agents interviewed me and recommended I come here for support."

"Two of our agents?"

"Scott and Emily," Agent Blackwood said. "They head up the scooper cases."

"Ah. Do you know a lot of the locals?"

Kate shrugged. "I guess. I know Earl because he was in support groups with me from earlier on, but I know Riley only by reputation. He's an old coot – he lives alone, hunts his own food, barricades his land, that kind of thing. You know how Ollie was worried about paranoia causing a riot?"

Chris nodded.

"Well Riley would probably be one of the starters. He'd spread the word like crazy if he thought the end was coming."

"Is he an abduct– I mean, a scooper as well?"

Kate shook her head. "Not that I know of. He treats us like we're spies for the aliens."

"Hence Sheriff Taylor telling you to be careful."

"Yep."

Chris looked at his partner. "He'll be fun to visit, like the Owens case, remember?"

"Don't remind me." The agent kept focus on her driving.

Kate paused. She tried to think of some other question to ask, but her mind kept returning to the same one.

"So, you guys get a lot of werewolf sightings being reported?"

"Tri-monthly," Agent Blackwood answered.

"That's across the entire globe," Chris added. "A lot of area to cover. There might be more that aren't reported."

The shock of the statement pulsed through her. They had other reports! And apparently they were regular enough to consider with callus. "Um, wow! D-Do you find any? Werewolves, I mean?"

She watched as Chris inquired of Agent Blackwood with his eyes. His partner responded in kind, only with a look. Kate was not in a position to see her expression, but the answer from Chris indicated a negative response.

"We can't go into any detail at this time, but we have made some… undeniable discoveries."

No way could Kate have expected this. These lukewarm answers spawned a flood of questions. Were there actually others out there? Where? What did they do with them? Was there any way to lift the curse? Fear tempered her excitement, for the answers could bring terror as much as ease. She would have to wait and see how they handled the case.

But hopefully it wouldn't take too long. Kate already stared at her desk calendar regularly, even more so as the full moon approached.

Tomorrow night was a full moon. No matter how she looked at it, time was running out.

<h2 style="text-align:center"><u>3</u></h2>

Earl Tippowitz lived in a simple apartment complex, neither gated nor painted nor otherwise maintained. Each of its three buildings stood two stories tall, encompassing at least five units each. The complex avoided a unique presence, and such was the case for most of its residents. Kate pointed out the apartment which Earl Tippowitz called home. Agent Blackwood parked the vehicle in visitor parking, in the shade of a row of trees. Though summer was beginning to make its presence known daily, it had yet to reach a point of discomfort. In line with Ollie's conditions, Kate stayed in the car as both agents disembarked.

The agents knocked on Earl's front door. Earl answered, looking indifferent until the agents introduced themselves. As he invited them inside Kate unbuckled her seat belt and shifted in the back seats, stretching out as much as she could. It might be a while for all she knew. Resting her head on her folded arm, she slightly bent one leg over the other and gently closed her eyes.

She started thinking about her family back in Serendipity. Maybe at some point she could apply for an imperial visitation permit. It would be nice to see her family again. She reminisced about their traditional places at the table, ready to eat the pot roast Mom and her older sister prepared. Ever so gently her conscious gave way to her subconscious as her breathing slowed, and a gentle breeze whispering through the open windows swayed her mind into dreaming.

Kate found herself driving an old pickup along an even older highway, en route to see her family. The media player started an ancient folk song about country roads taking the singer home, and the coincidence brought a smile. She looked on ahead into the night, noticing how the headlights complimented the abundant light of a full moon.

A deer stood in the highway up ahead. Kate tapped the brakes to allow the deer enough time to notice her vehicle, and to swerve around the animal if necessary. Suddenly the back of the vehicle sank. She glanced into the left side mirror, but saw nothing. She used the mirror on the right, and saw a shadow climbing into the bed of the truck.

Reinforced with knowledge of the deer, Kate pressed hard on the brakes. The screech of the tires startled the deer and it ran into the northern woods. And then, after the truck had come to a stop, the back rose. Whatever was hitching a ride back there disembarked. She leaned toward the right side mirror, trying to get a better view. In the bottom corner of the mirror she saw something moving. She froze.

Out from the darkness, a face appeared through the passenger window and glared at her with angry hazel eyes, rusted gray fur upon its lupine face. Its jowls bared white fangs among its teeth. It growled, and Kate vaulted to the other side of the cab, slamming her back against the driver door.

Kate shut her eyes as hard as she could, her breaths erratic.

After seconds of nothing happening, Kate opened one eye slowly, then the other. The face glaring at her before was no longer there. Ever so gently she pulled herself up to look over the hood of the truck, and saw nothing in the headlights. She peered across the moonlit landscape, and again saw nothing. She exhaled her breath in relief.

A furred arm crashed through the driver window, grabbing her shoulder.

Kate screamed out loud. But amongst her scream was another voice.

"Kate! It's all right! You're okay!"

Kate looked around, eyes wide with terror. She was in the back of the agents' car. After reaching back to wake her, Chris held his hands up in surrender.

"I didn't mean to startle you."

Rachel started the engine. "She's a scooper. You should have known better."

Chris dropped his arms. "Well, you could have warned me."

"No, you need to learn. And this was more entertaining."

Chris sighed and turned to Kate, assessing her status. "Must have been some dream."

Kate focused through her bemusement. "Yeah, bit of a nightmare."

Chris nodded. "Were you remembering your abduction?"

She shook off the fogginess. "What? Oh, no, I haven't had one of those in a year and a half. This was… this was something else."

"Wait a minute." Agent Blackwood looked back over her shoulder from the driver's seat. "You haven't had any recurring abduction dreams for over a year?"

Kate nodded. "Yeah, that's right. Why?"

"Did you report this?"

"No. I figured I was cured."

"What? What do you mean, cured?"

"Wait, Rachel, what's the problem?" Chris asked.

"Scoopers don't just stop having their dreams," She turned back to Kate. "Did you stop going to your support group too?"

"Well, yeah. Ollie suggested I take a break, so one day I did. That's when I stopped having the dreams, so I just… never went back."

"And that didn't seem the slightest bit significant to you?"

"No, not really."

"Rachel," Chris interrupted, "Calm down. What's the big deal?"

"Think about it. Kate left the group and the dreams went away. What if the support groups are prolonging the dreams? What if others want to be free of them?"

"Well, wouldn't we need to get more facts before we jump to that conclusion?"

"Absolutely, and we could have been investigating those facts a year ago if Kate reported it."

"Right, back off." His voice changed – there was a guttural quality now, his air almost as stern as his partner's. "If this needs further research, we'll call it in. But you're not here for that. Now, let's go and see Mr. Banks."

They both stared at each other, a silent battle of wills each reinforcing the points already made. Finally, Agent Blackwood broke the silence.

"Whatever." She put the car in gear.

Somebody needed to change the subject. "So, um, did you guys find out anything more from Earl?"

"Not really," Chris replied. His voice seemed back to normal. "He pretty much confirmed the report, except added a little more on what the creature looked like. It's been nearly six months since it happened, so his memory of the event might not be accurate."

"Well, don't sell him short. Some scoopers get training to remember dream details as clearly as possible. Earl signed up for it." Kate turned to the view out her window. "I didn't."

Chris nodded. "Good to keep in mind. Thanks."

Kate shrugged.

She continued the trip in silence, staring out the window at the familiarity of Loughlin. The nature of this new dream disturbed her. With all the others, Kate saw things from her own point of view - ensuring her home was safely secured, or bounding over a fence, or running off into the forest. This dream was different; the werewolf was outside of her, she was the victim.

Why did she have this dream? Was her guilty conscience replaying the incident from her victim's perspective? That didn't sound right–it wasn't like she killed Earl or Riley. In fact, she hadn't killed anyone according to the census. Surely a missing person would have been reported by now.

So the question persisted, why? Why this dream? Why did she view herself from Earl's view?

Earl's report. Ah, there's the answer. She skimmed through the report just before the agents arrived. Now she was taking the agents to Earl's place. Her subconscious merely added recent thoughts to her dream. It was known to happen with scoopers. What a cruel trick for her subconscious to play!

And relief set in, she could explain it away. But the recurrence of her lycanthropic nightmares still fertilized her apprehension. Also, the presence of these agents watered her unease. Fortunately Chris Hansen's personable nature provided some solace. It was not enough for her to trust him with her secret, but it provided a measure of hope. At this point she could use all the hope she could get.

A one-story home with little more than a roof and walls served as the abode of Riley Banks–at least, that's how it looked from the outside. Ollie sent deputies out here more than once, and they testified to the structural reinforcements as well as a large and varied arsenal. Although the quantity of arms raised alarm for many, Riley always had the appropriate licenses and certificates and kept them up to date. If there was ever an invasion, nearly everyone in Loughlin would try for Riley's house.

But Riley was not at all fond of unannounced visitors. Kate hoped Ollie called in advance to announce their arrival.

As the car came to a halt in front of Riley's house, Chris looked back at her.

"Kate, does Mr. Banks know you at all?"

Kate shrugged. "I'm not sure he'd recognize me, if that's what you're asking."

Chris frowned. "Things might go more smoothly if he saw a familiar face with us. I know we promised Sheriff Taylor you'd stay in the car, but how would you feel about coming with us on this one?"

Kate eyed him. "He doesn't like scoopers, remember?"

Chris inclined his head, acknowledging the point. "Right. Well, this time it may take a bit longer; you may be in the car for a while. I was just offering, because-"

"Because of a bad dream?"

Chris winced and cocked his head as he nodded slowly.

Kate flashed a weak smile, appreciating the concern. "Well, it would be nice to stretch my legs. I'll give it a try."

The three disembarked, making their way to the front door.

"That's far enough!" commanded a voice from inside.

"Riley Banks?"

"Who wants to know?"

"Rachel Blackwood from Department 118 of the Empire. This is Chris Hansen and Kate Crenshaw." She gestured to both.

"Ollie said you'd show up." So Ollie did call ahead for them. Good old Ollie. "What's she doing here?"

Rachel tipped her head in Kate's direction. "She knows where you live. We didn't. We're here to ask about your wild animal encroachment."

"No you're not. That's Dep:41. You're Dep:118. You're here 'cause I said it was a werewolf."

"That's absolutely right, Mr. Banks," Chris said. "We're here to let the facts speak for themselves. Unfortunately we don't have enough to support a conclusion. Can you help us with getting more facts on the case?"

"It's all in the report."

"Not true," Agent Blackwood contested. "The deputies didn't do a thorough job. We also want to get the story from your own words, not translated through biased deputies. Now do you want someone to take you seriously or not?"

Astounding. How could Agent Blackwood have so much aggressiveness and so little tact, and still be in a job dealing with the public? Yet even more to Kate's surprise, Riley's front door opened. He emerged cautiously, a shotgun held with both hands but pointed toward the ground. He peered at each of the three in turn, obviously uncertain how much leeway to grant them.

"You read the report. What do you think it is?"

"It's an unexplained creature," Agent Blackwood said. "Whether it was a werewolf, Chupacabra or some other creature remains to be determined."

"I know what I saw! It was a werewolf!"

"Then rest assured, the scratches and prints will confirm that," Chris added. "May we see them?"

Seconds passed by as Riley seemed to battle for control over his suspicion. "Follow me." He walked around the left side of his house.

"Owens case," Chris sang.

"Shut up, Chris," Agent Blackwood sang back.

They followed Riley, but soon Riley told them to stay back. He precariously stepped toward a small shack made from cinderblocks, much newer than the house. After Riley disarmed or manually set off several traps surrounding the shed, he waved to approach.

Agent Blackwood jutted her jaw at the shed. "What do you keep in there?"

"My kills. It's where I clean 'em."

"That explains interest in the building." Chris took a closer look at the metal door and its locks. "According to the first report, the creature crashed through the door."

"Yeah, that's right."

"So is this not the same door?"

Riley shook his head. "You kidding? The first one was nothin' but splinters after the first attack. I replaced it, reinforced all the hinges. The second time around it tore the latch off but couldn't get past the deadbolts."

"Looks like you got a shot off." Agent Blackwood pointed to a discolored indentation in one of the corner cinderblocks.

Riley nodded. "A few rounds, but never hit it. Damn thing was fast."

Chris stood from inspecting the markings. "Mr. Banks, what do you see when you look at these scratches?"

Riley shrugged. "Slash marks."

"Well, you'll be happy to know there's more to see." Chris pointed to the area around the locks. "Whatever did this slashed the door only after trying the locks. A wild animal couldn't understand to try the locks first. It shows high intelligence, so a wild animal is pretty much ruled out."

"What about a Sasquatch?" Kate asked.

"No claws," Agent Blackwood said. "And they're herbivores."

"So this creature is intelligent, has claws, and eats meat," Chris surmised. "Certainly narrows it down. What about the tracks you reported?"

"It's been a month. They'll be useless."

Chris shot Agent Blackwood a look which encouraged holding her tongue, at least that was how Kate interpreted it. "Mr. Banks, could you show me those tracks?"

Riley grunted, and took them behind the shack twenty meters into the tree line. He looked around to get his bearings, and led them to an area with disturbed grass. "They're here somewhere. You'll have to look around."

Both agents began looking for tracks, and it was not long before Chris found them. He squatted for a closer examination and then looked up. "Into the woods..." He mused. "Rachel, is my backpack still in the car?"

"Yeah."

He stood and exhaled. "I'm going to follow them. I might lose the tracks a few times–like Rachel said, they're pretty old." He looked at Rachel. "I'll call you if I need a pickup."

"Wait a minute," Riley interjected. "You're just gonna walk out there in the woods after a werewolf?"

Rachel sighed. "Three things: first, the tracks are a month old, and likely won't lead back to the creature's lair. If it does, Chris knows what to do. Second, he has items of protection in his backpack. Third, it's still daylight and the moon isn't full yet. We know what we're doing."

"But how is he going to contact you?" Kate asked.

Rachel looked at Chris. "Yes, Christopher. How do you intend to do that with no phone?"

He ignored her patronizing tone. "I'll make my way to town and borrow a vidphone, probably. In the meantime why don't you go over the events with Mr. Banks? You can fill me in when I get back."

She turned to Riley. "You mind going over the facts again, Mr. Banks?"

"S'pose not." He looked at Chris suspiciously. Kate agreed.

"Okay then, I'll go get my backpack and start on my way. Thanks again for your cooperation, Mr. Banks." Chris offered his hand to

Riley.

Riley accepted the hand and shook it. Then, with a smile upon his lips, Chris walked toward the car and left the other three to discuss the details of Riley's reports.

4

When Agent Blackwood's personality and Riley's paranoia met across the table, it didn't take long before deliberations broke into heated debate, and then became a flaming disaster. At one final point Riley stood up, his shotgun appearing magically in his hands, and demanded they leave. Agent Blackwood kept quiet all the way back to the Sheriff's office, which Kate appreciated. This agent was like a smart bomb, seeking out the weak links in a person's defenses and striking with overbearing force. It didn't encourage trust. Well, at least she'd be gone soon.

The past day, filled to the brim with worries and bad dreams, took its toll upon Kate. She clocked out at work, went home to change and then headed to the local tavern. In this town it was just about the only place to go when a person wanted to unwind, besides reading some second-hand books at Gary's little bookstore. Kate preferred the tavern.

She sat at a table with Ollie and a deputy named Fred, each enjoying a bottle of beer along with each other's company. The tavern was stuffy but not smoky, cozy but not cramped, offering welcome to any traveler. It had a finished wood décor, and a fire radiated heat from inside a pot-belly stove surrounded by tables. A low murmur of mingled voices and music hummed in the air. As Kate sipped her pint both men prodded about her excursion with Dep:118 agents.

"They're taking everything about it seriously," Kate reported, "and they seem to be objective about it too. At least Chris does–I mean, Agent Hansen." She noted Ollie darting a look when she used the first name. "It's like he investigates, but the other one interrogates."

"Ah, Agent Blackwood," Fred nodded. "Yeah, she's always that way. It's been a while since she was last here, though. I was hoping she changed, but guess not."

"Good cop, bad cop," Ollie said with a matter-of-fact tone. "It's a classic."

Kate shook her head. "But they're not playing it like that. It's more like she clears the obstacles and then he goes in to find answers."

"Is he finding any?"

"I think so. He ruled out wild animals at Riley's place."

Ollie furrowed his brow. "How'd he do that?"

"Now's your chance to ask him." Fred glanced his dark blue eyes toward the bar and jutted his chin in the same direction.

Walking up to the bar was Agent Hansen, looking around timidly as he approached. His hair—was it longer? No, it must be the light.

"That's him, right?" Fred asked. "He's not a local."

Kate looked at Ollie, her eyes inquiring if he was going to approach the agent.

"No thanks." Ollie sipped the animosity from his bottle.

"Alright, fine." Kate took a lasting swig from her glass and stood. "Then I will."

Kate felt Ollie's widened eyes follow her as she slipped out from between the chair and table. She twitched her head to the right, cascading her unrestrained chestnut hair behind her shoulders. She looked at Ollie once more, giving him a confident wink as she left.

Kate approached the bar on the right side of Chris, overhearing him confirm with the bartender that a certain beer was on tap. The agent ordered a glass and Kate repeated the request for herself. Steve, the bartender, gave her a knowing glance and then left to get both drinks. She looked over to Chris. "Hey."

"Hey." His eyes smiled along with his lips.

"I didn't expect you'd be back so soon."

Chris shrugged. "It only took a few hours. I lost the tracks about a dozen times, didn't find much more than an old carcass."

"Was it from the, um, creature?"

"Too decomposed to tell for sure, but the marks in the bone indicate something big fed on it."

"A werewolf?"

Chris cocked his head and raised his eyebrows. "Could be."

Kate tried to put on a false face, scoffing in disbelief. "So you honestly believe werewolves are real, don't you?"

Chris looked her directly in the eye, a shrewd smirk barely making presence on his lips. "As real as aliens."

While Steve provided the drinks and collected the tender, Kate thought about what Chris said. 'As real as aliens.' Chris knew she was a scooper. That was it; he was saying he knew werewolves existed as well. But if they were real, why the secrecy? What's more, what did they do once they found them? "Have you, um, seen any werewolves for yourself?"

Chris sighed. "I'm sorry, Kate, I can't say."

"Why not? I mean, if they're real, don't people have the right to know?"

"Certainly, in good time."

"What? You need to wait 'til they're ripe?"

Chris let out a weak laugh. "No, but we don't want to cause a panic either. Look, it took almost two centuries before we had definitive proof Sasquatch was real. When they announced it, what happened? A mass exodus to the forests, everybody trying to catch one. The Empire had to step in with heavy restrictions. They even had to use the GORE a few times. If we prove werewolves exist and make the announcement the wrong way, we'll get the same thing, only this time with guns and pitchforks involved."

Kate conceded the point. It made sense, but it still boiled down to the Empire withholding information in her opinion. "So, why are you on this case, anyway? Are you some sort of werewolf expert?"

Chris laughed again. "Oh, I wouldn't say expert. Specialist, maybe."

"But you're more than just an enthusiast for werewolf rights, huh?"

Chris once again looked her in the eye, and then returned his gaze to his drink. "Yes."

Finally, a direct answer! Kate was more captivated than ever, but from curiosity, not fear or worry. Chris was hesitant, reclusive concerning his knowledge, but something in his eyes said he didn't want it that way. Suddenly a theory came to mind. She had to find out, but discreetly. There had to be a way to ask the question without asking it.

"It's personal, isn't it? Something about werewolves happened to you, didn't it?"

Very slowly Chris picked up his drink and forcibly imbibed, taking time. He set the glass on the bar, looking down at the wood surface. His expression hardened for a second, and then his mouth began to open. Time froze as Kate eagerly awaited the emerging words.

"I never knew my parents. When I tried to find them-"

He stopped abruptly as Ollie's face appeared, staring from the left side of Chris.

"So Agent Hansen, you mind explaining your intentions toward Kate?"

Chris glanced at Kate, and then returned his attention to Ollie. "I- I'm sorry; intentions?"

"You heard me." Ollie's low tone was almost threatening.

Oh, this just wasn't fair! Kate stepped in before it was too late. "Everything's okay, Uncle Ollie. He's being quite a gentleman."

"Uncle?" Chris put up his arms in surrender. "Look, I'm only here for a drink. Kate had a few questions, that's all. I honestly have no intentions toward your niece, Sheriff."

Ollie leaned in toward Chris, a malicious smile upon his lips. "She's not my niece, Agent Hansen."

No, no, no; this wasn't right! Ollie was ruining everything at just the wrong time! She had to win back Chris' confidence. Kate gave Ollie a warning glare. "He means I'm not his niece by relation. Ollie and his family took me under their wing when I first got here. I became an unofficial member of his family, so I call him Uncle Ollie."

"Ah," Chris raised his eyebrows and nodded. "Actually I can understand that. Back at the office everyone calls our boss 'Dad', mostly because he treats us that way."

"How interesting." Kate raised her head and addressed Ollie. "See? We're just two people with mutual respect having a pleasant conversation. If it makes you feel any better I promise to go home alone, alright?"

Ollie smiled and perked up. "Good. See you tomorrow, Katie girl."

"Yeah, thanks Uncle Ollie." Kate couldn't tell if her sarcasm was audible.

Ollie gave an affirmative grunt, said farewell to the rest of the occupants, and left out the door. When Kate looked back at Chris. He was staring at Ollie's departure intently, his brows furrowed. Kate leaned toward him and spoke consolingly.

"Sorry about that. He gets a little overprotective at times. Besides, I think he just wanted to ruffle your feathers for fun."

"Then you'll understand if I start molting."

Kate laughed.

Chris drained the last of his drink, swallowing it down with a grimace. "On that note, I think I'll call it a night."

She was so close! She desperately searched for some way to repair the conversation, but to no avail. She simply *had* to find out more. Not tonight, though–not without looking like she was coming on to him anyway, and she wasn't about to go down that road. "Are you guys leaving tomorrow?"

"Uh, no. The day after, at the soonest. Tomorrow night's the full moon. That's why we came here when we did."

Oh, he just had to remind her. "Alright, well, if there's anything else I can do…"

Chris smiled. "I'll definitely let you know. And I thank you for all the help you've already provided, Kate. It was a blessing."

Kate smiled meekly. "Anytime."

With one last sincere look, Chris turned and exited the tavern, and Kate spent the rest of the night grappling with forgiving Ollie freely.

5

D-day. D-day. The phrase pounded in her head, chipping at her resolve in rhythm to her heartbeat. Tonight's full moon would define the rest of her life. Kate considered sedating and tying herself up as she did once before, but last time she woke up with the restraints severed, dirty paw prints leading into her house from the sliding glass door in her bedroom. Locking herself in a closet resulted in similar escape. Chris was right–she was pretty intelligent as a werewolf, and there seemed no taming the beast. But that was only as far as _she_ knew. Chris Hansen knew more.

Back at the Sheriff's office, Kate could do was anticipate the agents' arrival. Maybe some false report would get them in here sooner. Maybe she should simply turn herself in, but she still didn't know what their intentions really were.

The two agents finally arrived and went directly to Ollie's office. Kate didn't even feign an excuse. Trying to hide her agitated nerves, she followed them right in. Ollie, of course, objected to her presence. It was typical and expected.

"Come on, Ollie, you already let me help once."

"Once is enough."

Chris analyzed her with narrowed eyes, and then smirked. "Budding interest, or bored behind the desk?"

"The first one."

Chris continued his gaze.

"The second one."

His gaze did not falter, but he added one raised eyebrow to his smirk.

"Alright, both."

His smirk brightened into a smile.

Kate turned to Ollie. "Can't you let me stay in the loop just this once, please? Pleeeeease?"

Ollie put both hands to his forehead. "Great, I've created a monster."

"Monsters are people too, Sheriff."

Ollie looked up at Chris for a moment. He then sighed and looked at Kate. "Alright, you can sit in. But no more field work." He emphasized the stipulation with his finger.

"Thanks, Uncle Ollie," Kate said, and then gave him a big, embarrassing hug.

"'Uncle?'" Agent Blackwood inquired.

"The Raymond Collins of the Sheriff's office," Chris explained.

"Lovely." She didn't try hard enough to hide her annoyance.

Chris unfolded a map across the Sheriff's desk and explained their plan. They wanted to lure the creature in a way that would verify its identity and also allow capture. He pointed out two ridges and an imaginary line, and explained they needed to be sprayed with a special organic chemical used to simulate wolf boundaries. The boundaries would create a singular travel route, directly into the property of Mr. Banks.

"We already discussed it with Mr. Banks and he agreed–if for no other reason than to prove he isn't crazy." Agent Blackwood crossed her arms.

"We'll need the manpower to spread the chemical and be in position to flank it if necessary," Chris added.

Ollie continued to stare at the map. "You really think this will work?"

Chris shrugged. "It's worked in the past, it should work this time too, unless they've become self-aware."

Suddenly Kate was very pleased she took a chance at attending. This was almost too good to be true! "What do you mean, self-aware?"

"Well, most people believe a werewolf has no choice but to change form on the night of a full moon. So if a person actually becomes a werewolf, they submit to that idea. Their conscious mind retracts and the subconscious takes over, dominated by wolf instincts. We call that state 'primal.' But they're never a mindless, raging beast, because that's not a wolf's nature."

"So you're saying they'll act more like a wolf, not a monster?" Kate asked.

"Exactly. Once they learn to invoke the shift on their own, they become self-aware in their werewolf form. If they're self-aware, they'll likely see right through this trap. But if they're still primal, this will work."

A flood of possibilities threatened to overtake Kate's mind. It was actually possible to be in control, to be self-aware in her werewolf form! She just needed to know how to take control. Surprisingly, it was Ollie who asked the question for her.

"So if they're not tied to the full moon, how do they change?"

Chris looked at his partner. "They're interested. And they're taking it seriously."

She scoffed. "It's your funeral."

As Agent Blackwood closed the door Chris leaned toward Kate and Ollie, who responded in kind.

"What I'm about to tell you is confidential, but I'm willing to clear you for it. Even so, I need to make sure you won't spread it around."

Kate nodded in full anticipation, Ollie did the same.

"Alright. First off, werewolves prefer the term 'Lupan' as the name of their species, like how people are called humans. As to how they change, here's a toned-down version. Lupans can hear and adjust the frequency at which their body molecules vibrate. All they have to do is find the hum, think of the tone they want it to be, and the frequency will change accordingly. Their entire body will follow suit by changing physical form as their molecules respond."

"Then why do they change on the full moon?" asked Ollie.

"Their conscious mind doesn't know it can control the shift, let alone how, but their subconscious does. When the full moon rises the person surrenders their conscious mind, simply because they think that's what's supposed to happen. Their subconscious takes over and invokes the shift. Once they learn to control the shift, however, their subconscious doesn't take control anymore."

"So they get to be themselves in a werewolf body?" Kate asked.

"In a lupan body, yes. Of course, a huge amount of responsibility comes with this ability, but a self-aware lupan could lead a full life in the Empire, among the rest of its citizens, as long as they're careful."

The well of hope in Kate's heart flowed freely, watering the rest of her existence.

"So there could be lupans walking among us right now," Ollie commented.

Chris nodded. "You're right. There may be an unknown number of lupans walking among us," he brought up a finger to emphasize his point, "not causing any harm."

"That we know of," Agent Blackwood finished.

Chris let out an exasperated sigh.

Ollie leaned back in his chair, rocking slowly. "What about silver?"

Chris narrowed his eyes. "Why would you ask that, Sheriff?"

"Precaution."

Chris sighed. "Sheriff, this lupan is not a danger. Look at the facts: it's only been sighted by two people and it didn't attack either one. It went for the deer instead of Mr. Tippowitz, though he was the easier target. It went for Mr. Banks' food cache twice, but it didn't go after him."

"Fair enough, but I've seen wild animals cornered. If we're gonna try and capture it, we'll need precautions."

"We use tranquilizer rounds only," Agent Blackwood interjected. "No exceptions."

Kate tried to get more information. "But silver-"

"Is not an option," Chris replied, an uncharacteristically darkened tone. His resilience on the issue was unmovable, and that guttural tone came back. He turned back to Ollie. "I want your absolute word on that, Sheriff."

Ollie nodded, looking at Chris with an indefinable expression. "No silver."

Chris sighed in relief. "Thank you. Now, a shipment of our chemical should arrive in two hours, and we have sanction to use it on forest vegetation. It will dissipate over time; it doesn't have any lasting effects. We'll need to get it in place on the ridges by sundown. Can that be arranged?"

Ollie thought for a moment. "I'll call up Paul Krauss. He's got a retired duster but he maintained just in case."

"That should work nicely, as long as we distribute it in spurts, not a constant mist."

Ollie raised a finger. "One other thing: if you capture this…'lupan,' then what happens?"

Chris shrugged. "It's up to them. We can introduce them to other lupans, they can learn more about their heritage." He cocked his head. "But if they want to be a monster instead… well, that's how they'll be treated."

"We'll take action based on their choice, not ours." Agent Blackwood spoke with a solid finality.

"If that's all, Sheriff, we do have a few other things to prepare before tonight."

Ollie nodded slowly. "I'll get in touch with Paul."

Chris thanked him once again. He left the map with Ollie for reference on where to spread the chemical, and to plan the placement of his deputies. He then said farewell and followed his partner out of the office, closing the door behind him.

Ollie stared at his closed office door. His thoughts were clearly overwhelming his attention. Kate felt she knew what was going through his mind.

"You're wondering who it is, aren't you?"

Ollie looked at her for a moment, worry in his usual rock-like composure. There was something deep behind his eyes, but it vanished as quickly as it appeared. Ollie nodded slowly before answering.

"It could be anyone. It could be Fred, or Harold, or Steven… or even Janet. It doesn't have to be a guy werewolf. Hell, it could even be Riley, and his sightings are just meant to cover his own tracks. There's just no telling. But if it turns out to be someone from town, how will everyone take it?"

Kate sat in a chair in front of Ollie's desk. "Well, these guys seem to know how to keep secrets. I mean, they know a lot about werewolves and nobody else does. Maybe they have ways of keeping this secret."

"Yeah, that scares me too. This thing will be life-changing for whoever it is, as well as everyone else around them. What if whoever it is doesn't want their life to change?"

It bothered Kate to hear Ollie speak in such apprehensive terms. When she needed a sounding board, Ollie was always there for her. Countless times she considered confiding in him. Yet despite the desire to bear her burden, she just couldn't do it. She decided to wait until Ollie saw the change himself, so he could not deny it. She resolved to let things turn out the way they would. Why? Because she had to believe it wouldn't be that bad.

"I know how you feel, Uncle Ollie, but I really think it'll be okay. Whoever it is will learn how to cope with being a werewolf, and maybe even meet other ones. I mean, we already know Dep:118 supports scooper communities. Maybe they have werewolf communities somewhere out there as well."

Ollie lifted his eyes from wandering around his desk and looked at Kate. "Yeah. Yeah, maybe they do." He regained his usual rock-like composure. "Katie, I don't want you there when they catch this thing. It could still turn out to be dangerous. I promise to let you know what happens when it's all said and done."

Katie smiled. Boy, did Ollie have a surprise in store! "I understand. Just whoever it is, go easy on them, okay? I mean, they've been doing their best not to hurt anyone."

Once again Ollie smiled. "Unless it's Fred–then we'll have some fun before they take him away."

Kate smiled as well, and left the office.

D-day. D-day. The phrase returned to her head, but changed from a death sentence to a launching point for a new adventure, a new life.

6

At the end of her shift, Kate locked up her desk. She glanced at the paper mache dinosaurs, smiling contentedly at the Tyrannosaurus Rex. It stared back with yellow googly eyes and a toothy smile. She nudged its lower jaw with her finger. Finally she stood and made her way to the exit, waving a farewell to Ollie through his window as she passed by.

The air outside was comfortably warm, the sun sinking under the mountains along the western horizon. She scanned the sky for any sign of the full moon, which no longer held sway upon her fears. This was the first time Kate looked forward to seeing the full moon for many months. Once home she would explore listening to the internal workings of her body, and perhaps she would find the hum Chris mentioned. If she could do that tonight, then she could be self-aware and avoid their trap. The idea sounded ornery, mischievous.

And exciting.

As she left Kate noticed the agents' ground-bound vehicle in the parking lot. It seemed odd their car would be here when she knew they left earlier. She headed back into the office to see if something had happened.

Quietly she reentered the building, making her way through reception, trying to get a view of Ollie's office. As she passed through she caught a glimpse of Ollie's door, which was open, and Agent Blackwood standing just inside having an aggressive discussion with him. Kate heard more as she approached with stealth.

"She had plenty of chances, Sheriff. We know what kind of lupan she'll turn out to be, and we have to take action."

Oh, no.

"You don't know for sure!" Ollie shouted. "You're just making predictions!"

"That's right, and they'll be accurate. She knows what she is. It's only a matter of time before she uses it. People will be hurt." She emphasized every word in the last sentence.

Ollie shook his head vehemently. "She's not it. She just can't be!"

"Well she is, and we know what'll happen if we don't take her down."

Ollie's obstinacy made another appearance. "Enlighten me."

Agent Blackwood sighed. "Her self-awareness mixed with the primal freedom will intoxicate her. She'll feel unstoppable, and she very nearly will be. She'll test her abilities, which is what *you* said you wanted to avoid. If we can't capture her, we have to destroy her. And remember what I said about cooperating with me."

Ollie glared at the agent with a savage fierceness in his eyes. It frightened Kate, but apparently had no affect on Agent Blackwood.

"Get a new hire, Sheriff. Crenshaw won't be here much longer."

Ollie stood slowly and glowered at the agent. He responded with a cold voice, each syllable dripping with menace.

"Get the hell out."

Terrifying. He even had a guttural tone like Chris.

Agent Blackwood stood her ground for a moment, then relented and left.

Kate could barely think over the pounding in her head. Agent Blackwood just said the control would make her drunk with power. *Take her down*, she said. They intended to kill her? But what about everything Chris said? There had to be a way to stop this. There had to be a way.

She looked at Ollie once again and watched him stare at his

doorway, struggling with some internal decision. He picked up the receiver for his vid-phone, pressed a button, waited for a response, and then left a message.

"Katie girl, when you get this, pack a bag and get over to our house. If I'm not there, tell Nikki 'it's time,' she'll know what to do. We've been planning for this for a while, we just didn't tell you yet because… never mind, I'll explain later. Just trust me. Pack a bag and get to our house. Don't let anyone see you." Ollie hung up the vid-phone, stood from his desk and quickly left the building.

He knew. He *knew*! He knew and never said! He was probably waiting for her to come forward on her own. Stupid, stupid, stupid! There was nothing for it now. She had to get to Ollie's house as soon as she could. Forget the bag–she didn't own anything she couldn't live without.

Kate made for the back of the building. She pressed her code into the exit keypad, which unlocked the receiving door and the back gate. As she ran across the parking lot, Kate noticed the agents' vehicle was gone, but Ollie's craft was still there. What about climbing into his craft and waiting for him? No, if she didn't have control she might change form right there in the craft while airborne. That might be disastrous. The best option was to run for Ollie's.

Kate darted through the surrounding woods. Since Riley's was in the other direction, she didn't fear meeting the Dep:118 agents. Her mind raced with ideas and contradictions faster than she could identify them. She failed to take note of a fallen log. Her foot caught and she tumbled to the ground, putting bruises on her arm and a rip in her jeans. It didn't matter. None of it mattered. All that mattered was making it to Ollie's place. She stood and pressed onward.

It wasn't long before her run took its toll. She found a small glade with a large boulder on the edge and leaned against it, catching her racing breath. Every muscle in her body convulsed with her racing pulse, reverberating in her chest. She closed her eyes and took several deep breaths, filling her starving lungs with oxygen. Opening her eyes, she looked to the indigo sky. A large pale orb began rising above the cloud layer on the eastern horizon. At another time it would be beautiful, but now the doom it represented took precedence. Still, her other form might get her to Ollie's more quickly. Since he already knew, there was no point in trying to hide it.

Throwing caution to the wind Kate faced the full moon as it slowly emerged from the clouds, gleaming triumphantly in the night sky. She closed her eyes and raised her arms to each side, surrendering her existence to whatever fate lie in store. She stayed that way for many moments, feeling the moonlight meet her closed eyelids and caress her skin…

But nothing happened.

She opened her eyes and looked at her hands in confusion, a complete lack of understanding. Her mind began reviewing what she learned about werewolves. Since she was now mentally aware the moon held no sway, she would not forcibly change under its glow. And since she had not yet accomplished summoning the change on her own, the beast inside was effectively trapped. For now, she was safe from the change.

Yet how safe was she really? Could the beast break out at any time? What fate would be forced upon her?

There was a noise to the left; something stirred in the trees. Kate's eyes widened as she peered into the brush, trying to catch a glimpse of whatever was there. The rustle of dried leaves increased in volume. It was getting closer.

Suddenly a large furred beast emerged from the trees. It looked at her with knowing eyes, dark blue eyes which told of peace, not danger. It slowly circled in front of Kate, and she backed away until she was pressed against the boulder. The creature positioned itself directly in front, perhaps three meters between them. There they stood, staring at each other, an unknown amount of time passing as their eyes locked.

Intensely Kate gazed upon this werewolf, this lupan. Its ears were long and triangular. It had an elongated nose like a short muzzle, no doubt with large fangs under its jowls. Its coat was chocolate brown. The creature cocked its head to one side and then the other. Its tail swished in a carefree fashion, swinging left to right, but not really a wag. And then it sat.

It was clear this werewolf didn't mean any harm. Perhaps it sensed what she really was but did not understand why she had not changed form.

The creature's ears pivoted toward the right, and then its head followed suit. After a moment its dark blue eyes narrowed and it faced that direction on all fours.

Another werewolf with a frosted gray coat launched out from the trees. It rushed directly for the first one, its jaws open and flashing a vicious set of teeth, its claws ready to shred anything in its path. The brown werewolf rolled with the attack, and the gray werewolf stumbled as it landed awkwardly, quickly righting itself. It stood snarling at the brown, hackles raised and tongue lashing between brandished fangs.

Strangely enough, Kate noticed the brown werewolf was wearing some type of loincloth, whereas the gray was not wearing anything. She also noticed the brown kept a cool composure while the other threatened imminent attack.

The gray lunged at the brown, aiming for its neck, but the brown was too quick. As the gray charged once again the brown strafed to the left and pushed at the hind quarters of the gray as it passed, causing the gray to lose its footing once again. The gray roared in protest and reached around with a swipe at the brown, making no contact.

Once again they faced off, silently analyzing the other's prowess. The brown still did not expose his fangs, but kept defensive. The gray continued to show its fangs, tongue lashing between them, its ears folded against its head.

The ears of the brown swiveled once again, but its head did not follow. The gray one's ears also pulled up for a moment as well. Suddenly the ears of the brown pulled down, its jowls retracted to show his teeth. It hunched down, and its tail began swishing in a circular fashion.

The gray charged. The brown charged at the same time, getting its jaw below the gray as they met, and plowed into the gray with its full body weight. The gray flipped as it twisted and fell on its back, knocking the wind out of it. The brown dexterously hoisted the gray upright, holding it across the neck and abdomen. The gray frantically kicked its arms and legs, trying to break free, but to no avail.

Kate heard two hisses of air from behind her, behind the boulder. Two darts met the white chest of the gray, and it became even more frenzied in the hold of the brown. It did not take long before its attempts at freedom abided, and the brown lowered it to the ground gently and carefully.

From behind the boulder came Rachel Blackwood, holding a backpack in one hand and pointing a strange-looking gun at the gray with steady precision.

The brown leaned in toward the gray, whose tongue lolled idly with unconsciousness. The brown sniffed the gray's fur and nudged its neck, but the gray gave no response. The brown nodded to Agent

Blackwood and then looked up at Kate, meeting her eyes. It raised one of its eyebrows and added what seemed to be a smirk to its lips. Instantly Kate recognized the look.

"Chris…?"

The brown lowered his head with a respectful nod, and then used its right front paw to wave at her politely.

She knew it. She *knew* it! Chris Hansen was a werewolf himself! But who was the other one?

7

Agent Blackwood tossed the backpack to the brown werewolf. "Go change."

Chris picked up the backpack in his teeth and trotted off behind the boulder. After checking the gray, Agent Blackwood began holding up some sort of scanner to its chest. As she adjusted the scanner, she addressed Kate.

"Chris was right after all. Using you as bait worked."

"Bait? What?"

Agent Blackwood sighed annoyingly. "Chris figured out who the lupan was last night and decided to use you as bait to coax him into shifting on his own. It worked."

Confusion permeating her mind, Kate looked at the gray. "It's not me?"

Agent Blackwood reseated her attention. "You think you're lupan?"

Kate took a quivering breath and looked at the agent. She nodded with bemusement.

"Were you bitten?"

Kate paused. "Well, no. I just figured it was a side effect from when my mom was in those mutation projects."

"Lupans aren't from imperial experiments, and if you can't remember being bitten, you weren't." She returned to examining the gray. "Sorry, you're not in the club."

"But what about the tracks in my back yard, and the dreams?"

She looked at her again. "What dreams?"

Kate took another breath. "Every full moon I have dreams of being a werewolf. I saw my reflection in the window once. I can remember feeling hungry as I jumped over my back fence and headed for the woods. And when I wake up I find tracks in my back yard, sometimes in my bedroom."

Agent Blackwood looked off into the distance for a moment, apparently calculating something. She returned her gaze to Kate as she stood and approached. Standing directly in front of her, Agent Blackwood looked deep into Kate's eyes.

"Keep looking at me, and don't break eye contact no matter what. I'm going to ask you a series of questions. Answer with the very first thing that comes to mind, no matter how strange. Don't think, just answer. Ready?"

"I guess so," Kate replied nervously.

"How old are you?"

"Twenty-eight."

"How many fingers do you have?"

"Ten."

"What's the name of Chris' best friend?"

"Ted."

"What is the last number of your address?"

"Five."

"What is the apartment number on my door?"

"Fifteen."

"What color is my hair?"

"Black."

"What is the first name of Shannon's father?"

"Michael."

Agent Blackwood stopped, the content look on her face mixed with smug righteousness. "That settles it. You're not lupan."

Kate stood silent, hesitant to believe it. How did those questions decipher if she was a werewolf?

"You're a telepath."

"W-What?!"

Agent Blackwood returned to the gray werewolf. "Definitely under-developed. There's no way you could know the answers to the personal questions I asked unless you read my mind. You even used the incorrect answers I thought at the time. You're not lupan, and you're probably not a bona fide scooper either."

"I'm not a werewolf… *or* a scooper?"

Agent Blackwood put the scanner down again and looked up at Kate. "It's no big deal. You probably began picking up thoughts from a scooper in Aisleton, and your mind put them in your dreams. You came to Loughlin, the same thing happened around other scoopers. When you got away from them, the dreams stopped, remember? I bet the nightmare you had in our car mirrored what Earl Tippowitz was telling us." She gestured to the gray. "You probably picked up the thoughts of this guy whenever he came by your house."

Kate's mind was reeling, fervently clinging to reality falling away.

Chris emerged from behind the boulder, wearing jeans and a black tee shirt, but his feet were bare. He held his backpack nonchalantly in his right hand as he approached. His chocolate brown hair was shorter than it was when he originally arrived in town, but his dark blue eyes still held the compassionate sincerity Kate looked to as a beacon of hope. What hope could they provide now?

"I could really use a pizza or two," Chris mentioned rhetorically, and then turned his attention to Kate. "Hey, Kate."

She merely nodded. Words were having a difficult time forming in her throat.

"Did I hear things right? You're telepathic but you thought you might be lupan?"

"I…guess…" Kate methodically returned her gaze to the sleeping werewolf.

Chris smiled with comfort. "If it's any consolation, we know a few other telepaths who can help you with your ability, and you won't be in any danger from the Empire exploiting you, either."

Like the click of a switch, something came on in Kate's thoughts. A previous conversation blared in her mind, begging for explanation. She looked over at Agent Blackwood. "Wait a minute–you told Ollie I was the werewolf, and you had to take me down."

She looked at Kate and smiled teasingly. "Why, you naughty little eavesdropper! No wonder you bolted."

"Don't worry," Chris assured her, "we're not going to take anybody down. We were simply trying to make the Sheriff invoke the shift on his own so he'd be self-aware. Our people call it 'awakening.' It's considered the first step a lupan should take. And it makes learning our culture a lot easier too, believe me."

"Wait, wait, back up. Are you saying that…" and she slowly pointed to the gray.

Chris smiled and laughed. "That's your Uncle Ollie, yes. Since we told him how to invoke the shift, I figured he might try it on his own to protect you." He turned to his partner. "See? I was right."

"Don't let it go to your head. It's still a full moon. He might not have figured it out."

"Oh yes he did." Chris turned back toward Kate. "Anyway, when I saw you running out the back, something told me I should follow you. Looks like I was right on that, too."

Apparently disbelief bore upon Kate's face.

Agent Blackwood sighed. "Look, we could prove it to you but he'd be naked."

"Oh, wait–I've got a towel in the backpack. Hold on." Chris rummaged through his pack. He pulled out a towel with the number forty-two on it and draped it over the werewolf's midsection. He looked back up at Kate.

Kate was still trying to process all of this. She was not a werewolf after all, and she was apparently not a scooper either. She was a telepath who was picking up on the mental images of Ollie, who was a werewolf, and periodically checking in on her. He must have severed her bonds when she tied herself up, and brought her out of her closet as well! It was all so difficult to accept.

"Tell you what," Chris said. He repositioned himself at the back of the werewolf and squatted, and then gestured for Kate to join him. "It's okay. Come here."

Cautiously Kate took a step toward Chris, and then another, all the while keeping her eyes on the sleeping creature. She carefully knelt down next to Chris. Chris took her left hand with his right, and placed it on the gray pelt. The fur was coarse and thick, but the inner coat was oh so soft and warm to the touch. Her right hand touched the soft skin and hair over the ears. As she ran her fingers through the fur, the creature took a deep contented breath. Its chest expanded and contracted, the ribs and muscles under its fur no different than any other animal.

"See?" Chris said softly. "It's real. He's real."

"But... Ollie?" Kate whispered.

"We'll show you," Chris said through his smile.

"If this piece of crap will work," Rachel added. "What did you do to this thing, Chris?"

"Let me see it." He took the scanner from her hands.

Kate continued to run her fingers through the fur.

"No wonder–you're not using the auto detect. First you detect the current frequency and then adjust to the second one, see?" He showed her the display. "That's his lupan frequency. Human is lower, lupan is higher. So we start going lower, and… there. There it is. See?"

"Whatever. Just make it go, will you?"

Chris turned his attention to Kate. "Are you ready?"

Kate shrugged.

Chris pressed a button. The scanner made an alarm sound, and after a few seconds the lupan twitched in its sleep. Chris ran his own fingers through the fur of the werewolf, and an enormous clump of gray hair came away with his hand.

"Here we go," he announced.

Kate looked on as the creature's legs began to shrink and reshape. The pops of joints were clearly audible, sometimes accompanied with a twitch from a limb. The muzzle of the werewolf retracted and the skull began to expand, making the shrinking ears appear like they were sliding down the side of his head. All the while more and more fur fell away, exposing hot red skin. The two darts in his chest pushed out and fell harmlessly to the ground. Kate watched the tail recede, and the digit grade paws twisted into a more human form. The reddened skin cooled, showing a farmer's tan. Finally, there in a bed of fur lay Uncle Ollie, still unconscious with a towel draped across his waist. Incredible. Simply incredible!

Ollie began to stir with a moan.

"The shift purged the sedative from his system," Chris announced. "He's coming around."

Agent Blackwood casually shot him twice.

Chris twitched with reflex. "What the-? What the hell did you do that for?!"

"He's unrestrained. I don't want to chase him around all night."

Chris grabbed his forehead with his hand in frustration, and took a deep cleansing breath. "Alright, fine."

"So what happens now?" Kate asked.

Chris looked at her and took another breath. "Well, now I'll take him to a tribe of our people so he can learn our ways, learn how to be lupan."

"And then he'll come back?"

"That's up to him," Agent Blackwood said. "A lot of lupans don't come back. They like what they find."

"But what about his family? What about Nichole, and Tristan?"

"It's best if they don't know in case he doesn't come back. That way they can chalk it up to a missing person or an animal attack."

"What?"

"I know it sounds harsh," Chris said, "but believe it or not, sometimes it's the best way for the family to deal with their disappearance. It's a lot easier than explaining the real reason, no matter how much we hate to lie."

Kate's eyes widened as the message Ollie left for her came to mind. "But what if they already know?"

8

Chris and Kate lifted Ollie out of the car, careful not to disturb the towel tied around his waist. They hoisted him to the door as Agent Blackwood rang the doorbell.

"This is gonna get ugly."

"Why?" Chris asked.

"She's loyal. She won't be cooperative."

Chris sighed. He turned his head toward his partner. "You know, you're definitely a winter. A bit of faith applied to your cheekbones would really bring out your eyes…" and he batted his eyelashes, accompanied by an insincere smile.

"Two words. 'Dog,' 'muzzle.'"

"Five words: 'Bite,' 'my,' 'furry,' 'lupine'…"

Scuffling from the other side of the door indicated it was about to open. A few seconds later the door gave way to a woman in her late forties, curled blond hair meeting the shoulders of her closed robe. Her blue eyes widened when they caught sight of Ollie, and so did the door. They brought Ollie into the living room, and gently placed him on the couch.

"What happened?" the woman asked Kate.

"Is Tristan in bed?"

"Y-yes, of course. What happened?"

Kate looked at her with loving concern. "Nichole, do you already know Ollie's secret?"

Nichole's eyes narrowed with scrutiny. She glanced at Chris and Rachel. She looked back at Kate, who did her best to convey sympathy and assurance. Nichole straightened her posture. "So you know too?"

"I just found out." Kate gestured to the agents. "This is Chris Hansen and Rachel Blackwood from Department 118. They don't mean him any harm."

Nichole looked at the agents in turn. "Can you help him?"

"Yes, absolutely." Chris radiated confidence.

"Hang on, Chris." Rachel looked at Mrs. Taylor. "What do you mean by 'help'?"

"*Can you cure him?*" Frustration quivered in her voice.

"Why, is he sick?"

"What?"

Rachel crossed her arms and dropped her shoulders. "What makes you think being a werewolf needs a cure, Mrs. Taylor? You'll offend other lupans in the room, like Chris."

Nichole looked at Rachel with astonished disbelief. Her gaze shifted to Chris, who meekly smiled and waved.

"Hi. No offense taken. And we do prefer the term 'lupan,' just so you know."

"L-lupan?" Nichole stuttered.

"Yes, that's what we're called. At some point in the past your husband was bitten by a lupan and eventually became one himself. I am too, but I was born one."

Nichole looked upon her sleeping husband. Then she looked at the night through a living room window, and returned her gaze to Chris. "But he's… and you're…"

"Not in lupan form?"

Nichole nodded.

"I have control over my shifting ability, and now your husband does too. He'll be able to shift form whenever he wants, full moon or no. And if that wasn't good enough, he'll be self-aware from now on. You see, when a lupan shifts form, often times his subconscious-"

"Save it, Chris," Rachel whined.

Ollie groaned, and his arm moved. Chris immediately looked at Rachel and gave her a warning stare, no doubt protesting the use of further tranquilizers. Rachel raised her hands up in surrender and rolled her eyes.

Both Kate and Nichole immediately moved to Ollie and knelt down, waiting to greet him. When his eyes opened they focused on Nichole, and then Kate, both of whom were smiling with loving concern.

"Where am I?" he asked.

"You're home, baby." Nichole gently stroked his salt-and-pepper hair. "You're safe."

Ollie looked at Katie. Awareness coursed across his face.

"I'm fine, Uncle Ollie. You didn't hurt me or anyone else."

Ollie frowned. "They said you were a werewolf."

"It's okay, you never bit me or attacked me or anything. All you did was protect me. They told you all that to make you shift form on your own. You did. Everything's okay."

Ollie sighed awkwardly and looked around the living room. His countenance fell when his eyes met the agents. "I take it the secret's out?"

Chris nodded. "Not to worry, Sheriff. Your secrets are safe with us, as long as our secrets are safe with you."

Ollie frowned at the comment, rubbed his temples and sat up. After becoming aware of his current attire he was very careful when doing so. "So who was that other one?"

"Uh, that was me," Chris raised his hand.

Ollie sized him up, then huffed. "Specialist my ass."

Chris shrugged. "Well, I'd be a fool to claim I knew everything about our people."

Ollie looked at him curiously. "Our 'people'? We have a people?"

Chris nodded, refreshing his smile. "Your world is about to shift form just like you do, Sheriff."

9

The summer heat made a full appearance the next day. Kate tossed Ollie's shoulder bag into the back of the white ground-bound vehicle, and then looked back at Ollie and Nichole's house. Just outside the door Ollie was squatting down, talking to his nine-year-old son, Tristan. Ollie put his hands on Tristan's shoulders, reinforcing his eye contact with a smile.

Kate admired the loving, gentle way Ollie had with Tristan, Nichole and herself, but also recognized his fierce loyalty and protective nature, no doubt intensified by the wolf nature of his lupan existence.

Tristan gave his father a great big hug, and then stepped back inside. Ollie stood and gave his wife a hug and a kiss, and then spoke with her for a while. As she looked on with admiration, Chris approached.

"Are you sure you don't want to come along?"

Kate smiled. "Yeah, I'm sure. I don't think the sheriff and the clerical assistant should leave the office for two months at the same time."

"I see your point. Still, you probably wouldn't be gone as long as he will."

Kate shrugged. "Better safe than sorry. People in this town love gossip as much as they love conspiracies. I'll wait my turn."

Chris nodded. "Tell you what: if you'd like, I'll have a friend of mine swing by. She's been a telepath for years. I'd imagine she can give you all kinds of tips and pointers. Let's face it, the more you know about your abilities the better off you'll be, just like Uncle Ollie."

Kate thought about the offer. As long as it was on her terms, perhaps it would be a good idea. "Maybe in a few weeks, after Ollie's been gone for a while. Things might be a little awkward until we get used to all this. One thing at a time, you know?"

Chris smiled. "Oh, I know, trust me."

Ollie walked up to the car. He quickly glanced at the items in the cargo area, verifying everything was packed. Finally he turned to Kate and gave her a hug.

"I'm still sorry for everything I put you through, Katie girl."

"Will you stop it already? It's not your fault I was picking up on your brainwaves."

"Yeah, on that note," he took a glance at his approaching wife and son, "Nikki knows but Tristan doesn't. I think it's best for now."

"Got it. You take care of yourself, okay?"

Ollie shrugged. "It's only a couple months, I'll be fine. If you guys need me, you can relay a message. I already confirmed it with their Overlord." He narrowed his eyes. "And that doesn't need to be the only reason you call, either."

"I know, I know!" Kate groaned, pretending to be irritated by the nagging.

Ollie hugged his family and kissed his wife one last time, then climbed in.

Chris shook Kate's hand. "Don't worry. I'll bring him back safe and sound."

Kate smiled. "Why, Agent Hansen, you read my mind."

Chris smiled too. "Take care, Kate."

She nodded, and Chris got in the vehicle. Kate's eyes followed the car's progress as it pulled away. Her mind, however, looked to the future with hope instead of doom. They lived in a town of scoopers. She was telepathic, the sheriff was a werewolf, and his wife knew both their secrets. Loughlin had become a small pocket of oddity, alone in the wilderness away from the Empire's vigilant eye, living its own reality.

But Kate didn't mind. Well, at least not yet.

IN THE MOUTH OF THE WOLF, WOLF MANIFESTO, & WOLF VARIATIONS
MARK TREDINNICK

Mark Tredinnick, winner of the Montreal International Poetry Prize and many other honours, is the author of a dozen works of poetry and prose, including The Blue Plateau, The Land's Wild Music, *and* Bluewren Cantos. *He lives on the Wollondilly Rive in Southeastern Australia. His latest work is* Almost Everything I Know. *A new book of poems comes out from Hip Pocket Press in 2016.*

In the Mouth of the Wolf

A line came to me, like thunder to the valley, my love,
This morning, while my head, seeking wisdom
And good fortune, rested in the mouth of the wolf,
As if it were a pillow I would never rise from:
When will you not be afraid of your life?
I wish you wouldn't talk with your mouth full,
I said. But the mouth of the wolf was a forest
Of oracles, and so it went on, Don't act
Without your heart's consent; without your heart,
An act is all your life can be. With your heart
In my mouth, each moment is sacred, a holy day,
A truth become a tree. Each day, a way.
Mmmmhhh, I said, for the fight had gone out
Of me. Your body is a house—the wolf went on,
Indistinctly, her mouth a sepulcher—where your heart is
A guest, and your heart, like me, is free and wild, and time
Is a wilderness yet. For your body is a creature
Of the earth, and it knows what you came for and where
Your hunger wants to fall and where your feet must follow.
Hear the thunder from the ridge? It could be your death,
Or it could be the rest of your life calling the rest of your name.
See the lightning flaring from the ridge? It is the Beloved
And see how she has been coming all along? Your work
Is love, and it starts beyond the valley where you are known.

Wolf Manifesto

Write because

you got nothin' to say

and you might as well

say it. You never know just who might be dying

for want of the wild sweet

nothing he can hear

from no one else

but you.

Write because there's a wolf

in your mouth, and it wants to run off with you.

Let her out

before she eats her way all the way

down to your belly, where you keep

everything you love. Free her

to find her mate; free her

to wake the world she hungers

for—to leave love like scat,

like a manuscript of paw

prints, everywhere

she treads.

Write because there's a wolf

out there, and it's tired and looking

for somewhere to stop. It's been

coming for years. Across deserts

it's come, across rivers; across

tundras and mountains, all along

an archipelago

it came, where it grew older than time

among

unforested trees. It brings lines

and chapters and sorrows in its belly,

and hymns. It carries you

in its mind. Let your mouth be where it lies, then—

a den for songs the world wants

sung, a refuge and a voice

and a world.

Wolf Variations

1.
Blue wolf at the edge
Of spruce woods, snow on the ground:
This is how she misses him.

2.
Memory is a wolf
                    in the mouth of the morning,
Blue in the first light and lost a moment,
Like a child, inside the elegant
                         ecology

Of winter's mind. He stands
                    like silence at the edge
Of these spruce woods, studying the wind
For word of her and
              reading the snow for sign.

3.
I should be a pelt, he thinks,
By now, a skin on some hunter's floor,
A prize. What he's come through
Might have ended another,
Taken his life, (and some of his lives
It did end, some of his selves
It stole), but it's borne him
Again. It's run him wild. Greyed
Him and taught him nothing
But here and her, wherever
That may be, and delight.

4.

I howl the night down in wait for you,
Love, my voice soft
        with years and deserts, my cry
Slender and tender and lonely as a vanishing grey
Tribe, as a child in a cage, made afraid
By his parents of every last one
            of the 83 wolves left in the wild.

5.
Others see a threat in his brow,
A studious look in his eye. She notices,
When she comes to his shoulder,
The delight in his eyes, the snow
On his forehead, signs of play, a new
Lightness in his touch. His voice,
Too, she thinks, has deepened
And it carries farther than it did.
There is new timber in it, she thinks.
Alder and aspen and pine. Hickory. Snow
On some of them, doubt fighting with
Hope in his eyes. Before, he looked;
Now, he is. With her. And she sleeps
Against him at last.

IN PASSING
AMY HAKANSON

Amy Jean Hakanson, an English—Creative Writing graduate from San Francisco State University, lover of writing, and a published poet, grew up with the love and protection of her dog Sandy, and today watches the same characteristics flourish in her pup Honey. Her love for canines drew her to the fascinating story of the return of wolves to Yellowstone National Park. Seeing their struggle to thrive in a human dominated world, she felt compelled to bring into words the light and good she sees in such majestic animals. She hopes her small poem will join the voices of many who feel the same way to one day make a difference.

summer fades in smoldering rain
sun burning translucent drops
into honeyed amber tears
accompany my ponderings
of all gains soon to be lost
within the soft fold of autumn's encompassing wing
but still
the crinkle of dancing padded paws striking leaves
a ritual of sorts during these last easy days
pointed ears emerging through the thicket of tall grass
bellies full
evident by a satisfying
unifying pant
coats cleaned by the gentle rainfall
their progression quiet compared to my footfall
I catch a glimpse
I feel a tug
to know these guardians of the natural world
where they are trotting

so proud and aware
their silver, black, white, tawny fur
all glinting against this settling turn
they move so swiftly
the wind whips at their tails
carrying them to a new place
I am unaware
I clutch my wrists
it's a bit of jealousy
to live day by day embracing what is and not what one thinks it should be
it is more living than I can ever foresee
look back
          just once
                    so I might understand the secrets you heed

KAI, LITTLE RED CAP, & WERE DANCE
ISIS RAYE

Gothic/fantasy artist Isis Raye, resides in Queensland, Australia. Her formative art skills were gained during years of private art tuition. During her Secondary high school years, Isis first gained notoriety in the local community as an artist, being awarded with the Youth Rotary Award for excellence in the field of visual arts. International travel across Europe bewitched her soul, and the artist was born. Her passion for animals, myth, and legends are weaved into her paintings, and, with each artwork, a story is told. For Isis, the subject matter of her paintings remains much the same solemn, somewhat haunted images that are immortalized with Gothic romanticism. Isis is inspired most by the artwork of the Pre-Raphaelites; while her range of artistic mediums vary, she is drawn to water color paint, pencils, ink, and charcoals.

Kai. Watercolor paint, ink, and pencil.

Little Red Cap. Watercolor paint, ink, and pencil.

Were Dance. Watercolor paint, ink, and pencil.

THE LAST CALL, SPIRIT OF THE WHITE WOLF, & WORDS WITH THE WISE
KELLY WALFORD

As an artist, Kelly Walford tries to capture her passion for her subjects in her work. She enjoys using acrylics, charcoal, graphite, but her favorite medium is color pencils. Earlier this year, she began needle felting, creating 3D sculptures of animals using the natural fibres of wool. Sculpting over wire armatures enables the animal to be posed in ways that showcase its natural characteristics.

Kelly has been able to indulge her passion for wolves and help support them by having her artwork published in the previous anthology Wolf Warriors. *When she's not in her studio, Kelly enjoys exploring the countryside on her motorcycle, riding her horses, and enjoys reading.*

Kelly Walford resides in Taupo, New Zealand, with her partner and their menagerie of dogs, horses, and an assortment of other animals.

The Last Call. Acrylics on canvas. Photo reference permission Paul Danaher.

Words with the Wise. Color pencil on colored paper. Photo reference permission The Endangered Wolf Center.

Spirit of the White Wolf. 3D sculpture, Needle felted over a wire armature.

LET THE WOLVES RUN FREE
RATTY

Performed by Ratty and the Watchers

Your amber eyes and coat of ashes, I see sorrow in your face
With the pain a young one thrashes, a trophy for the human race
Hunted down I feel the heartache, from ancient dens the wolves must flee
Misunderstood beliefs we must break, education is the key.

I saw a pack when in full flight
Brothers / sisters chasing starlight
Their hearts are yearning to be free of our world

In the night an Alpha male howls, it's a song of such beauty
All they hear is Hollywood growls, and not the call to his family
Never safe on the lonely mountain, the guns are heard in the deep valley
Another notch on the butt of a rifle, a pup added to the death tally.

Shadows dancing on moonlit skies
Leave them be don't wave them goodbye
All they want is to be free of our world

Look in his face, Look in his eyes, there's only grace, there's no disguise
Look at their life, what do you see, don't give them strife, let them run free,
Let the wolves run free

THE LINE
FOREST WELLS

Forest Wells was first inspired by the events of 9/11. Though he didn't know anyone involved, the day lit his passion for writing, beginning with poems of emotion, transitioning to works of fiction. Wolves, and really all wild canines, are his second passion, which Forest put into his first published short story "The Line," as well as a longer, wolf focused novel currently undergoing final revisions. When he's not writing, you can find Forest cheering for the San Diego Chargers, the Arizona Coyotes, and either playing League of Legends, or watching the professional matches online. He also spends much of his free time volunteering with a local Girl Scout troop. Forest currently lives in his hometown of Thermal California. For more information about Forest Wells, check out his website at www.forestwells.com.

A prime reason I'm not a father.

I shook my head at the commotion that broke what had been a calm morning in the village. A small group of children were following an older boy in low-quality brown pants and dark red tunic out of the stable. The boy tried to get away, but the mob wouldn't let him as they continued to fling insults at him.

Pity for the boy turned to anger when I saw the mob was led by the short, round headed kid I knew as Cantso. The little brat had tried to make trouble at my place, only to feel the sting of my whip instead. I never did hear from Marshil, his father, except for the drop in orders I noticed soon after. An attempt to talk with the man had gotten no results beyond an understanding of how much he thought of himself. I got little more than cold conversations from him, and smug looks from his son, from then on. The latter left me not at all surprised to find him at the head of this group of bullies.

I left my shipment of nails in the care of the village baker, then stomped toward the mob. I adjusted the sword on my back in case I needed to make a point. Not quite the glory it saw during the wizard rebellion, but then, those days were long behind me. Meanwhile, the insults in the present grew worse. I began catching words in time to see the older boy whip around to face his attackers.

"Leave me alone!" he shouted. "I don't want things to turn ugly!"

A boy wearing a worn vest sneered while pretending to swoon. "Ohhh, he doesn't want things to get ugly. What are you going to do, throw hay at us?"

Another boy, whose smooth hair and clean appearance spoke of little labor, quickly added, "Nah, he won't do that. He'll use the horse poop he just shoveled instead."

The group laughed, drawing a breath of fury from the boy. I had to give the young man credit. At fourteen, I'd be throwing punches by now. I hastened my pace before the boy's control ran out.

He made another attempt to retreat, but the mob followed. They continued to drown out my own calls with insults I couldn't believe children their age knew. The things I heard got *my* blood boiling.

Just as I got close enough to be heard over the insults, one of the bullies threw something that hit the older boy in the head. The boy stopped, drew up his shoulders and clenched his fists. When he turned around, the mob froze as if they'd turned to stone.

I stood in front of the mob but faced the boy. I froze myself when I saw his eyes. They had turned to animal amber. The color combined with a glow beneath to make a glare I have never seen before. Then, his shoes vanished, though his clothes remained intact, as the boy grew into a solid white, smooth furred, werewolf. His ears were fully forward with a snarl on his lips as he now stood as tall as I did.

Before I could recover enough to act, the werewolf grabbed the smooth haired boy, and threw him into his compatriots. The boy tumbled through the group, knocking them and me to the ground. The werewolf swiped at Cantso, leaving shallow cuts on the back of his thighs. The children screamed in terror as they sprinted away, leaving their whimpering leader to the mercy of the wolf. Cantso started sobbing as the wolf held him to the ground with a snarl that rattled within my chest. He inched his fangs closer to Cantso's neck as if he were about to rip into it.

I rose to my feet, drew my sword, and prepared to face the beast. As much as I hated bullies, I couldn't let the werewolf kill him. When I stepped forward with my sword raised, I suddenly doubted to the wolf's intent. The beast had had ample time to kill Cantso however he liked. Yet, he'd stopped his fangs just short of Cantso's neck. For the first time I saw careful thought in the werewolf's eyes. I stood close enough to act while praying I didn't regret my hesitation.

A painful moment passed, then the werewolf closed his jaws while lowering his snarl to a low growl. I got the shock of my life when the wolf spoke in a raspy, but no less clear voice.

"Next time you bully me, I won't stop."

He let Cantso go, who promptly sprinted away as fast as his wounded legs could carry him. The wolf's glare turned to me, where it was replaced by cold fear. His tail tucked between his legs as his ears fell against his skull.

I stood frozen, trying to process what I just saw. Of all the werewolf stories I'd heard, none mentioned concentrated control, nor speech, nor fear of any kind. Yet here stood a werewolf showing all three. When he cowered with a soft whine, I saw nothing more than a scared pup.

I sheathed my sword while raising my hands. The wolf's ears eased forward as his eyes met mine.

"Easy," I said. "You have nothing to fear."

Slowly the wolf rose, though his tail refused to come out.

"Don't I?" he asked with no rasp in his voice. "Most people don't react well to werewolves."

"I am not most people. I won't harm you, provided you don't harm anyone else."

The wolf's tail shot out as his growl returned. A hand not unlike mine, yet still mostly paw, pointed after the bullies.

"Talk to them about doing no harm! I tried to ignore them, I tried to get away, but I might as well have turned away the sun!" He took a pair of heavy breaths, then his ears went back while his eyes pleaded with me. "Please. I tried to control myself. I just couldn't. I acted before I knew what I was doing."

He lashed out. That's all it was. He'd reached his boiling point, and lashed out. I couldn't believe it. Were all werewolves like this one? Do they merely use their form as I might use my sword when enraged? Did it matter? This one had, and I didn't feel he deserved punishment for it.

My mind took hold of that thought and wondered, has any werewolf deserved what they got? Society claimed they were aggressive, lethal, and out of control. The king had tried his best to keep them safe with law, but fear remained strong. They continued to be seen as monsters with little thought and less honor.

Yet, as I looked at my first living werewolf, I saw none of it. His actions, his words, his emotions, all stood in contrast to what I'd heard. In light of what I saw I had to ask myself, what are people so afraid of?

The wolf's growl became a whine, bringing me back into the moment. He withdrew into himself while his hand went to his shoulder with a cringe. Before I could wonder about his pain, cries from behind told me what my eyes soon confirmed. The fathers of the children were charging our way. Most were carrying staffs or farm equipment, except for one who carried a sword, flanked by a tall, well-built bowman dressed in fine clothes.

Marshil. The high and mighty father of Cansto. That's just what I need. I glanced at the wolf with a sigh, and found him retreating against the wall of the stable, looking every bit like a cornered animal.

All hesitation vanished. A line had been drawn, and I stood at the gates. With more conviction than I've ever felt, I drew my sword while placing myself between the wolf and the fathers.

As they approached at a more cautious pace, I looked back at the wolf. "Stay close, and listen for my orders."

He only cowered tighter as the mob stopped several feet away. There was fury in their eyes, though a few held fear as well. I did nothing but lower my blade at them. The next move was theirs. I had to let them make it.

The two with real weapons stepped forward. I got my first good look at the rust bitten shell that used to be a sword. I looked past it to see the thin and short carpenter I knew as Wallace. Good customer, questionable business leader, and a very poor swordsman. That left me with an old, though well-kept bow, and superior numbers.

That's more than enough, I reminded myself.

The two weapon holders collected themselves to face me.

Wallace raised his sword almost straight up. "Step aside, Binlit. We just want the werewolf."

I pointed my sword between them while casting a wry smile at them both. "Yes, I know. Tell me, what do you plan to do with him?"

"We plan to punish him for attacking Mashil's son."

"Punish him? There's a lot more than lawful penance on your minds. I can't allow that."

Marshil's eyes burned with the rage I heard in his voice. "He injured my son! I demand justice. No one hurts my boy, especially not a filthy werewolf."

The father of a spoiled brat. I almost wanted to hit him myself. "Justice. You might want to talk to your son about justice. Starting with the concept of-"

Wallace swung his sword out, missing Marshil's leg by inches. "Enough! We're taking that beast. Stand aside, or join him in his fate."

"If that's the way it has to be, then I'm sorry for the blood I must spill."

The men huffed at my comment, then Marshil pulled an arrow out of his quiver. I faced him directly, hoping to avoid what I had planned. When he set the arrow against the bow, I realized they were committed.

I waited for him to nock it into place. It would provide the most inattention I was going to get. But before either of us could take the next step, an arrow streaked between us and embedded itself in the stable wall. We all looked for the source, and found three paladins, the king's elite soldiers of honor and justice, on horseback and in full armor, minus helmets. Two of the three sat ready for another shot, while the one in the middle glanced back and forth between me and the mob.

"He who moves first gets the next arrow." The center paladin called out.

Everyone lowered their weapons. I, more than the villagers, knew the wisdom of that act because of the war. The image of a paladin brushing off a fire spell, followed by the quick and violent end to the caster, was forever branded in my memory. We remained still, except for the wolf who, to my surprise, managed to cower tighter as the paladins approached. His hand was just as tight on his shoulder, which seemed to draw another pained whine. Something I would have to address, somehow.

The armored trio dismounted in one, uniformed motion. One took the horses away while the others stepped between us.

The leader looked at both sides, then straight ahead with a deep breath. "I want one person from each side to come forward."

Marshil and I stepped forward. The mob gave us some room while the wolf just stuck to his corner.

The lead Paladin looked us over, then pointed to Marshil. "You first. What's this all about?"

This should be good.

Marshil pointed at the wolf with all his fury. "That beast attacked my son! No provocation, no reason, he lashed out and left deep cuts on my son's legs!"

The paladin's head eased to the side. "I see. Is that all?"

"Yes sir."

The paladin hummed annoyance, then turned to me with a hard gaze that left me worried.

"Your explanation?"

I took a deep breath to settle my emotions before replying. "Sir, the werewolf did attack his child. However, the boy was one of several children that were teasing and mocking the wolf. He tried to get away, but the children followed."

The paladin's eyes raised. "That's why the wolf attacked?"

"No, sir. He lost control when one of the children threw something that hit him in the back of the head."

"Did you see what they threw?"

I began to answer no, but was interrupted when the other paladin walked past us to the wall of the stable. He dug through items leaned against the wall until he tossed a rotten apple to the lead paladin. He turned it over in his hand with another annoyed hum.

While my heart fluttered, the man carefully approached the wolf, trying his best to assure him he meant no harm. After several whines, and an added assurance from me, the wolf allowed the paladin to get close. The paladin proceeded to examine the back of his neck and head, at times digging into the fur.

I could only watch and pray. Paladins were said to be divine protectors of justice, as well as the kingdom. Their code demanded the highest level of duty and honor, including a strict mandate to find the truth, and protect the innocent. If these paladins were the followers of the code they should be, then the wolf should have nothing to fear. If not, then his life could be lost, as well as my faith in the paladin order.

The search went on forever while my heart stopped, uncertain how to take it. A few seconds later, the leader stood with a pat on the wolf's shoulder, to which the wolf flinched with a whine.

The leader flinched himself, but in curiosity. He gently tested the wolf's shoulder, probing mostly the joint itself, getting whines and cringes in reply every time. He knelt in front of the wolf and asked, "What's your name?"

The wolf's ears rose, though only halfway. "Thintal sir."

"Hello, Thintal. I'm Jilsar. Tell me, what happened to your

shoulder?" Thintal's ears went flat as his gaze fell on the fathers. "Thintal. It's not polite to ignore a paladin. It's bad for our image. Please, tell me what happened."

Thintal again looked at the mob, then back to Jilsar's soft smile. "Sir, his… Marshil's son…. He startled a horse while I was cleaning its hoof. It kicked the leg I held. Its hoof hit the outside of my shoulder."

"That's a lie!"

All eyes went to the corner of the stable where the young man in question had appeared. His father looked furious. Jilsar just grumbled.

"I never went near your stinking horse!" The boy said.

"Cantso!" Marshil said. "I told you to stay at the inn."

"But, dad. I want to watch you beat the lowly, werewolf, stable hand-"

"Cantso! Go home!"

"But dad—"

"NOW!"

"Do not move young man." Marshil's face lost some color as Jilsar stood and motioned for Cantso to come to him. The boy obeyed without question, though he glanced at his father with each step.

Jilsar knelt before the boy while his armor took on a soft glow. "The village can be boring, can't it?"

Cantso nodded with a smug look. "Yeah. The grown-ups won't let us do anything out of town."

"Too many bandits. I understand. So, you went looking for fun?"

"Yeah. Fran had a great idea for a joke."

Jilsar raised an impressed eyebrow I almost believed. "Oh really? What was it?"

The boy looked around, then whispered into Jilsar's ear. Jilsar nodded and hummed, sounding genuinely interested. I watched and waited, realizing that Cantso had been snared by the paladin's storied talent for getting the truth. Though the stories never spoke of magic being involved, the glow of Jilsar's armor was unmistakable.

Cantso soon leaned back with a full grin. "It worked better than we could have hoped. When the horse kicked him, he jumped right into the hay and spread it all around."

Jilsar nodded apparent approval or agreement. "Improved the effect." Cantso nodded. Jilsar nodded with him again, then let his gaze turn hard with a matching deep breath as the glow faded. "If you ever, do anything like that again, an angry werewolf will be the least of your problems. Am I *CLEAR?!*"

Jilsar's last word was more felt than heard as it echoed off the stable wall. Cantso looked more afraid than the wolf as he nodded his full and complete understanding. Jilsar turned him around before giving him a push toward his father. As he took cover behind Marshil, I noticed the cuts on his legs were only lightly bandaged. Deep wounds. Heh. Probably wouldn't even leave a scar. Guess Thintal had more control from the start than I thought.

Jilsar stood to face the mob with no less anger in his voice. "Go home, all of you! This werewolf has done no wrong here."

I breathed a deep sigh of relief. As last, I could stop thinking about what to do if the paladins called for Thintal's hide.

Marshil on the other hand, suddenly remembered his courage, or forgot who he was dealing with. His eyes were wide with anger and shock.

"No wrong? That beast assaulted my son!"

"After your son assaulted him," Jilsar said with his own inner fire, "which does not include ringing a bell in the ear of a horse he was working on. Thintal's lucky a bruise is all he suffered. As for the damage Thintal did," Jilsar looked at the still cowering werewolf, then back to the father with a long sigh. "I think you've done the same if not more damage to him. I'm calling this issue resolved. Neither side owes the other anything, am I clear?"

"Sir paladin—"

"*AM I...* clear?"

Marshil seemed ready to continue the matter, until Jilsar made a point of going for the hilt of his sword. Fear then seeped into his eyes, followed by furious acceptance.

"Perfectly, sir." Marshil spat.

Jilsar released his blade with a nod. "Good. Now disperse your mob. You'll get no pound of flesh today."

Marshil gave another deep breath of fury before turning to his already splintering group. I sheathed my sword with a sigh of my own, though mine was all relief. With the conflict indeed over, I was able to go to Thintal's side to provide true comfort.

I knelt beside him and rubbed his uninjured shoulder to get his attention. "Hey. You can relax. You're safe now."

Thintal allowed only his eyes to acknowledge me. "They might come back."

Jilsar stepped to my side while patting the hilt of his sword. "Not if they value their lives they won't. Not after showing so much hate for so little reason."

"But, I attacked his son. I injured-"

I put my hand on his nose to stop him. "Thintal, relax. You stand behind the line of innocence. So long as you do, I will not allow any harm to come to you." I rose and extended my hand. "Come on son. Reclaim yourself."

Thintal looked up at me with flattened ears. I just held my gaze and waited for him to come out of it. After a long moment in which I feared he would stay afraid forever, his ears rose as he took my hand. I helped him to his feet... er... paws, with a warm smile he soon returned. I stood beside him and put my arm around his shoulders, careful to avoid his injury. His only response was to let his tail float calmly out behind him.

"That's better." I said.

"I should shift back," he said softly.

"Why? You look fine, elegant even, uh, minus the soiled cloths I will admit. Being in this form doesn't hurt you does it?"

"Well no, but—"

"But nothing. You are a werewolf. As long as I'm here, you will not be anything else just because society is irrational. If you like this form, then retain it. I don't mind," I narrowed my eyes while forcing my voice to go deeper. "and no one else will either."

Thintal's smile grew and his tail gave a single swish.

Jilsar stepped in front of Thintal with his hand out, but whipped around with sword drawn as an arrow panged off of his armor. I redrew my own while latching onto Thintal's hand before he could move.

"No more Thintal! You have cowered for the last time!"

I don't know what my stare conveyed, but I saw Thintal's eyes switch from fear to trust. His ears still went down, but his tail was straight up. I smiled approval while handing him a dagger I used more as a tool than a weapon.

My charge ready, I looked past Jilsar to find Marshil as the one who had fired. Behind him stood the original mob, some of whom carried what appeared to be parts of tables as makeshift shields.

From his first, echoing word, I knew Jilsar was furious. "What is the meaning of this? You were told to disperse!"

Marshil drew another arrow and nocked it into place. "And we will, once that beast is dead. He is a threat to the world and must be put down. No one will stop us, not even you, betrayer."

A deep breath from Jilsar spoke of great fury under fading control. He wasn't far from growling when he spoke again.

"You will not harm this wolf. I won't allow it."

Marshil just huffed at him. "We'll kill you if we must, Jilsar. I only want the beast."

I stepped forward to add my body to the line. "Don't be a fool, Marshil. You're facing paladins here. They'll tear you apart if you threaten them."

"Like those werewolves did to my brother? He and his friends knew what they were. They saw through their false promise of peace. They tried to snuff them out before they came after our children. They failed. By his blood and that of my son, I shall have my vengeance! First the beast, then you for protecting him, then all others that dare stand in my way!"

Marshil raised his bow. He drew his arrow back, but before he could gain enough tension to fire, something zipped past my head and into Marshil's chest. As the man crumpled to the ground, I glanced back to find Thintal glaring at the mob, empty-handed.

"No one threatens my pack!" he growled.

I smiled my pride at him with a nod of the same. "Much, much better."

"Indeed." Jilsar said with the smallest of smiles. He returned his focus to the mob. "The same awaits you all if you do not disperse immediately!"

The fathers looked at their fallen leader, then ducked behind their "shields". They marched our way, and Jilsar tapped his lieutenant's quiver. The man traded his sword for his bow, nocked an arrow into place, then fired into one of the shields. The owner dropped the table top while jumping away as if it had bitten him. The mob stopped and stared at the man's shield, or rather the paladin's arrow sticking through it up to the feathers.

Jilsar's lieutenant took more careful aim at a second target. He made a show of pulling the arrow further back, suggesting the first shot was not at maximum pull. "Last chance."

The mob looked at the dropped shield, to their fallen leader, then back to us. Jilsar and I pointed our swords at them. The lieutenant pulled back even further. They looked at each other a moment longer, then splintered once more.

Jilsar and I watched them go long after the street had cleared. Once we felt sure they were gone for good, we sheathed our blades and turned to Thintal.

"Where did you learn to do that?" I asked.

"Have you ever tried to chase rats through a stable?" Thintal said. "Wolf or not, you often end up in the muck pile."

I chuckled while Jilsar shook his head. He looked over at Marshil's body with a sigh.

"The only thing I truly hate in this world is hate," he said. "Its cost is too high."

"I agree." I said with a look of my own. "But he chose his fate. Maybe his son will learn from this."

"I fear he will not. Thintal, I must suggest you gather your belongings and come with us. Relax. I suggest it because I fear your life here is over. I doubt those… people, will let you live in peace. Don't worry. I'll make sure you find a good place to live before I leave you."

Thintal nodded his understanding, then looked at me. I gave a nod of my own, for I had no words to offer.

Thintal's ears moved back for a second before he faced Jilsar. "I won't be afraid. So long as Binlit comes with me."

Jilsar looked at me with the silent question. I tossed the idea around while considering the effects.

"I'd be giving up a lot. I have a calm life here I rather like." Thintal gave me a pleading look mixed with fear. Very lost puppy. My heart decided without hesitation. "Then again, business hasn't been that good lately. After today, I imagine it will soon get worse. I might as well make sure a young wolf stays safe. Perhaps we can find a new place for both of us. Once you've packed, we'll head to my place so I can do the same."

Thintal's ears went up and his eyes brightened. "Thank you! Thank you so much."

"Don't thank me yet, pup. I expect you to pull your weight."

"You won't be disappointed."

Jilsar patted my shoulder with a chuckle. "I'm sure he won't. We'll tend to our horses while you pack, Thintal. Then we'll all go to your home Binlit, for your turn."

I thanked Jilsar for his escort, and his help, then motioned for

Thintal to lead me to his home. I walked beside him, feeling so good I couldn't resist a gentle tease.

"You don't have fleas do you?"

Thintal only smiled in reply, his tail gently swishing behind him.

LUNA
JASON LIMBERG

Jason Limberg was born in Marinette, Wisconsin in 1982. Limberg works predominantly in the medium of drawing with an emphasis on pen & ink. Limberg is primarily self-taught with a concentration on drawing at UW-Green Bay in 2005. He has had solo shows throughout the Midwest, exhibited Internationally, included in multiple publications, and has collected numerous awards.

Limberg is the Director of Art on the Rocks. He lives and works in Marquette, MI. Inspired by the natural surroundings where he resides; Limberg creates drawings that pull from his imagination and the visual beauty of the wild.

Luna. Pen and ink.

THE MASSACHUSETTS BAY COLONY IN RELATION TO WOLVES AND OTHER NATIVE WILDLIFE
JUSTIN HILL

Justin Hill is a wildlife advocate and history enthusiast living in North Carolina, where he spends his time researching, hiking and studying the surrounding wildlife.

When the Spanish began their conquest of the Caribbean and Hispaniola, they were introduced to a new world of wildlife they had never encountered. In turn, the Spanish brought with them soon-to-be invasive species upon the Americas. Livestock, particularly European pigs, would soon overrun entire Caribbean islands (Tindall). While livestock would change local ecosystems, the introduction of the horse would have a much wider effect upon the ecosystem.

While it had been outlawed by the Spanish for Native Americans to own horses, the Pueblo Revolt of 1680 granted Pueblos access to these coveted animals. Through trade with neighboring tribes, horses quickly became a way of life for Natives spanning the Great Plains of North America. This allowed greater mobility for some tribes willing to uproot themselves and become nomadic. This would also have an impact on American buffalo populations on several fronts. One in particular was that riding horseback increased the success of buffalo hunts. Native Americans began surplus killing herds faster than they could recover, largely for trade—an all too recurring trend (Tindall)

For centuries, Native Americans had been altering the landscape for their needs. A noted method employed was a slash-and-burn system in which they would burn down forest land to create ideal agricultural fields, as well as creating ideal lands for game to graze on (Tindall). However, using the lands and hunting grounds on an as-needed basis, these alterations were not permanent fixtures on the landscape in the way Europeans were accustomed to establishing.

Well before the Pueblo Revolt, Europeans were fleeing religious persecution, and in the 17th century, one of the most attractive places to escape this persecution became New England. While the Plymouth Colony was founded with the intent of establishing a pious and true Christian settlement, the Massachusetts Bay Colony was initially chartered as an entrepreneurial endeavor. However, through the savvy legal maneuvering of John Winthrop, the governing headquarters for the colony would not be in London, but in Massachusetts itself. With this shift of governing power, Winthrop would alter the colony from being a "profit-making enterprise" to a Christian-based establishment. He would bring his "city on a hill" declaration to reality (Tindall).

Religious conviction or not, payments and debts still needed to be paid. The Plymouth Colony real estate would be sold in 1628, and a new charter would be written granting it to William Bradford, but the merchants back in England needed to see profit ("Charter"). The rocky New England landscape did not lend itself to bringing about large amounts of commercial cash crops such as tobacco in Virginia, so to earn their keep, Massachusetts colonists instead turned to industrialization, such as ship-building, and exploiting the local wildlife through ventures such as fishing, whaling and the fur trade(Tindall).

While whaling by Native Americans in the Pacific Northwest is well documented, for New England Natives, whaling was not a definitive practice. The whales utilized by northeastern tribes had either beached or died at sea and drifted to shore. In either case, whales were not actively pursued off the coast of New England until European colonization (Symington).

From the time of colonization through the turn of the 20th century, whale parts, particularly whale oil, were in high demand. Whale oil, a byproduct of processing whale blubber, held a number of uses, from lighting fuel, to lubrication for mechanical devices, to creating wax products, such as candles and cosmetics. In addition, whale bones and teeth were used, especially in women's fashion items, and were a substitute for ivory (Symington). Massachusetts understood it was in prime position to capitalize on its proximity to such a valuable resource. Nantucket would become a major whaling hub on the New England coast.

The most prized was the bounty of the sperm whale, which, in addition to the oil processed from its blubber, also produced a wax known as spermaceti, which was used for higher end candles and

Goods (Symington). Another whale hunted off the coast was the Atlantic right whale. The animals were hunted to abysmal numbers, and today, both the sperm and right whales are designated as threatened and currently under the protection of the Endangered Species Act ("Endangered Species Act").

When whaling first began, the animals were abundant along the coast; however in a relatively short span of time, their presence began to dwindle. Whalers would have to venture out farther into deeper arctic waters to find a target. The Boston Non-Importation Agreement of 1768 actually makes note of the poor fishing and whaling prospects encountered as excuse of inability to make payments, stating of the whale fishery, "by which our principal sources of remittances are likely to be greatly diminished..."

As whaling required hunters to venture out into colder, deeper waters, whaling became something of a job European-Americans did not want to do. The whaling industry was one that lent itself to diversity, employing largely Native Americans and African Americans on sloops. But the industry hardly ended with the whalers themselves. In town, the whaling, fishing and shipping industries brought employment to ship builders, rope makers, as well as a line of processing from raw material to merchant.

One such raw material enthusiastically received back home to England was fur. Beaver fur in particular was greatly desired, and the North American beaver even more so as it had a thicker and longer pelt than its European relative. Beaver coats and hats were very fashionable and a symbol of status at the time. As a result, the European beaver had been hunted to near extinction, so the discovery of a land populated with this animal was a major score for fur traders, and some Native Americans would profit (Tindall).

The primary forces behind the beaver fur trade were Native Americans and the French. The Native Americans were expert trappers and hunters, and beaver became a major form of currency. Pursuit of these animals became so intense that gaining the upper hand, specifically in the interest of the Iroquois, spawned what would be known as the Beaver Wars. As a result, the Iroquois would hunt regional beavers into extinction (Tindall).

In John Winthrop's journal, many references are made as to payment by means of beaver. Winthrop recalls an incident in which a ship was lost at sea, and several people aboard drowned; however, where the loss of human life was mentioned almost as a blurb, the loss of beaver cargo goes on for nearly a full paragraph. He writes, "Plymouth men lost four hogsheads, 900 pounds of beaver and 200 otter skins, The governor of Massachusetts lost in beaver and fish, which he sent to Virginia, etc., near £100. Many others lost beaver..." (Winthrop).

Like the buffalo skin trade, the New England fur trade relied heavily on Native American hunters. To engage in trade with Europeans, these hunters diverted from a "take only what you need" way of life to essentially becoming commercial trappers. The North American beaver would be depleted from the eastern United States and migrated westward (Tindall). For as much as other animals may have been hunted to the brink, none seem to have been hunted with such contempt as the wolf.

Europe had long held an unfavorable view of the gray wolves native to their own lands. By the time Massachusetts was receiving her first settlers, wolves in England had been effectively exterminated, and the rest of the British Isle and mainland Europe were on their way to doing the same (Beeland). In the time that passed, the rarity of wolves gave way to their gaining a somewhat mythical status among Europeans.

The wolf had become a staple antagonistic villain in European folklore. They circulated stories including a "big bad wolf" that would become favorites in the Grimm Brothers' collection, such as "Little Red Cap" and "The Wolf and the Seven Goslings," with their contemporary adaptations known as "Little Red Riding Hood" and "The Three Little Pigs," respectively (Grimm). Additionally, mainland Europe had tales of werewolves as early as the 15th century.

But as John Winthrop, William Bradford, and their respective companies were devout Christians and believers in scripture, perhaps part of the distaste for the wolf would come from a misinterpretation of scripture. As followers of Jesus are often referred to as regarding a flock of lambs and Jesus as the Shepherd, verses such as Luke 10:3 ("Go; behold, I send you out as lambs in the midst of wolves") and the warning of "wolves in sheep's clothing" may leave some unable to recognize the use of metaphor. Additionally, Paul uses a similar analogy in Acts 20:29 saying, "I know that after my departure savage wolves will come among you, not sparing the flock" (*Bible*).

Wolves didn't entirely have bad press in Christian culture however. The Catholic tradition of "St. Francis of Assisi and Brother Wolf" depict an animal that is not inherently evil, but has the capacity to repent and subject himself to God through the righteous. But any inspiration emanating from the "Brother Wolf" story would be lost on Europe and America.

Cultural folklore and religious traditions were rooted indeed, but the colonists of Massachusetts Bay were not without firsthand reason for at least being annoyed with the American wolves. Many folks settling in Massachusetts would have found themselves not as the lambs amongst wolves, but as the shepherds themselves guarding their livestock against the wolves.

Livestock was and continues to be an important part of American culture. John Winthrop notes in his published journal several instances of wolves taking cattle, especially young calves and pigs across Massachusetts. In his early settlement book, *New England's Prospect*, William Wood opines of the region's "greatest annoyance," the wolves, musing that if only all of the wolves could be replaced with bears, how great it would be. He states the three greatest annoyances of settling around the Charles River were rattlesnakes, mosquitoes, and wolves.

Wood, although referring to wolves as "ravenous rangers" and "devourers," also makes honest efforts at adequately describing and understanding their behavior. He observes that the American wolves are not like wolves of other countries: they are not aggressive toward humans and tend to stick to smaller prey, avoiding cows and horses. He even notes that when the wolves take a calf, they tend to be red calves, which he concludes are mistaken for deer (Wood).

Indeed, Wood was correct in his assessment. Today, it is believed there are four distinct wolves native to North America. There is the gray wolf, the largest of all living wolves whose historic North American range spanned from Canada and encompassed the Midwest to western United States. The Mexican gray wolf, a subspecies of the gray wolf, historically found along western Mexico and southwestern U.S. The presently critically endangered red wolf once held a historic range spanning the southeastern United States from Pennsylvania to Texas. The eastern wolf, morphologically similar to the red wolf, ranged to the east of the Great Lakes, including New England. The eastern wolf's taxonomical rank is somewhat murky, with some designating it its own species, others as a subspecies of the gray wolf, others considering it may be a red wolf (Beeland). Whatever the scientific community decides, what is today known as the eastern wolf is most likely what Wood and those settling Massachusetts encountered.

Massachusetts Bay had not been settled long before there would be an actual bounty placed on wolves. On November 9, 1630, it was officially written as law that "[every] Englishe man that killeth a wolfe in any p'te within the Lymmits of this pattent shall haue allowed him..." It then states revenue on these bounties will be collected through livestock tax (Court of Assistants)/ This would be the first colonial bounty on wolves, but others would follow. Bounty payment would eventually increase to about an average month's pay per animal. Displaying societal contempt for the animals, wolves that had been killed in more brutal ways, such as mauled by dogs, would take a larger bounty than a cleaner kill such as gunshot (Beeland).

In Charles Upham's book, *Salem Witchcraft*, he gives detail of the means by which colonists would trap bears and wolves. For bears, a corridor was fashioned in which some bait was placed at the end. When the bear would remove the bait, a cord would be attached to the trigger of a gun, and the bear would be shot in the head. Wolves, on the other hand, would be trapped with a dug-out trench, known as a "wolf pit." The trench would be scantly covered, and the wolves would fall through into a steep trench. Upon being found, they would be killed. Upham also mentions another animal, a cat, smaller than a wolf, but more ferocious by his account known as a "lucifee." This animal would be later known as the lynx. He writes that to kill this animal was considered a "useful public service" and that they were only "taken by the gun." The Canada lynx is presently listed as "threatened" under the Endangered Species Act.

While the depletion of some native New England wildlife and forest land was a relief for those settling livestock and setting up towns and suburbs, the fur industry of the colonies would need to make adjustments. Like the whaling industry, which saw hunters venturing farther and farther to earn their living, the quest for beaver and otter became a driving force behind Western expansion (Sleeper-Smith).

Just prior to the 19th century, several treaties were made between the newly established United States and various Native American tribes, stating that United States citizens settling or poaching areas in a tribe's agreed territory would be "out of the protection of the United

States" ("Charter"). These agreements would not hinder the commerce of the fur trade, and Western expansion pressed forward. The Louisiana Purchase and the expedition of Lewis and Clark would officially unlock the West and prospects of gold, with the idea of "manifest destiny" added to the hunger of conquering all land to the Pacific Ocean.

Over the course of American settlement, Massachusetts and the rest of what would become the lower forty-eight states would see dramatic changes to the landscape, flora, and fauna. The historic ranges of native animals such as the gray, eastern, and red wolves, grizzly bears, beaver, right and sperm whales, bison and lynx would be dramatically reduced due to the effects of both over-harvesting and the sprawl of American society. All aforementioned animals are currently or have previously been allotted protections under the Endangered Species Act (Endangered Species Act). While these animals are a vital part of American history, they should not be resigned to the pages of history. With sincere and coherent conservation efforts, perhaps forestland such as those in present day Massachusetts may someday hold a better testimony to the lively landscape described by William Wood. Otherwise, we may find ourselves lamenting the same disappointment as Massachusetts native Henry David Thoreau when he wrote of his state: "But when I consider that the nobler animals have been exterminated here-the cougar, panther, lynx, wolverine, wolf, bear, moose, deer, the beaver, the turkey, etc., etc. - I cannot but feel as if I live in a tamed and, as it were, emasculated country" (Thoreau).

Works Cited

1. _____. "Charter of the Colony of New Plymouth Granted to William Bradford and His Associates: 1629". Web. Yale-Avalon.

2. _____. "Boston Non-Importation Agreement, August 1, 1768". Colonial Society of Massachusetts: 1768. Web. Yale-Avalon.

3. _____. *U.S. Fish and Wildlife Service*. Endangered Species, 2015. Web. February 20, 2015.

4. _____. *New American Standard Bible*. Anaheim: Foundation Publications. 1997. Print.

5. _____. Court of Assistants of the Colony of the Massachusetts Bay 1630-1692. Boston: Suffolk County. 1904. eBook.

6. Beeland, T. Delene. *The Secret World of Red Wolves*. Chapel Hill: UNC Press. 2013. Print.

7. Grimm, Jacob, and Wilhelm Grimm. *Household Stories*. London: Macmillan. 1882. PDF.

8. Hittell, Theodore H. *The Adventures of James Capen Adams, Mountaineer and Grizzly Bear Hunter of California*. San Francisco: Towne and Bacon. 1860. eBook.

9. Sleeper-Smith, Susan. *Fur Trade and Empire: The Epic History of the Fur Trade in America*. Journal of American Studies.(May 2011):381-382. Web. February 20, 2015.

10. Symington, Timothy. *Leviathan: History of Whaling in America*. Historical Journal of Massachusetts. (Winter 2008):92-93. PDF.

11. Thoreau, Henry David. *The Heart of Thoreu's Journals*(edited by Odell Shepard). New York: Dover Publications. 1961. eBook.

12. Tindall, George Brown, and David Emory Shi. *America: A Narrative History*. New York: Norton. 2013. Print.

13. Upham, Charles W.. *Salem Witchcraft: An Account of Salem Village*. Vol. 1. Boston: Wiggin and Lunt. 1867. PDF.

14. Winthrop, *John*. *Winthrop's Journal: The History of New England Vol II* (edited by James Kendall Hosmer). Ebook.

15. Wood, William. *Wood's New England's Prospect*. Boston: John Wilson and Son. 1865. Google eBook.

MEXICAN GREY WOLF
TI'A GORUP

Ti'A Gorup is a potter and self-taught artist.

She combines her love of painting with her love of nature—in particular, the wide open spaces and focuses much of her work on endangered species.

She is committed to donating a portion of any sales to those organizations that educate and inspire others to save the wolves, wild horses, and other subjects of that endeavor.

Her home-based studio, New Earth Pottery Works, is located in the breathtaking beauty of the Sonoran Desert outside Tucson, Arizona.

www.newearthpotteryworks.webs.com

Mexican Grey Wolf. Pastels.

NO REGRETS & WOLF CHILD, MIRROR CHILD
SUE CARTLEDGE

Sue Cartledge has been writing fiction and poetry since her early teens. After spending much her life in Tasmania—Australia's smallest and most beautiful State, she now lives in Sydney. Sue has been active in fighting for the environment since 1966, when as a student she marched against a hydro-electric dam being built high in the mountains of South-West Tasmania, flooding Lake Pedder and its unique aquatic denizens.

No Regrets

I plead guilty, yes guilty, to the act
of eating red riding hood and her granmamma.
Furthermore, I'll admit, not without some pride,
that it was my honey tongue
that seduced the girl – altogether
too trusting, too naïve, too unaware —
so easily I convinced her to stray
from the straight and narrow way to walk
among primroses and strawberries.
And yes, it was that same clever tongue of mine
fooled her granma, silly old biddy,
shortsighted no doubt from years of sewing fine seams
and knitting and cooking up
moral fables to scare the youngsters with.

But I object! I am not the villain
or evil personified — wolf in gran's clothing
though I may be!
I aver, ladies and gentlemen, boys and girls

of the fairy tale reading public — judge and jury all —
that in my defense I need only point
to my lupine nature. I simply did
what a wolf naturally does. Nature
red in tooth and claw, someone has written.

Well, this wolf's not so bloody. I obligingly
swallowed them, my victims, my prey,
swallowed them whole to spare them the pain
and for my gentleness
was shot, disemboweled and skinned.
And while I plead my case, let me remark
that I am NOT that wolf
that bullied and threatened and in the end
was outsmarted
by those three smarmy smart alec pigs,
(though I believe he was a distant cousin
on my father's side.)

I know you all clapped and cheered when
the huntsman oh so conveniently appeared
in granma's cottage to shoot me,
slit me open
and let the ladies out. But please remember
I am just a creature of nature. Any evil
imputed to me is branded on my skin
to serve as awful warning
to those who want to stray.
Let's hope that pretty little missy
has learned her lesson well!
As for me, I am condemned
to eternal scorn and infamy;
worse, to an ignominious existence
as a rug on the huntsman's floor
forever trodden under the feet of my enemy.

Wolf Child, Mirror Child

Grief and loss have been my constant companions since first I could feel. They are burnt into my shadow; wherever I walk, they walk with me. My path is crowded, my sisters and brothers—fear, doubt, terror, courage and tenacity—dog my footsteps. I walk invisible, unseen, overlooked. My face may be familiar, my clothes and hair clearly recognizable, but I am nowhere to be seen.

Why do the two oldest siblings—grief and loss—stay so close to me, the baby of the family? They are closer to me than my skin, my mouth, my breath, my heartbeat. Though they are a part of me, I know they are not me. I am separate, vulnerable, treasured. All my invisible family cluster around me, hiding me, protecting me, caging me, teaching me.

Where have they come from, my dark and shadowy family? Night visitors, glancing at me from dim spotted mirrors in dusty hallways, they recognized me at once, the baby girlchild wandering alone in the empty night. I caught their eyes, glittering in the dark, and at once they took hold of me, their arms and legs, eyes and mouths entering me. Walking with my feet, touching with my hands, seeing though my eyes, but never uttering a single sibilant word.

Later, their younger sisters entered me during solitary daylight walks or lonely hours in my empty room. Courage and tenacity walk hand in hand with doubt and terror, and teach me to deny and defy the everyday world. They are with me everyday, but daylight cannot lift the stain imprinted on my soul by grief and loss.

Though I live in a big bleak house, dark and cold and echoing, I'm not sequestered from the everyday demands of life in a provincial town. I'm not hidden behind graying gauzy curtains thick with dusty cobwebs and shredding in the slightest draught. I may be locked away, but my duress is not physical. I must go to school, to music lessons, to Sunday school, to church. I must walk down the main street, observed by prying gossipy eyes, but still I walk unseen, unmarked, overlooked.

At school, church, Sunday school, how quickly I am made to learn just how other I am. Such lessons come daily, hourly. Not just from God's Word and His Laws, but equally from the social conventions and expectations my enforced companions have drunk in with their bottled formula. I am judged and found unacceptable for being what I am. The fierce ghost that no one sees. The clumsy girl that everyone sees, passes judgement on. Even the few adults who vaguely apprehend my shadow family clustered around me cannot reach through.

One grief I am fully aware of, one loss which I cannot comprehend—my body. Why do I have this body? Why not that one? Or some other one? Why am I even human? Where is my fur? My gleaming eyes, my sharp fangs? I did not choose this! Where am *I* in this alien body?

The mirrors fascinate me, threaten me, entice me with their bewitching, dangerous entrapment. You might not like who you see in the mirror, who looks out at you when the lights are off, and only a stray gleam of starlight or the beam of a passing car's headlights cracks it open, and you see who or what waits within. Some of these mirror folk are my shadow sisters and brothers, but there are others lurking in those glittering icy depths—wolves, warlocks, witches, ghosts, beasts, lost and abandoned souls, unnamed and unnameable entities trying to find their way out. Fused with my visceral dread of these mirror beings is an equally overpowering hunger, a ravenous desire to find my way in, to where I will be recognized, known for what I really am.

Alice climbed through her looking glass and entered a world of paradoxical reversals and comic mirror imaging. That's not the world I will come to when finally I break through that skin of glass and plunge into the peat-black pool beneath. A submerged world of multifarious shades of darkness yet crystal bright, flashing diamonds of hard white light.

Where am I? My unfamiliar body is still trapped on the physical side, endlessly walking down a cold, dark, empty hallway. A hallway stretching on forever, mirrors at regular intervals winking at me across the void, trying to lure me into staring into their eyes and release the wolves or the witches or warlocks, or something else. They want me so much they send waves of yearning, of desire, in flashes of light: over here, over here; look here, look at me! I keep my eyes firmly on the floor and go on walking, walking, walking through the night until dawn wafts me away with birdsong, trees, and sunlight.

Every night, I traverse that endless hallway, always hoping, but never reaching the door at the far end. Never daring to look any mirror full in the eye, barely doing a quick sideways shuffle with my eyeballs as I scuttle past. On and on, night after night, dawn releasing me from the danger I desire to face, the world I yearn to enter. Can I get there?

How can I get there? How can I break out of this daylight world of alien existence into the diamond hard light of my mirror-self?

In the depths of that darkness that is also light we will all be gathered—all the lost souls and abandoned bodies transformed: the beasts who would be human, all the humans who have become animals and birds, or half and half, or gods or devils, or neither. Where, finally, I will become the wolf within me—sleek, gray-dark as smoke, swift, supple, with mighty crunching jaws and joyful, triumphant howl.

THE MONTEXAN
ALAN GOOD

Alan Good's writing has appeared in Timothy McSweeney's Internet Tendency, The Legendary, Atticus Review, ExFic,Bookslut, *and* Word Riot. *His first novel is* Barn Again: A Memoir. *He can be stalked on Twitter:* @TheAlanGood.

I've always had trouble relating to people, I think because I wear my heart on my sleeve and my heart is shriveled and putrid, smells like a soggy cow carcass. (That's a specific smell, and if you've never encountered it, be grateful.) Somehow I took to the Montexan right away. We were instantly old friends even if she was loud and vulgar and incomparably yappy. She is so earnest and goodhearted it got to where I didn't notice those things after a while.

If there's one thing I hate, it's a stativist, or state nativist, the type of American who thinks his state is the greatest and never misses any opportunity to remind you, the type who also believes that people who didn't have the privilege of being born in his glorious state should not have the opportunity to move there. Fortunately, there are no such arbitrary strictures about how many things I can hate, so I am free to rage against not only state nativists but hypocrites, tailgaters, fanatics, poachers, and, if it is a long car trip and I need some aggression to keep me awake, the Machine. Montanans are a proud lot. Next to Texans and Alaskans, they are the most stuck-up about their state. One of the nice things about being from Oklahoma, unless you're from Oklahoma City, in which case there is nothing nice about being from Oklahoma, is that you get all the pretension knocked out of you at an early age. I am pretty happy no matter where I am as long as it's not Oklahoma.

Occasionally, if you can stand to be around a person long enough, or if you are trapped together in a moving vehicle for an extended period of time, you might be able to see past the things about that person that drive you crazy and find the person's redeeming qualities.

Most people have some, although they're buried deep in a lot of us. I say most, which is a gross and unfair generalization. I can think of too many exceptions. So I should say *many* of us have redeeming qualities. Or some. On the surface, Yalda Zandi and I were natural enemies. She was the worst type of state snob: a transplant. She loved her adopted state with the passion of a convert. It didn't help that she was originally from Texas and retained a passionate fondness for her native state. If Oklahoma and Texas ever go to war, Texas will win. They outnumber and outmoney us. But it will be a pyrrhic victory. In fact, linguists would have to change the expression to "a Texan victory."

I picked her up on 191, about halfway between Jackson and Moose, on a drizzly evening. When I first saw her, I thought she was just a tree stump. Then she moved, and I thought she was an elk. I slowed down in case she was going to jump in front of me and saw that she was actually a human: medium height, athletic build, long curly black hair, doe-scat-brown eyes.

I slowed to a stop, pulling along beside her. I rolled down the window and she stuck her head in.

"Nice ride. I've never seen a dude driving one of these."

This is a sore spot for me. Where did people get the idea that the Jeep Liberty is a car for females? It is in fact a car for mechanics. Every time my mail finds me, there's a new recall. They'd recalled the suspension. They'd recalled the headlamps. They'd recalled the lower ball joints and the door locks. The motors for the rear windows broke so the windows wouldn't stay up without duct tape, but if you asked Chrysler about it they couldn't recall. If my Jeep was a child, it would have been born with a cleft lip, a club foot, and spina bifida. I still would have loved it. Mine was black, a 2005 diesel that I ran, whenever possible, on biodiesel. I responded, rather testily, "And I've never seen a woodland caribou, yet I know they exist, in Canada and northern Idaho. Did you want a ride, or are you just doing thumb exercises?"

After an hour of riding together in the same car, I knew just about everything about her, a lot of it quite personal, her weirdest secrets (she called them secrets, but that was just a formality), her college GPA, her preferred sexual positions. She was Yalda Zandi, an Iranian-American Texan who had reinvented herself as a Montanan. She had a skull tattoo on her left bicep, a fist with a raised middle finger on her right forearm. I'm ready for the tattoo craze to subside, but I guess they're good for the economy if nothing else. Her father, an Iranian who moved to Texas and converted to Christianity for business reasons, was big in petrochemicals, and her mother, a housewife from east Texas, was just big. As if being from Texas was not bad enough, she was from Houston, a city I am proud to say I have never visited, although it did give us Townes Van Zandt, a pretty redeeming quality. I told her I was sorry for where she grew up, but she did not act as if she heard me. She was busy explaining the geography of Houston. If I am pathologically shy, as I have been told my entire life, Yalda was pathologically extroverted, meaning if she did not have someone to talk to she would die of panic. She had been talking to her fifty-pound Mystery Ranch backpack when I showed up. She was a good hiking partner: you don't need a bear bell when you have a Yalda, not that I advocate bear bells. I hate them.

She had just broken up with her boyfriend, who had called her an unpleasant name, the one they can't say on television, on the way to the Gros Ventre Wilderness for a seven-day backpacking trip.

"And he just left you on the side of the road?"

"I told him to pull over and let me out, and he did."

"He didn't follow you? He didn't offer to take you into town?"

"He did for a while, but he gave up."

"You made the right decision leaving him." A gentleman would have given her the car to borrow and found his way into town on his own. "On second thought, you should have stuck it out for a couple days and pushed him off a cliff."

She leaned forward nervously in her seat and drummed her fingers on the dash. "I've made a huge mistake. Huge mistake."

I thought she would talk about her boyfriend, maybe her decision to hitchhike at night along a poorly lit rode frequented by gun-crazy, beer-guzzling anti-feminists, but no.

"I wore a hat that says Montana on it."

She took it off and stared at it, as if to see if it really said Montana on it or if she was just paranoid.

"So?"

"You don't advertise the state when you leave it."

"It's probably not a big deal."

"You just don't do it."

"Should I unscrew my license plate?"

"Are you being sarcastic?"

"I think so."

"I can't seem to tell whether you're being sarcastic."

"I have the same problem sometimes," I said, but my reply was lost to her, trampled down like our civil rights after a terrorist attack.

"Dude, listen to this. My friend told me I have this thing called Resting Bitch Face. Like last week she said this. My face just sets in a natural sneer, I guess, and people think I'm giving them nasty looks but I'm not. Everything I say comes off as sarcastic but it's not."

"RBF," I said. "I think I saw a pharmaceutical commercial about that. Talk to your doctor about Smileagra from Pfizer."

"I'd never heard of it before but I think she's right. I mean like I don't mean things to sound mean but most of the time they do. At least now I have an excuse. It's a medical condition so if I ever offend you just know that I didn't mean to. Thanks for picking me up, by the way."

"Most of the blond girls in Bozeman have the same thing," I said. "Or maybe a variant disorder. I'm not sure what the name for it would be, but they all walk around looking like they just swallowed a fart."

She snorted. "Oh my God, have you met Elisa Ackerman-Offerman-Mann? You just described her to a tee. Is it tee or teeth? Are you armed to the tee or armed to the teeth? I've never known which one is right so I usually just say teeth but I make the 'th' part really quiet so you're not sure if I said tee or teeth. That way I don't look stupid. By the way you totally are armed to the tee^th. What kind of guns are those back there?" She had been examining the interior of my vehicle all this time, peering in all directions as if searching for an escape. There was a 20-gauge shotgun and a .44 rifle behind her seat that she must have seen when she tossed her pack in the back. There was also a Henry AR-7 survival rifle, but she couldn't see it. It was stored in my pack. And a Sig Sauer .45 under my seat.

"All those guns are loaded. Don't touch them unless you're fixing to shoot someone."

"Oh my God, is that a bow? Like a real bow that shoots arrows? Are you serious? I think you just became my new hero. You are like literally Robin Hood. On the hunt for a mad killer. I guess that's not really like Robin Hood but it's all in the name of truth and justice so in a way it is. Can you shoot that thing? More important, can you show me how to shoot that thing?"

Why not? The rain had stopped, and I needed to stretch my legs, and it was late. We could have pushed on, made it into Bozeman by midnight, but what's the point of driving through the park when you can't see any of it? I knew a good primitive campsite nearby. We hadn't entered the park yet, so we didn't need a permit or anything.

I'd bought my bow off a guy who needed money for child support. It was set to fifty pounds, and I'd never messed with it. I wasn't going to hunt elk with it. I just like to shoot, and archery is a lot cheaper and quieter than shooting guns. I figured she might be strong enough to draw it back. I'd seen her haul that big pack of hers off the ground like it was nothing.

I set up my target, lit up by the Recall's headlights, on a little hill so if she missed I wouldn't lose my arrows. I showed her how to hold the bow, how to stand, how to aim, how to breathe, how to draw, how to use the release: "Never put your finger on the trigger until you're ready to shoot." If she took a deep breath and closed her eyes, she could just draw back the string. She was wild on her first five or six shots, missing ten feet to the left, then to the right, then five feet high, then straight into the dirt, but she finally found her zone and got to where she could reliably hit the target. I left her on her own and went off to set up my tent and boil some water for tea. By the time I was done, she'd hit the target twelve times in a row. Her last shot was a bullseye.

Yalda was a good camper, not one of these pyromaniacs that believes you need a raging bonfire and a mountain of marshmallows to go camping. The stars and the moon and my effusive glow were light enough.

She sneered at me. "A tent, Molnar? I'm from Montana. We don't use tents. I just sleep under the stars."

"This is a decoy. I set it up here, sleep over there. Any bears or bandits come looking for me in the tent, I've got the drop on them."

"A lot of bandits come looking for you in the middle of the night?"

"Not a lot. But once is enough."

Yalda pulled a giant contraption out of her pack that allowed her to boil water in something like seven seconds. Then she poured her hot water into some astronaut food in a titanium pot. I felt like I was in the space station. I gripped my cup a little tighter so it wouldn't float away. When her gruel had cooled, she dug in.

"Want some? Beef stroganoff."

"No."

I'd eaten trail mix for supper. I don't mess with backpacking stoves. I'll make a little twig fire to boil water for tea, but I generally stick to cold food.

"You like a vegan or something?"

"I just hate cows."

"Seems like if you hate cows you should eat them."

"But then the cows keep coming, filling the rivers with their filth and killing off the predators."

She had wheedled the basic details of my case out of me. "So are you going to let me come along on your secret mission?"

"Maybe that's not a good idea. It could get dangerous. Whoever I'm looking for is a maniac with no scruples."

"I can handle it, dude. Did you see me shoot that bow? And anyway . . . ."

She had powers of persuasion. Talk a man near to death and you can get him to agree to anything. "OK," I said, "you can be my sidekick."

"No. Not sidekick. Partner."

It would mean splitting my take, but I didn't mind. I would have better luck with a partner. It's not a world for introverts. Even menial retail jobs these days require outgoing, vivacious go-getters. Now hiring friendly people. Introverts need not apply. Someone should file a lawsuit. Computers analyze our personalities when we apply for jobs, screen our voices for our potential relatability. I am not a people person. I could fake it when I was with Wilder West. With its weight behind me, I could approach someone, start a conversation. Freelance, different story. Yalda would come in handy.

I woke up early and slunk into the woods to take care of some personal matters. Yalda was still asleep when I got back, so I made some tea, drew an arrow in the dirt in the direction I would go, and hiked up to Fictional Lake, whose name I've changed to protect the innocent. It was about a mile off. I spooked a couple mule deer when I got there and thought I saw a moose. I sat on a fallen log on a rocky bank and quietly drank my tea. Twenty minutes after my arrival, an osprey tore down from its invisible perch in a pine on the other side of the lake and swooped down to steal a fish, then flew back to its hideout. With any luck, the bird he snagged was an invasive brook trout, but more likely it was a cutthroat. That's how it works on this planet—the things that need killing thrive and take over while the things that are worth protecting get eaten.

This was a good way to start a day. It would take a lot to top the osprey's surprise attack, so I finished my tea and headed back down the trail. Yalda was awake, doing yoga on a boulder. She smiled in acknowledgment but did not, to my surprise, say anything. I wondered if there was a yoga routine she could do in the car so I could enjoy some quiet.

A while after we had entered the park, we noticed a funny thing: there was a massive herd of elk on the east side of the road, a massive herd of mule deer on the west. Yalda snapped her fingers and sang, "When you're an elk you're an elk all the way." She was entertaining, which was convenient because I'd listened to all the books I had out from the library.

Somewhere down the road in the middle of a story about Yalda's friend who had been attacked while jogging by a mountain lion that turned out to be a golden retriever in estrus, my confounded cell phone rang. There's some technology I like, and a lot that I hate. Compound bows, electric drills, and Bowie knives I like; cell phones and computers I hate.

"Why do I even have service?"

We were still in the park, maybe twenty miles from the north entrance of Yellowstone, and I'd assumed, or wished, that cell phones just stopped working once you got in the park. I didn't want to answer. Only one person had the number, and I didn't think I wanted to talk to him. It would only be bad news, like another wolf had been butchered, or a grizzly. I was surprised to hear Alex Percy on the other end, saying he had a lead for me.

"Greetings, Molnar," he said in a nasally semi-robotic voice because he thought my name sounded like an alien's. He did it every time he talked to me, his hilarious joke. He got back into his regular voice: "Just saw a picture this yokel posted online. Bragging about killing a wolf."

"I didn't know you were in on this."

"Russ told me. I'm not trying to horn in on your action. God knows you need the money. Just think of me as like a consultant."

Russ could tell anyone he wanted since he was bankrolling this operation, but if he'd asked me I'd have told him to leave old Percy in the dark. Percy and I were on the same team but not the same wavelength. After the incident in Ritchey, he had wanted Wilder West to cut me totally loose, leave me to rot, disown me so my trouble wouldn't come back on the organization. I shouldn't know this, but I do because he felt the need to tell me after I got out of jail.

"So where is this child of the Enlightenment?"

"Frontier Days."

"Cheyenne?"

"I'm going to text you his name and some pictures. You should probably head that way."

Cheyenne. Some people say that human beings are the most comfortable in flat, savannah-like settings because that is where we originated. Not me. I was born a flat-lander but didn't spend a comfortable moment on the plains in eighteen years. I'm only comfortable in the mountains. I like the beach, but the plains give me the jimjams. Maybe I am a snob in my own way. I don't like the artificiality of saying one state is better than another one, but I'll take the Rocky Mountains over anything on earth.

"What was that about?"

"You like rodeos?"

Yalda, as usual, was talking: "So get this, I know eleven people who have been mauled by bears. I mean none of them have died but three of them lost their eyes. The funny thing is they all still love bears and they all still go backpacking and hiking and flyfishing. I guess it's not that strange; it was never the bears' fault. These guys are all, like all guys, idiots. This one guy, he's kind of an idiot really, like even more of an idiot than the rest, thought it would be a good idea to defend himself against this massive grizzly he'd wandered up on by saying, 'No, bear,' in a really stern voice, and pointing at him like he was a child he was telling to go sit in the corner. The bear just reached over and ripped his eye out. That's what the bear thought about that guy. Oh my God, back in Texas, blah blah blah . . . ."

Something didn't smell right. About the case, that is. Yalda smelled fine, and I'd bathed only two days ago—in a fountain in Jackson. I couldn't understand why someone who had taken the trouble to hunt down three wolves in three separate areas and shoot them, always in the same spot, the mouth so they couldn't eat, and leave no traces or footprints, would turn around and post evidence of his crime on his public vanity page. We didn't even know what gun he was using. No one had found any casings or slugs. The cynical part of me was starting to think old Percy had sent me on an ivory-billed woodpecker hunt, that he knew right where the butcher was and did intend to horn in on my action and cut me out of the reward money. I didn't really care about the money that much; I'd wash dishes for a couple months. I just wanted him caught. I did not want to go down to Cheyenne. I needed to be up in the mountains searching for signs and slugs. They didn't even know precisely where two of the wolves had been shot. They'd all lived a few days before starving or bleeding out and could have wandered any number of miles.

"Oh check this out, Molnar. Molnar. Molnar? Molnar!"

Yalda breaking into my reverie like a hacker into a big retail chain's secure database.

"It's my favorite Yellowstone game. It's called Whatcha Lookin' At? You pull over, get out of your car, and stand on top of a ridge gazing out in front of you. Then you wait till about forty people have pulled over next to you and take off."

"I'm still going to pull over."

I was glad I did. We'd abandoned Bozeman and headed for Cheyenne by way of the Lamar Valley. Traffic wasn't too bad, but as we approached a big pullout in the north end of the valley we saw a swarm of cars disgorging eager wildlife watchers with binoculars and spotting scopes. The moment I stepped out of the Recall, I saw what the fuss was about: maybe one hundred fifty yards off the side of the road two grizzlies, a sow and her yearling, were noshing on the carcass of a wolf-killed elk. That must have been a sight. I'm not a dedicated wolf watcher. I do it from time to time, following the wolfers around the Lamar Valley as they follow the wolves around the Lamar Valley. I love them, but I don't need to see them every day. I'm just happy to know they're out there. But I would have loved to see them take that elk—and to see the grizzlies take it from them. It was enough, though, to get to watch the tail end of the affair. Wolves are great, but the grizzly is closest to my heart. I dug out my old spotting scope because I heard someone say some of the wolves were lingering in the brush a few hundred yards toward the Lamar River. Then I noticed a burly baldy guy, a thirty-something easterner, at least if you believed his Red Sox ballcap and Bruins jacket. He'd stepped over the guardrail and was making straight for the griz, camera in hand.

"You probably shouldn't get any closer."

"No worries, bro, I'll just walk slower."

One less fool in the world would be one way to look at it, but that fool was going to get the bears killed and ruin a lot of people's days. I followed and grabbed him by the arm, put myself between him and the bears.

"Seriously. Nobody came here to watch these bears eat your intestines and then get killed by Smokey the Fuzz."

"Back east you'd get your head cracked for this."

"Out here you get your guts ripped open."

And that sneaky easterner sucker-punched me right in the nose. It hurt, too, moderately, like an intense ice cream headache. Blood hurled out so I could barely see. Half-blind from the blood and throbbing, I lowered my head and barreled toward him, wrapped him up in a bear hug and pushed him back toward the cars until we tripped over the guardrail. I gave him a few elbows before I got up, and Yalda strolled over and finished him off with a long squeeze of bear spray.

"Careful," I said. "That stuff's expensive."

We got a standing ovation from the bystanders, a bored but threatening glance from the mother bear. I packed up my scope, and we rolled off with Yalda driving, me holding my nose in the air, clogging it with tissue.

Aside from the thing up in Ritchey, which was an anomaly, I lived my whole life without fighting. Two days as a private dick or bounty hunter or whatever, and I'm fighting at the drop of a hat.

"Does this stuff happen to you a lot?"

I was raised not to fight but to solve my problems through reason and dialogue. That was my parents' way, and it was the way I tried to live my life. I do fail sometimes, though. I wouldn't normally hit a man when he was down—I wouldn't normally hit anyone at all—but I wanted to make him think carefully about how close he wanted to get to those bears.

"I really wanted to see those wolves," she said. "I've never seen one. Not in the wild. I've seen them in the zoo, obviously," and off she went.

It's a long haul out to Cheyenne, not that Yalda seemed to notice. She's a good traveler, doesn't get bored or complain, just talks, talks, talks, and asks the occasional question, like, "Yo, what was the scariest thing that ever happened to you? Mine was this time . . . ." Yada yada Yalda. "So what's yours?"

I had to think for a second. Dangerous move. You've got to be ready to pounce with her.

"Scariest moment? Molnar?" She looked ready to keep going, so I said, "Probably this time I was nine and the tornado sirens went off. We ran outside to the fraidyhole, but it was full up of water. My dad was for getting in anyway and treading water until the storm had passed, but I was convinced it was full of water moccasins so I wouldn't get in. I ran back inside and hid in a closet. I knew I was going to die."

"But you didn't die."

"I don't think so. The tornado passed three miles outside of town. Stonewall's so little the only way it would get hit by a twister is on purpose, like God or the universe just wanted to destroy it."

"Hey what's a fraidyhole?"

"Storm cellar."

"Oh my God, that's hilarious. I've got to write that down." She undid her seatbelt and crawled into the back seat to root through her pack, keeping up her end of the dialogue the whole while. "I bet you're full of hilarious Okie slang. You know, I don't think I've ever met anyone from Oklahoma. I didn't know people still lived there."

"I love being from Oklahoma. I hate being in Oklahoma."

"Hey, don't take this the wrong way, but you speak really well for a guy who didn't go to college."

"You don't have to go to college to be smart or well-spoken. The problem is most of the people who don't go to college don't take the time to educate themselves. The bigger problem is most of the people who do go to college don't take the time to educate themselves."

"Ha! Another gem. Got it!"

"It also helps," not that she heard because by this time she'd crawled back through to the front holding a little notepad and was writing down my gems, "that my dad was an English professor."

Yalda was a talker the way the Mick was a ballplayer. (Aside from my dad, Mantle is my favorite Okie. I loved my mom, too, of course, but she wasn't an Okie. She came from Florida.) It's what she was born to do. Yet she had a way of drawing me out, getting me to reveal things I generally keep to myself. She asked a lot of questions and was genuinely interested in the answers, even if she had a compulsion to interrupt them. Really, I think my mouth just wanted to give my ears a rest. So I told her most of my life story.

I moved up here at the age of nineteen and worked two summers at Yellowstone, taking reservations for one of the hotels in the north end of the park. At the end of the summer, I would drift west out to Oregon. My parents were dead, and I had nothing keeping me in Oklahoma. It's beautiful down there, but too hot for me, and Oregon has not only the ocean and great birding and hiking but abundant wild blackberries all along the coast.

The third summer I got a job with Wilder West, a nonprofit conservation group. It's known as being mainly a wolf advocate, but it supports conservation and reintroduction of many species, black-footed ferrets, wolves, etc. For an uneducated curmudgeon, I was surprisingly good at my job. A lot of black people say that they have two voices, or ways of speaking. There's the way they talk around black people, and the way they talk around white people. What most people don't understand is that everyone does this, white people, black people, pretty much everyone else. Even rich people do it. There's a way they talk to rich people, and a way they talk to the rest of us, if they are forced into our company. I figured out how to talk to ranchers and hunters and other groups that might be unfriendly toward wolves. I played up my Okieness. It's not that I put on an act—I just let my inner Okie come out. I'm always slow-talking; growing up in the heat just does that to you. But I was looser with my grammar, sprinkled in some colorful colloquialisms. You've got to humanize yourself. You can't go to a ranch dressed in yuppie clothes, or even worse some alternative outfit and half-dollar-sized ear gauges, and expect to get them on your side. These tend to be people who think that environmentalists and conservationists are misguided and out of touch at best, evil minions of Satan or the federal government at worst. They see us, because that is how we are presented to them by our real adversaries, as people who don't know the value of work or family, as wingnuts trying to destroy both their livelihoods and way of life. But they are also usually people who respect the land, even if it's in their own sometimes incomprehensible way, and identify with wild creatures because they see themselves, even if they are squarer than the Fifth Avenue Apple Store, as wild. There are always a few people who won't listen to anything they don't want to hear. They don't care if nonlethal control methods have been proved cheaper and more effective. They want to kill wolves, and that's it. It's hard to know the reasons because all the ones they give are known to be false, and they won't give any other ones. Until Google invents the software that looks into people's hearts, probably by next fall, we only have conjecture. As far as that goes, I'd venture those types are stuck on habit, tradition, inertia, superstition, plain laziness, stubbornness, vengeance, distrust of outsiders, and sometimes old-fashioned orneriness—any combination of the above. But they're in the minority. If you can figure out how to talk to the people who will at least halfway listen then you've got a good chance of convincing them.

In my first year as a community liaison for Wilder West, I convinced six initially very unfriendly ranchers to drop their opposition to wolf protection and incorporate, with our group's financial assistance, non-lethal wolf management practices. We provided them with trained guard dogs, helped build and pay for fences, brought out biologists, researchers, and other ranchers who had been successful using non-lethal methods. We also took them out on free guided wolf-watching trips in Yellowstone. I took one sheep rancher to the Yellowstone Association store in Gardiner and showed him how much it cost to buy a stocking hat made out of predator-friendly wool. Six isn't a big number, but that number represents six fairly large ranches where a wandering wolf that would have been shot on sight now, thanks to electric fences and fladry (bright cloths hung along the fence), probably doesn't wander at all. And if he does, he won't get shot, just run off, maybe shocked if he gets too curious.

I worked there for nearly three years. It was the best thing I ever did. My ultimate achievement, had it come to fruition, would have been our sponsorship of the bull riding events at the Big Sky Pro Rodeo Roundup in Great Falls, Montana. I wanted to show people that we weren't adversaries, that we didn't disrespect them or their culture, that we weren't trying to harm them, that we shared common ground. Percy had hated the idea. He wanted to apply more radical methods. His type, more interested in perception than progress, loves to be thought of as radical. But we were moving forward with it, and it would have been successful if I hadn't gone to Ritchey.

I'd met with a rancher in the morning, finished early, and was on my way back to Bozeman. I wanted some coffee so I stopped at the gas station in Ritchey, a blip of a town with a population that one bad car wreck would decimate, and when I came out some yahoo was driving down Main Street with a dead wolf strapped to the hood of his truck. It was bloody and its tongue was hanging loose. I knew the driver, a small-time rancher named Marty Fields. His ranch was going under, and he blamed the wolves when he should have blamed himself or maybe his parents or the education system. He was thoroughly unintelligent. I've squashed bugs with more brains than him. He had no head for business or ranching, just killing and drinking. If he hadn't spent all his money on wolf traps maybe he could have saved his ranch. He had pointed a gun at me outside the high school after a community meeting one time, threatened to shoot me if I ever stepped foot on his property. He was honking his horn now like his team had just won the Super Bowl, hanging his head out his window like a happy dog. I climbed in the company truck I was driving, spilling the coffee all over the seat, and peeled out after him. I bullied him off the road and into the post office parking lot. He wouldn't get out of his truck so I reached in and dragged him out. "Fight me," I said. "Fight me, coward."

"You like my new hood ornament, hippy?" He was drunk. He wasn't going to fight me so I started cutting the wolf loose until I heard a click. I turned around, and he had a gun on me. I stepped up to him and knocked the gun out of his hand. I punched him in the right shoulder with my left just to get him facing me, then threw two hard jabs with my right. He was dazed and wobbly, and I put him down with a gut punch that I put my whole body behind. He was puking blood as I cut the wolf loose. I put it in the truck, covered it with a tarp, and drove back to Bozeman, where the cops were waiting for me.

I broke all the rules. Never get rattled, but if you do, don't let it show. Never lose your temper. Always be respectful. Never let yourself feel like you're better than whatever idiot you're talking to. I was fired, but Wilder West's lawyers got me out of jail.

I was driving south on the interstate and therefore in foul spirits. It was raining again. Even if it takes six times as long, it always pays to go the back way. Ten miles before Wheatland, we got bogged down in a massive snarl-up caused by a sleepy trucker driving too fast on a wet road. I hate interstates more than a fat kid hates himself and was cursing like a comic's comic when this quadcab, coal-rolling Dodge diesel duelly with Idaho plates zoomed past and wedged itself in front of me right before traffic stopped. The truck was lily white like its passengers. Call me racist, but there's something wrong about a white truck. I would have been angry that the truck cut me off and irritated and amused that it rolled coal at me in the process. Coal-rolling is when a truck spews black smoke from a big pipe after modifications to the emissions equipment. People pay big money to have this trash installed because they think it looks cool and makes them look tough and rebellious. Everyone wants to see themselves as rebels, especially conformists. I don't see myself as a rebel or nonconformist. I'm just maladjusted. Of course, if anyone ever told me I was well-adjusted to this malformed society, I would kill myself—or probably the no-good mangy varmint that called me well-adjusted. The most conforming people make the most annoying rebels because they rebel against meaningless things or things that are good. Coal-rollers are rebels against science and environmentalists. They'll rebel against clean air, but let a Republican president talk up a war, and they're bending over like a Goofy Goony drinking bird. They act this way for a number of reasons, primarily because they feel like they're the minority group that it's safe to hate. I would have rolled my eyes, but I would have cooled off once the black smoke cleared if not for the decal on the rear glass. It was all in white: a howling wolf and the words "Idaho wolves. Shoot, shovel and shut up." I tried to ignore it by focusing on the other sticker, which said, "Horses are proof that God loves us."

"Before you buy a bumper sticker, think it through. If it's true that 'Horses are proof that God loves us,' then aren't horseflies—and probably humans—proof that God hates horses? And what kind of God would hate horses? Write down that license plate. Maybe God loves us and put our psycho right in front of us." All bumper stickers say the same thing—that their purchasers crave attention. I try not to get worked up over them. I try.

I would have sat there and stewed, fantasizing about murdering all four of the truck's brain-dead inhabitants—it is not immoral, after all, to murder a zombie—but I wouldn't have got out of my vehicle if an empty beer can hadn't whizzed out of the driver's side window.

"What are you doing?" Yalda said with concern. "This is not a good idea. I know this girl who . . . ."

But I didn't hear anymore about her friend because I was out the door. I ambled up to the can, picked it up, and tossed it in the truck bed.

"You dropped something," I informed them as I headed back to my Recall.

Those boys stepped out of that pasty truck grinning like they were about to lose their virginity. If you guarantee a four-to-one ratio and offer a choice of an unfair fight or a supermodel sex party these guys would pick the fight every time as long as they're on the unfair side.

A wiry guy who looked to be in his forties and was wearing a cut-off tee shirt that said "Keep Calm and Shoot Something" said, "What'll we do with this one, Charlie?"

Charlie, a little fatty with a face that had been knocked around too many times, said, "Don't know, Dingus. But it'll be fun."

Dingus said, "Maybe we ought to take him out in the weeds there and teach him a lesson."

"Can teach him a lesson here, Dingus," one of the others said, this one the most muscled-up of the group, the one I was least interested in fighting when it came to that. I heard one of them call him Nuts.

"I mean like a"—he scatted the *Deliverance* tune—"lesson he'll remember."

"Jaysus, Dingus. Let's just get the kick the crap out of him and get back to drinking that beer up."

Yalda beeped the horn at them, and the Liberty possesses a pathetic horn. She hollered out the window for them to get back in the truck. I don't know, maybe I'm out of touch, maybe those dudes are more feminist than I am, less hung up on antiquated, sexist notions of chivalry and respect, but I was taught that there is a certain way a man should speak to a woman that was very, very different from the way they spoke to Yalda then.

I had a two-month-long career as a bullfighter when I was eighteen. It was after my parents were dead. I remember a line the announcer used about us: "There's a fine line between bravery and ignorance, and most of these guys can't tell the difference." I was proud when I heard that. Ten seconds later, I got slammed to the ground by a flailing bull while trying to lure it away from a dazed cowboy who was having trouble getting to his feet, and then I got stomped by that same faunching animal. I broke my collarbone and was lucky that was all. But it was the end of my rodeo career. I wasn't much of a rider, had never ridden a horse before that summer—we were too poor to keep one—but I'd been holding my own against the bulls, learning the craft. It was just as well; if I'd kept bullfighting I wouldn't have gone into conservation.

I wasn't that caught up in cowboy culture. I just liked to get close to the bulls. In the arena, I was only in the arena, not thinking about anything else. I was never the cowboy growing up. If I played cowboys and Indians, I was an Indian, although I told the neighbor kids that I was a Cherokee, not an Indian. I'm too simplistic, too black and white, to want to be the cowboy, can't convince myself that the guy who is obviously, even to a six-year-old, the bad guy is really the good guy. (True, the cowboy isn't necessarily the bad guy, more like the pawn of the bad guy.) I also don't like the uniform. Cowboys are still popular because the cowboy is the American psyche. Everyone involved in every dispute wants to be the aggrieved party. There is no one more put-upon than the aggressor because he has to come up with a way to live with himself, and that way is often to make himself the victim.

That line about ignorance and bravery probably applies to what I did next: "You idiots had better apologize to the lady, and then listen to her. Just get back in the truck, drink your beer, and enjoy your little daisy chain."

These were the types of men who would sooner beat their brother man into the ground, then spit on him and cut his throat if there's no one looking, than shake his hand. I knew better than to egg them on, but it was like it wasn't really me talking, like I was just a spectator watching someone else, someone crazier, controlling my body and my words. I was almost as angry as I'd ever been in my life.

I heard a door slam behind me as bulgy, veiny Nuts stepped toward me with clenched fists and, to judge from his expression, a pipe up his rear.

"You filthy hippy," he was saying before he froze. His friends started shouting and squirming, and I turned around to see Yalda with my bow. She was aiming an arrow at my aspiring assailant. She looked at me and said, "This thing is getting heavy."

"Point it down, for God's sake," one of them yelled. "Point it at the ground."

She pointed it at the speaker: "I want all you rednecks to get back in the truck."

"Don't call them rednecks. They're not good enough to be called rednecks."

"What should I call them?"

"Jackwagons."

"What's a jackwagon?"

"A fake redneck with more blisters on his johnson than brains in his head. A redneck drives a pickup. A jackwagon spends four thousand dollars to lift a pickup."

"Ain't you full of fun of facts, hippy?" said Nuts.

"Shut it," said Yalda. "Shut your chawhole you jackwagon or you'll be full of—hey, what are these arrows made of?"

"Carbon."

"Carbon. Carbon? Everything's made of carbon. Seriously, this thing is getting heavy. I can't hold it much longer."

"Point it down," I said, and she did, "and just ease it back to resting," which she didn't do. She let the arrow fly—her finger had been resting too close to the trigger—and it bounced off the asphalt and careened up into the biggest brute's kneecap. He howled and dropped to the ground and curled into a ball. I needed that arrow; I didn't have arrows to waste and it could probably be traced to me if anyone wanted to take the trouble to do it. So I kicked him, lightly, in the kidney to get him to uncurl, and yanked the arrow out of his knee. It just had a bullet point on it, not a broadhead, but it still must have hurt, pain I don't want to imagine. I said I was sorry. You never heard such a miserable sound. The trapped wolf I found in the woods, the one they were calling Stumbler because of his limp, had nothing on this guy. His buddies had been shocked into submission, but they stirred back to life and came after me. I waved my arrow at them; it was like it had magical powers, because it stopped them.

Yalda had put the bow back and returned with my big rifle. It was a lever-action .44 Winchester and kicked like Doug Bruce. It holds five rounds and if I empty it I've got a bruise on my shoulder five minutes later. It would have knocked her flat if she'd fired it.

"I'm going to blow out their tires."

"Please don't do that," I said.

"Why not?"

"Listen, girlie." She swung the rifle toward the speaker, the guy who hadn't made any noise yet except to spit and pound his fists together, and I was sure the next thing I saw would be his head splattering. He had the same feeling as me, evidenced by the growing stain around his crotch.

"What did you say to me?"

"Nothing. Ma'am."

"Get on the ground."

"You don't have to do this."

"All three of you on the ground. Lie down. You, Venice Beach, just keep writhing but do it quieter."

They complied. I pulled out my boot knife, a fixed blade Smith & Wesson I'd picked up at an auction in Ada, and slashed their back four tires so they couldn't come after us right away. I got in the driver's seat of the Recall and Yalda backed her way into the passenger's, pointing the gun at them until I had turned around and crossed the median and sped off into the night. In spite of its many problems, I'll always love that Jeep because it got us out of that tight spot: we were nearly bumper to bumper with the duelly and about the same with the tailgating Honda behind us, but the Recall can turn like a contortionist. I didn't make it look easy—it just was easy. I spun the wheel all the way to the left and inched up against the duelly, spun it back the other way and backed up a few inches, turned it back left as hard as I could and squeezed right out. I raced north on 25 and turned off on the first road that went east and took the detour to Cheyenne through Nebraska and Colorado.

We camped in the Pawnee National Grassland in northern Colorado. Out of the mountains I was out of my element, felt like a grizzly bear in a pen. I let Yalda drive once we hit the dirt road and followed behind with a big pine branch, sweeping away the tire tracks. I wasn't sure they'd report the incident to the police, who hadn't seen any of the action, being so busy with the accident, and we hadn't seen any lights behind us. I was still paranoid. There was no way to camouflage the Jeep so I set up my decoy tent about a hundred yards off and set myself up farther off in a patch of tall grass. I felt like a lion.

Just as I was drifting off to a fitful, unsatisfying sleep, I heard Yalda's voice.

"Hey, Molnar."

"Yes?"

"Come over here."

"I just got comfortable. What do you need?"

"Bring your bag over here. Or crawl into mine. It's big enough."

"No thanks."

"Come on. After all that excitement and adventure—let's bone."

"Bone? I've never heard a woman say that."

"Just sex. No expectations."

"Sorry, Yalda. I can't. It's hard to explain, but you're like my spirit sister. It wouldn't be right."

After a silence: "Spirit sister? I can't tell if you're being sarcastic or not."

"Neither can I, but I think I mean it."

I did. Don't think I'm some iron-willed ascetic. Part of me was screaming out to accept her offer. But it would have ruined our partnership. She may have been OK with casual sex, but I would have been a mess. She's a beautiful woman. I've never been able to go to bed with a woman I didn't love. A lot of men are perhaps wired to bed as many women as possible, certainly a lot of men like to think they're wired that way. Maybe they are. Maybe I'm more evolved. We like to blame our flaws on our wires, our instincts, but we can be better than our instincts. I don't believe morality is biological—otherwise there would be more moral people in the world.

"All right, spirit brother, your loss. But do me a favor and don't listen to what I'm about to do over here."

NATURE IS BORN ON FOOTSTEPS OF WOLVES
JUDIT BIRÓ

Judit Biró is an applied zoologist turned textile artist.

She is a Hungarian girl living in Madrid, the busy and fizzy capital of Spain. She thinks of Madrid with a lot of grace: it gave her huge changes, great experiences, some amazing discoveries, loads of books, a best friend (her dog), and the love of her life. And wolves! Meanwhile, she misses her beautiful country, the wilderness of nature, the sounds of the forests, and the friendly little spring just by her house in Szombathely, close to the Austrian Alps. She was raised to love nature, or as her Mom says, maybe it just came with her; she's been loving nature since she first opened her eyes, as drawing and later on sewing. As a teenager, she was thinking too much about what she should be and what she should study; arts or biology... Finally she opted for the latter, and after earning her degree in zoology in Budapest, Judit traveled to Madrid to begin a new life. For some years, she worked in education, but she realized it was not the right path for her; it let her submerge in the magical and many times forgotten world of children's imaginations. That was an impulse for starting her new project, like her homesickness for arts, for drawing and biology. So by the time Judit discovered she did not have to choose between arts and her beloved animals, she just needed to understand how to link these two fields into something she always wanted to do. That's how Poppy Seed Cake was born, a textile-art project inspired by nature, but this project is still a newborn; Judit hopes that as it grows, day by day they will make her dream come true together: get people's attention on animals, on endangered species, and on nature itself using the art that comes from her fingers... And regarding wolves, she is a volunteer member of the group Accion Lobo, working for changing the situation of the iberian wolf in Spain. Besides other things, she is contributing with her illustrations and articles in the online magazine of the group. Now, she invites all of you with pleasure to visit her online, to show you all her work and inspiration: you can find her on Tumblr: Poppy-Seed-Cake, and as she is preparing her Facebook page, so soon she will be available there too as Poppy Seed Cake.

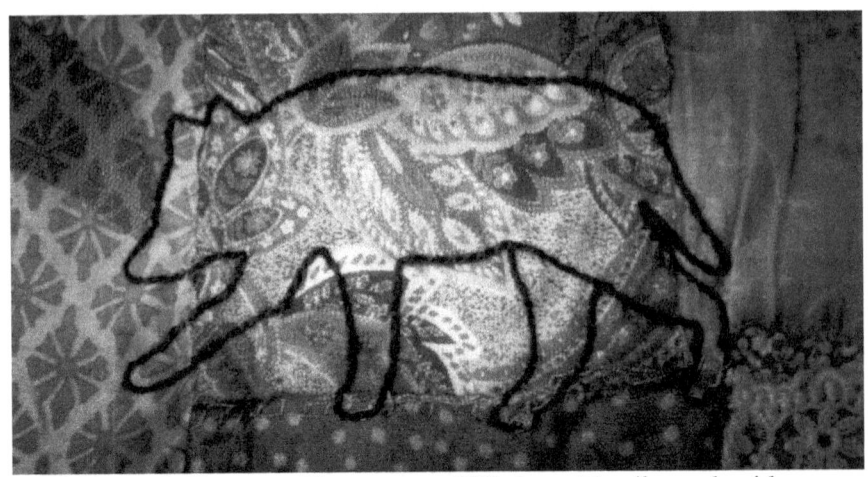

Nature is Born on Footsteps of Wolves. Textile, embroidery.

NIGHT OF WHOLE MOON
MICHAEL E. HAYNE

Michael E. Hayne lives in Tujunga, CA, with three rescued dogs and three rescued cats.

'It was not my intent to frighten you or your dog last night.'

That statement startled me. I looked around for who had just spoken. The only other customer in the coffee shop at that early hour was a man wearing a battered old hat, seated at the counter eating breakfast, and drinking water. His back was to me so I could not see his face.

"Excuse me? Did someone say something?" No reaction from anyone. Ok. I went back to my own breakfast.

'Your dog is named Lady. I like her.'

This time I knew I had heard that voice: clear, crisp, male, and rather soft actually.

Watching the restaurant staff go about their work without even a casual glance in my direction, I focused my gaze at the back of the man at the counter. He was almost finished with breakfast and I watched him use several slices of toast to sop up lots of bloody juice on his plates. Then he drank all of his glass of water and quietly sat there for a moment.

'As I said, it was not my intent to frighten you or Lady last night. I'm sorry.'

The man stood up, about six feet tall and rawboned, holding his check in one hand and a wad of money in his other. He put a bill on the counter and turned around. He saw me staring at him, tipped his hat, gave a brief nod, then walked to the cash out desk. He handed the waiter several bills. They exchanged smiles and he headed for the exit.

His hand pushed the door open. Then he paused and looked directly at me. He knew I was still staring. No challenge in his eyes, nor weakness. More one of sorrow, perhaps hope.

'It was me.'

His lips did not move. He did not speak. Yet I heard his voice. Or that voice, again. I blinked a couple of times and started to go after him but he was already gone. I hurried outside to give chase and stopped. Nobody in sight. What?

That evening, arriving at home from work, I was eager to let Lady out of the house so she could run around and be silly, as only she can be. My home is on a dead-end overlooking a flood plain arroyo, so no houses can be built. A full view of the expanse and distant foothills. Like me, Lady took to it right away. So I fenced the yard in chain-link, gate across the cement driveway. Lady has full run and she loves to play and chase her Frisbee. Her motto: eat, sleep, pee, poop, run, play, be silly. She excels at all.

Lady is a street rescue mutt. A mix of miniature poodle and who knows what else. Off-white and a tail that likely had been cut off when she was a puppy, leaving just a short stub.

But this night, when I opened the front door, Lady was not to be seen. Usually she is right there, dancing on hind legs, that stub a blur of fur. Tonight? Our home is deathly silent.

My heart lodged in my throat. What has happened? Where is she? "Lady?"

A whimper from our bedroom. I rushed down the hallway and found Lady cowering on the floor beside the bed. I quickly squatted down, stroking her fur to calm her.

"Lady girl. What's the matter?" I used my hands to gently probe her body. She did not react with any pain tremor, only rolled onto her back and limply wagged her stubby tail. "Come on, Lady, let's go outside. It's ok, I promise."

Lady slowly rose to her feet and followed me outside. She stood on the stoop and looked quickly around, repeatedly. Perhaps a visitor had come while I was gone? A visitor with not a very nice nature? That restaurant man? I long ago gave up faith in humans, so I walked around our home, checking any place that might have been a point of entry for someone. All secure.

Later, Lady ate her dinner very slowly, and kept looking up to see where I was. Usually her food disappears almost as soon as I put the bowl down to her. I had stayed in the kitchen to be near her, to watch her actions.

She finished, and lapped some water. Then, tail tucked under, she came over. I knelt down to her and she pressed her head, hard, against my chest. I just started to stroke her fur when her ears pricked up and a low growl rumbled in her chest. She stepped away from me and stared at the front door. Now the hairs on my neck were standing up. What, or who, did she sense?

I looked through the door peephole. Nobody there. Lady stayed back about ten feet from me, her growl now a bit more of a whine. I unlocked the door, grabbed the flashlight kept by the door, flicked it on, and carefully opened the door enough to look out. Still no one in sight. I stepped into the twilight. The waning full moon was just cresting, but I could still see fairly well.

"Lady, come on." I looked back. Lady's hackles were standing up and she was poised, as if to leap. "We can both go out." She did not move, just stared. "Ok, you guard the fort."

I swept the yard with the light, swept it again very slowly. Moving out on the lawn, I swept the roof, then panned the front of our home. Moving quickly, I shined the light at the gate and fence enclosing the ten foot breezeway between home and garage. The gate was closed; latch on the outside was hooked, so that area was clear. To the front of the garage, then quickly around to the other side of my home, all the while keeping that light trained ahead of me, lighting up areas I had not checked as yet. Once more, not a thing.

Inside, I double locked the door this time, and gave Lady a biscuit. She took it and stood staring at that front door. Then she raced into the bedroom, a whine in her throat. I followed her.

Lady was hunkered down flat near the bed, the uneaten biscuit lay between her front paws. I brought the flashlight into the bedroom and placed it beside the bed, easy to reach.

Later, as I was about to turn off the light for sleep, Lady's ears perked up, her back hair stood on end. She stared at the curtained window overlooking the breezeway. I grabbed the flashlight, pulled back the curtain and shined it into the breezeway. Nobody. I closed the curtain.

"Ok, Lady, there is nobody out there. So no growling, whining or barking. It's bedtime."

Lady did not look at me, just kept staring at the curtained window. I turned out the light.

"BARKBARKBARKBARKBARK!!! WHIMPERBARKBARKBARK!!!"

I bolted upright in bed, grappling to find the light switch, my heart pounding.

"BARKBARKBARKBARK!!!"

"SHUT UP LADY! BE QUIET!!!"

Lady ceased all but a soft whining. I clicked on the light. She was standing near the bedroom door, again staring hard at that curtained window. The clock radio showed just after one in the morning. I turned out the light, picked up the flashlight and, using my hand to shield the light, turned it on, allowing just a narrow beam of light. I made my way to that window, turned off the flashlight, and pulled the curtain aside.

Two red rimmed yellow eyes stared straight at me from about three feet away, from inside that closed-off breezeway. The eyes seemed to throb from some intense inner longing. I froze in place. That coyote— it had to be a coyote—it must be standing on its hind legs.

'Home. The heart and trust of my People are yours.' His forlorn voice cried in my brain.

I could only drop the curtain back in place and stand there shaking. Right then, the coyotes starting howling in the arroyo, more than just several of them. I flicked on the flashlight and put it against the window. The breezeway lit up bright as day.

Nobody was there. No glaring eyes. Nothing.

The coyote baying took on a different sound. Not one of the hunt, or of calling. This time I could feel, more than hear, terror in those voices. I looked around for Lady. She was cowered down low, at the door, tail tucked tightly under.

Outside in the arroyo I heard the horrible sound of animals fighting and screaming. Then the hard silence of killings. Farther up the arroyo I heard other coyotes howling as they ran away.

Call 911? Right, and tell them what? I opened the bottom dresser drawer and took out the 9mm semi-automatic pistol. One full clip inserted and a round in the chamber.

Donning a pair of tattered old shorts, I picked up the gun, flicking off the safety. Leaving all the lights off, and with flashlight in my other hand, I headed for the front door. Lady curled beside the bed, with a continuous low and barely audible whimper.

I had to pause a moment before opening that front door. I clicked on the flash as I swung the door open and quickly aimed the gun at anyone, anything, that may be there. As it was earlier, all clear. I cocked back the hammer and stepped out.

Again, a complete search revealed nothing. Whatever or whomever those strange eyes belonged to, it was now gone. The coyotes far up in the arroyo had also stopped baying and yelping. The only sound was the soft night murmur of the distant city. Still, those haunted eyes, and especially the desperation in his voice, captured my mind.

'Home. The heart and trust of my People are yours.'

I awoke startled. Lady stirred, lifted her head to look at me. The clock said 8 in the morning. I sighed in relief. This is my day off. I had forgotten about that.

Lady enjoyed her breakfast while I had my usual very big mug of strong black coffee. I strolled outside, last night's events momentarily forgotten. That's when I saw Randy, who owned the property that made up the arroyo. He was talking with a man in uniform. Randy saw me and waved, motioning me to join them. I refilled my cup and walked down to them.

"This is Officer Munger, he's from Fish and Game."

Officer Munger said local animal control contacted them about several coyotes that looked like they did not die a natural death. He led us up the arroyo about twenty yards and pointed. Two torn coyote bodies were splayed all over the ground. Whatever killed them had very sharp teeth, very sharp talons, and was very strong. Another, fifty yards farther up. Randy and the officer started walking in that direction. I looked again at those two butchered coyotes.

'Yes, I did that. The other as well.'

That startled me. I looked at Randy and the officer who continued on. Then I saw him. That man from the restaurant, standing on the arroyo rim in front of my home, hands behind his back. His old battered hat shading his eyes from the morning sun.

"Randy! I'll be along shortly." Randy looked back and nodded.

I did my best to act unconcerned, but failed. He watched me close the driveway gate and walk over to face him. He did not remove his hat.

This time he spoke aloud. "Perhaps we should get out of the sun, it's going to be a scorcher today. Although not inside your home, I don't want to possibly upset Lady, get her agitated. I hope I can meet her, with you here."

"I don't care if the sun burns you to death. Who, or should I say 'what' are you?"

"This will sound utterly insane. There is no way for it not to sound that way. All I ask is for you to hear me out. Please. I need your help."

"Help, huh? Then explain the coyotes. Explain your 'Yes, I did that. The other as well.' And your other intrusions into my head." It was difficult to keep my anger from showing.

"I will do that. If you will please keep an open mind to what you will hear."

"Any time I stop you, that is it. So if you don't mind sitting on concrete, we can sit in front of the garage. Sun won't reach there until after eleven. Coffee? A bit old, I can reheat it."

"That would be very nice, thank you. I appreciate it."

To be safe, I locked the front door. I paused and looked at the phone. Do I call 911 about this guy? And again, say what? Lady watched me nuke two coffees. Leaving Lady inside, I carried the cups out and handed one to him. He lifted it to his nose and inhaled slowly and deeply. He did not taste it.

"Forgive me, please, I don't drink coffee anymore, but I do love its aroma."

"Tell me who you are and what all this—that morning in the restaurant, last night, the night before—what is it about? It was you I saw in the breezeway last night. I know it was you. Your eyes are quite different in daylight. Not as…" I waved my hand around, perturbed.

"Reddish yellow. I know. I suppose it would be called a natural side effect."

"I am still listening. Or do I go call the psycho police to haul you away?" I am embarrassed to say, but after all of these events, I did want to know what this was about.

He took another deep inhale of the coffee. Finally he sat on the cement, legs folded akimbo, keeping the coffee cup close at hand. I sat the same way, but facing him from the side.

"I told the coyotes to stay back. They are distant brothers who believed I had invaded their territory and tried to stop me from going up into the canyon. The three died honorably, and I deeply regret that it happened. But I wanted you to see me.

"Why?"

"To give you a glimpse of what this is about. Because I need help to get back home. To the People who know what to do. You have never heard of them, they are mostly unknown to this outside world. They live high up and well hidden in the mid-south Andes."

"Did you do something to them? What did you do?"

"I violated their trust. Their sacred tribal Honor. Everything about who and what they are. For that, I have been on the run since 1965."

"Whoa whoa whoa." I had to interrupt him. "Now you sound like some vampire movie, living forever until somebody drives a stake through your heart or you die from the sunlight."

"Nothing like that. I can, and will die, just like any living being."

"Ok… so what are you? Why did you run?"

"I was an accident. What happened should never have happened. I didn't even know for certain such a tribe truly existed in that mountain area, nobody ever reported seeing them. For certain. These People were said to vanish in front of your eyes, literally. They would still be there but you couldn't see them. They blended so well with their surroundings.

"A great part of their religious worship is the land, nature, certain creatures. Especially the wolf, which they consider a Sacred Being, never to be harmed. The worst evil of all was to kill a wolf, even in self-defense, because the wolf is only living its life, in harmony with nature. You can defend yourself against a wolf, but once you are safe, you leave that wolf alone. Unless that wolf is sick or mortally wounded. Only then can one be killed. That is considered a blessing for that wolf, and for the person who helps the wolf cross over."

"You killed a wolf that was not sick or injured."

"Worse. I killed their Spirit Wolf."

He paused, struggling to keep his composure. I let him struggle. It took several minutes before he was able to speak.

"I picked you because of Lady. I know what she has given you. The joy and compassion you have been missing for so long. Don't deny it, please. Just listen. Or if you prefer I will leave now. It is your choice. You can even call the psych ward if you want. Okay?"

He did not look at me, just hung his head, avoiding my eyes. I don't know why I didn't tell him to get out but I did not. For a moment I felt I was again looking at Lady, in those initial seconds, standing on that busy street, before she started to trust me, and finally came over to me. "Please. I am glad Lady helped you. In whatever way she helped."

"Thank you. When I killed their Spirit Wolf, I did not know then that is what it was—what he was. I was camped high up in the Andes. It was late, camp fire damped nicely. I was in my blanket, struggling to sleep. I realized I was on edge and I didn't know why. Just twitchy about something. Perhaps it was all the sounds, and the deep shadows from the brilliance of the moon. I certainly was not expecting what happened.

"It was full, third night of it. The moon is truly only full for a brief moment in time, but the night leading up to it and the subsequent night's fall off, those three nights, are important, as you will learn. As did I.

"Rustling in the underbrush and odd noises startled me awake. I had just dropped off to sleep and suddenly I was fully awake, my pistol in hand, a .45. Reflex action. This was wilderness, you remember. I heard a deep heavy rumbling noise just outside of my camp, opposite the fire.

"An animal emerged from the darkness. It looked like a huge dog, or a wolf. But then… then it slowly rose up to stand on its hind legs. Creature must have been at least seven feet tall. It did not move to attack me, but just stood there, that thick restrained noise coming from deep in its massive chest. To say I was terrified doesn't even come close. I thought I was a dead duck.

"I lost my nerve and fired my pistol repeatedly, hitting the creature directly in its chest. It started to turn away and I kept firing until the gun was empty. That was when the creature roared in pain and rage and leapt across the fire to land on top of me, knocking me to the ground, almost crushing me with its massive weight. Its hot blood splattered all over me and it clamped its huge sharp teeth in my left shoulder. I could feel my bones being crushed. But then, the pain eased. The creature reared back and howled at the moon, shrieking. I could see what looked like tears streaming from its eyes, and it ever so painfully slowly collapsed on its side, freeing me.

"The creature lay there, in great pain, and knew it was dying. It reached a massive paw, like a hand, toward me. Not to claw me, but more to need the touch of another being. I failed again and did not reach out. The creature gave a heartbreaking almost human sob and died."

Suddenly he stood up, so quickly it was startling. One moment sitting, the next standing. I jerked back in surprise. He wiped his eyes. After a moment, he again sat down.

I shifted away from him, staring. "You can move rather quickly."

"I did not mean to scare you. I'm sorry. It's just that ever since that time, I have lived with that memory every moment of every day of every year. But back then? I was proud of myself, for how I had handled a very dangerous situation and, although wounded in the engagement, likely had discovered a previously unknown species. I even thought I would name it after me. I would go down in history, be famous, give lectures around the world. Have that body stuffed and taken on tour. I was the great hunter.

"Then, just as I squatted down beside my... trophy... the change happened. It was so startling. I felt very light headed, I sat back on my butt and I could only stare. My monster, his blood still seeping from all the bullet holes in his chest, slowly transformed itself into a fully grown human man no bigger than me.

"Oh good grief! A werewolf story? That is what this is all about? Cut it out!"

He just hung his head. From inside, Lady wailed as I had never heard before, like the coyotes from last night. Another howl. Then silence. That upset me more, yet calmed me.

"It seems you have an ally. Okay, go on."

"After I ran from the People, I made my way back to Buenos Aires, caught the first ship out and came home. I was fortunate the cycle was not in force and I made it here safely, as did the crew of that ship. Ever since I came back to America, I have searched for a connection like the one you and Lady have."

I was incredulous. "That's a lot of years, since 1965, to be searching, as you say."

"Oh, believe me, I found other companion dogs who wanted to help, but their humans would not—could not hear what I was trying to say. I never pushed. Once I was turned away, I immediately left. Fortunately, disbelief prevented the humans from reporting anything about me.

"Like you, I don't like asking for help. But I need to ask. If you choose not to help, that is ok. I will simply disappear and continue my search, for however long as I can."

"Search for what? Wait, I am trying to understand. Tell me why you came here, what do you need from me? Or from Lady? Straight up. No nonsense, because I will know."

"I know. Lady told me a lot about you. Simply put, I need you to trust me, and to accompany me back to the People. I was not from their People. To heal both our Peoples, theirs and mine, I need one of my own People, of you and me, to be with me, to witness the surrender, the joining, being one. And I will need a keeper, in case we mistime it and the cycle happens."

"Keeper? Cycle?"

"The moon. Unfortunately, like the fairy tales, ghosts and goblins and that, the moon is key. The three day cycle. Right now we have twenty eight days before the next cycle happens."

"You want me to accompany you where? The Andes in South America? I can't do that. I won't leave Lady here for however long a trip that would be. Besides, I have my work, my job."

"Lady can be boarded, I will pay. You must have vacation time, and the trip would not take more than a couple weeks, maybe three. I don't want another cycle to happen here, in this country. It is no longer safe anymore for me to be here."

"Even if I wanted, it would take me at least a week, maybe two, to arrange time off, take care of Lady. I appreciate your offer, but sorry."

"May I see her?" His eyes were filled with hope.

I sat up straight and glared at him. "Why? What are you going to do?"

"I'm not going to hurt her, at all, ever. I love that little girl. You don't know this, but there were many nights I came here, and outside the enclosure you built around your back patio, I would sit with her. Talk with her. She really loves you. You saved her life. She told me."

"If that's true, why did she react as she did? The nights you came here and you were…"

"Different. Changed. Yes. I have tried to explain to her but she is so protective of you that she would not listen. She was not certain I would not harm you, or worse. No matter how I tried to convince her, she would not give an inch in that regard. She was ready to die to defend you and your home. She told me this is the only home you ever had. Her home, too. This is the only home she has ever known. Her only family. Did you know that?"

"No. When I managed to coax her out of the street, she was just a lost and terrified little dog. I was amazed that traffic had actually gone around her. Usually I am just taking the shattered and crushed bodies of all sorts of creatures off the streets, the roads, the highways."

"Lady told me. She is your guardian wolf, Spirit Wolf, if you will. You are hers."

I stared at him. He stared back. After a moment, I stood up and went to get Lady.

I opened the front door and found Lady right there, waiting, her stumpy tail wagging. I stepped aside and Lady dashed past me, yelping and jumping, straight to him. Frankly, that made me jealous, a bit angry in fact. Who was this loon ball to come in here like this? Knowing so much about me? I walked out, leaving the door open, and stood so I could watch them.

Lady was rolling around on the ground and he was playing with her, rubbing her bared tummy and laughing, while she made squealing noises, utterly enjoying herself.

"Ok. Enough. Lady! Back inside. Now!" Lady recognized the angry tone in my voice and jumped up, looking from me to him and back to me. "Alright Lady, you can stay out here with us, but I need to ask this gentleman some serious questions."

Lady waited until I came over and sat on the driveway concrete. Then she lay beside me. He paused, looking at us both, a gentle smile on his face.

"My name is Louvel. I am asking you for your help, your trust, and your faith, if you will, because as I said, I cannot do this alone. If I could, I would have been gone long ago."

"What is so compelling about getting back to... you called them the People?"

"Living there for countless centuries. Always with their guardian who keeps them safe, their Spirit Wolf."

"But you screwed that up for them. You killed that wolf."

"Yes, and I have regretted it ever since, in more ways than I can describe. The elders told me of the wolf, and what lay ahead for me, both for the killing and for the mark it left on me."

I nodded. "When you were bitten."

"Yes. You see, when I killed Spirit Wolf, I took away their power to connect with their Spirit World, their protection. When the elders explained all this to me, it was too much. I ran. I abandoned them. As fast as I could. Several members tried to catch me, but the elders stopped them. I know why. Becoming Spirit Wolf was a personal decision only I could make. As it has always been through the centuries. The one who offered his, or her, heart and soul to become the next Spirit Wolf needed to do it for the People. To sacrifice for the People. A venerated decision. I ran from that. I had told them a number of times that I had not willingly made that decision."

"I can understand that."

Lady got up, walked over and pressed her lowered head against his chest, rocking against him, pushing. He dropped his head and rested his cheek on her head. Tears ran from his eyes. I was speechless at the familial intimacy. He looked up as Lady licked his face. He smiled at her.

"I was wrong. In fact I had made that decision. When I entered their world, I consented to become a part of it, and all that their world was and is. Taking the life of their Spirit Wolf was my agreement to abide by the laws of their world.

"I was told this by the elders. I listened, but did not hear. I would not hear them. I did not want to hear them. When I ran, I knew I was running from their truth. My truth. My life. They needed me. At the time, I did not know how much I also needed them. Now I know.

"It has taken all these years to have the courage to face what has been shadowing me. To trust the People. The way Lady trusts you. The way you trust Lady. I know I must trust them, return to them. If not, I will die corrupted. The People will die. We are tied together. My life, our lives, emanate from there, and have since that fateful night. I know now there is very little time."

"Are you saying I am your last hope? I don't appreciate getting put on that kind of spot."

"Lady told me to tell you. She said you would not believe me, that you really only take in four-legged strays. And birds. Any creature not human. That made me laugh, when she described you. That's why I let you get only a glimpse of me last night, and spoke to you."

"Why then just the glimpse, if it is so important for me to know?"

"If you had seen more of me, I know you would not be here talking with me now."

"It still comes down to why I should trust you and not call the cops?"

"I can't make that decision for you. I need help and I have never liked asking for help. From anyone, especially a stranger. But I cannot live with it anymore, my time is running out. I want to die with my People. And I need to pass this along to another who is willing."

I stared at him, horrified at what he just said. He turned and looked at me, his eyes flicking from me to Lady.

"It is not the horror that you think. It is now, because of what I did when I ran."

"I am not your volunteer."

He chuckled, then busted up laughing. "Thank you for the laugh. I would never ask you, or anyone, to volunteer to be Spirit Wolf. And the People will never allow another outsider, like I was—am—to take that position. Even if it meant their own destruction, they would not allow it. They learned a hard painful lesson in their experience with me."

I needed a break. I sipped my coffee, then drank all of it. Louvel took the time to inhale another long sniff from his own cup.

"You ran in 1965, how do you know what they know or learned or whatever, since?"

"I cannot explain it. I just know. As you heard me inside your head, I hear them inside my head. Not all the time, mind you. But enough to know these things."

We talked for another hour. Mostly, Louvel talked. Occasionally I asked questions, and I answered all of his. He dropped out of college to avoid the Viet Nam war draft, and sailed to Rio.

"The ironic part is that when I came back, I flunked the physical. Bad heart. When I told my dad and mom, they hugged me. I wish they were still alive. I wish I had any of my family still alive. Another sin to atone for. All that suffering I caused."

After a moment, he continued his story. Down the coast until Buenos Aires. There, local superstitions and tales of the tribes in the Andes intrigued him, especially the stories of the phantom People and their wolf guardian. A number of expeditions had gone searching, but found nothing. He decided to try his luck on his own. Foolish he admitted, but he was young and reckless about such things.

"So now what, more recklessness?" I could not keep from snorting aloud. "You are saying I have no time to think on this, or consider all the ramifications of this madness?"

"Sorry. There is no more time. I need to know right now if you are going to help me, to trust me. Does any of this make any sense?"

"Lady, is he mad as a hatter? Do I call the cops? Psych ward?" I reached a hand to touch her head. She did not immediately respond. Then she curled up in his lap, head resting against him. "Well, ok. I trust Lady, implicitly. Looks like this is a go."

Louvel held up a hand. "One other thing. My own personal request. But I believe it will be most important to you after all this is done. Bring along some journaling materials and pens."

That was too much. "A video recorder would be simpler and more accurate."

"The elders will not allow that. They gave permission for this, and this only. It is your personal engagement in what is to come that will be important. I want you to keep as complete a record as possible of what you see, hear, feel, think, all of it, through all of this. Not for me. For you. Your journals I hope can help you find what you are looking for. And perhaps many years from now, these journals can be revealed to others who need them. I hope so."

How prophetic of him. Without those journals, what follows would not be possible to tell.

The next three days were a whirlwind. Fortunately my passport and visa were current and clear. Lastly I called a friend in my area. I asked her to stay at my place, to care for Lady for the time I was gone. I told her I had to fly to Buenos Aires for up to a month. I would be in cell phone connection as much as possible, but I doubted any service was available in the Andes and I could be out of contact for at least a week, perhaps ten days. I was so grateful she agreed.

Louvel told me which airline, he would pay the fares, and arrange everything in Buenos Aires. Since I did not speak Spanish, I realized I would need to rely on him. This was nuts.

As the first leg flight lifted off, I mentally told Lady how much I loved her and hoped I would see her again. Seated beside me, Louvel spoke:

"You will see Lady again. This is the only thing I can guarantee you. The Elders know you are coming with me, they were quite moved by your generosity. And knowing their Spirit Wolf was returning, they extended their power around Lady and your friend."

It was an experience unlike any I ever knew before. Those four weeks and three days are a kaleidoscope in my memory. So much happened, so much change, so quickly. It was more than just going from crowded, noisy Buenos Aires into the wilderness and altitude of the southern Andes. Yet that was a powerful indication of the transformation to another time and place.

The last leg of our trip was just me and Louvel. We climbed higher and higher. I had no idea where we were and I knew I could never make my way out on my own. The vegetation was thick, but Louvel led the way, walking as if he knew a path. Perhaps he did.

He stepped out into a small clearing and stopped. He motioned me forward to stand beside him. He smiled through the tears that brimmed in his eyes.

"I am home. Welcome to my home. My People."

I looked around and saw only dense foliage. Certainly not any people. Then I did see them. The People. Standing in a circle around us. I started to step back, but Louvel put his hand on my shoulders and nodded to me. He walked forward a few paces, stopped, bowed his head.

Drums began a heartbeat rhythm, a heartbeat filled with joy and gladness. Two men stepped forward to greet Louvel. The Chief and Medicine Man. They were followed at a distance by the Elder Men and Elder Women. Louvel looked at the two men and then he broke down and they wrapped their arms around him, holding him close. I could see the tears on their faces.

A signal must have been given because the Elders rushed around the three, followed by the People. Louvel somewhere in the middle of all those joy filled souls. Although I was standing outside of this gathering, I felt part of this fateful occasion.

After a few minutes, a path opened in the People, from Louvel and the Medicine Man to me, and the Chief, head held high and his face wet, walked to me. I did not know what to do or say. It was not necessary. Chief opened his arms and gave me the best bear hug I have ever had. Now I almost cried. The People gathered around me, welcoming me into their Society.

The People had prepared a celebration meal for that evening. Lots of singing, drumming, dancing, their Sacred Resin burning throughout the event. The Spirit Wolf Child was brought out to meet Louvel, and me.

This time it was a young woman, Sandalio, no more than twenty years old. Louvel put his hands out to her. Throughout that evening, and through the following events, Sandalio was always close to Louvel's side.

In the following days prior to the Cycle, there were many Sacred Rituals to which I was allowed to witness, and especially those very few in which I was taken in to participate. Sacred Symbols and Emblems were hand made by the People. I was allowed to make several for my own. About most of those events I shall not speak here now. I gave Louvel my word.

Some things were kept from me, and only later did I understand why. It is those moments that are the most painful to carry in my heart. It is for Louvel that I have now accepted all that happened. For Louvel that I now understand what he told me about his own beginning.

On the return flights, I was beyond exhausted. I slept each flight leg. Even sleeping in the waiting areas before the next connection. Dreams filled my sleep. Intense dreams alive with the brilliant colors, scents, sights and sounds of those events. All these experiences are seared permanently into my soul.

When the flight touched down early afternoon in Burbank, I found I could finally and fully awaken. I was home, and Lady was waiting. As the craft taxied to the gate, and passengers started gathering their things, I unexpectedly broke down. I shielded my face from any and all. Finally, everyone had deplaned and I was that last passenger. I stood up, as tall as I could, clenching my teeth to keep myself together, and walked to the exit. The stewards watched me, each visibly concerned. I smiled and nodded my appreciation.

Someday in the future I will transcribe fully from the journals all that happened. For now, this is what I will write. The three most important periods of the Moon Cycle.

Night of Approaching Moon

The ritual of the old Spirit Wolf meeting the new Spirit Wolf Child, a preparation to understand and again agree to what lay ahead, the final acceptance of their fates. The People made a wide circle in a sizeable meadow, obviously a sacred gathering place. In its middle, giant fires were built at each Sacred Direction. The Fire Keepers were diligent in their duties.

As the moon began to break the distant horizon, Louvel was brought to the center of the field, into the center of those fires. Then Sandalio was brought in to stand opposite him in the center. He wore only a waist wrap, while she wore a bare shouldered wrap that just covered her torso. Sacred Resin smoke flowed, surrounding everyone.

The Elders made a circle around them, while softly beating small drums. The Chief and Medicine Man moved around them. The Chief carried the Sacred Blade. The Medicine Man rhythmically shaking his Sacred Rattle and moving to the drum beat.

Approaching Moon fully cleared the mountain peaks. Grandmother Moon. Reflecting Grandfather Sun's light to illuminate this ancient and solemn ritual. That Moon light galvanized Louvel, as if he had been struck violently in the back. His arms shot up in surrender and he slowly sank to his knees, finally curling forward to touch his forehead to the ground.

The air felt full of electricity. All the hairs on my body vibrated. The drums grew in strength and intensity. Sandalio stood her ground, the Chief and Medicine Man close behind her.

A bloodcurdling roar erupted from Louvel and he reared his head back and howled at the Moon. I watched him struggle to his feet, watched him change, become Spirit Wolf. He grew to at least seven feet tall, his muscles massive. And hair. His body sprouted a coarse thick coat. Talons sprang from his fingertips. His hands, more like elongated paws now, reached for the Moon, his mouth opened to roar again, exposing long fangs, saliva dripping. But no roar.

He spun to face the Chief, Medicine Man, then Sandalio. This was her first experiencing of the Change. All three stood unafraid. I did see the Chief holding that Sacred Blade ready. It was not necessary. Spirit Wolf turned his head and stared at me for a very long moment, his eyes pulsating. With a scream of power and conquest, he sprang past all of us so fast he literally vanished. In the surrounding circle, an opening materialized and he disappeared into the night, into the wild. I could hear his roar echoing across the valley.

Night of Whole Moon

As it was the previous evening, the People made a Sacred Circle around the meadow. The Four Directions fires were lit. The inner circle of Elders quietly beat their drums. Chief and Medicine Man stood in the middle, waiting. The Whole Moon just peeking over the horizon.

Louvel stepped into view, the flickering light of the fires making him appear to glow as he walked to the inner circle to stand where he had the previous night. As before, he wore only a waist wrap.

In a few moments, Sandalio passed through the outer circle and walked directly to her place opposite Louvel. She was also dressed as before. She displayed no outer emotions, simply locking eyes with Louvel.

Chief held the Sacred Blade at his side. Medicine Man shook his rattle more forcefully than the previous night, moving to the rhythm of the drums, matching their growing intensity. Although the electricity in the air was definitely alive and intimidating, I felt at peace. Perhaps it was Louvel's obvious serenity and anticipation of what was to come. I found my feet were moving in unison with the Medicine Man. I was dancing where I stood. I wished I had a rattle.

As if I had spoken aloud, the Medicine Man danced to me and vehemently held out his Sacred Rattle to me. I knew I needed to take it. Whatever was to come, this was a powerful part of it all. When I grabbed that rattle, there was a moment when he held it tight, forcing me to literally take it from him. I did. He stepped behind me and pushed me into the inner circle, to stand near the Chief. I felt spooked. Who was I to be there?

The drumming grew louder, the smell of their burning Sacred Resin filled the night, overpowering all other scents. Chief turned to Sandalio, and Louvel who watched all this. At the horizon, the Whole Moon came into reality. Grandmother Moon again reflecting Grandfather Sun. Reflecting on the Surrender, the Joining, the being One. The Sacred Rattle in my hand moved on its own.

Louvel reacted almost as before. Almost, because tonight it was obviously much more intense, more painful to him. He did not fall; he just stood there, trying not to show the agony, taking it all and letting it happen, his body visibly throbbing. The Change was more obvious now with him standing upright.

Sandalio watched. Her eyes staring directly into Louvel's, all through his Change. Louvel was standing there, then he was the other, Spirit Wolf. The drums ceased. The burning resin smoke even more intense, blanketing the entire meadow in the mist of its intoxicating fragrance.

Spirit Wolf stepped forward, close to the young Woman, the Spirit Wolf Child. He towered over her, yet she did not lose eye contact with him. Chief and Medicine Man moved closer to her. I followed. I don't know how I knew to do that, but I did.

Spirit Wolf grabbed Sandalio just above her waist and slowly lifted her up, bringing her eyes level with his, holding for several long seconds, then lifting her as high as he could. All the while, their eyes remained fixed on each other.

I realized Chief held the Sacred Blade at the ready, and Medicine Man now also held a narrow long-bladed knife in one hand. I forced myself to breathe, and watched Spirit Wolf slowly lower the young Woman to bring her close to him, to his face, those long glistening incisors. Sandalio never flinched when he sank those fangs into her shoulder. I was startled to remember that it was the same shoulder on which he said he had been bitten.

She was held in that embrace for more than a minute. With a jerk, he pulled his head back from her. Blood oozed from the punctures. She had not flinched. He brought her face right up against his face. It was then he roared, mouth wide enough to swallow her entire being. As before, she never wavered.

His roar settled into a growl from deep inside. He held her out to arm's length, still in the air. Then slowly, I could not believe how slowly, he lowered her until her feet were on the ground, and he released her. At that moment I realized that the Sacred Blade was now in her hand of the uninjured shoulder. Sudden fear surged through me.

He reared up to his full height, looked at that magnificent Whole Moon, and keened in triumph. In that moment, Sandalio quickly brought up that Sacred Blade and drove it straight through his chest, through his heart. Outraged, I started forward, but the Chief and Medicine Man held my arms in a tight grip. I could not move. I wanted to scream in anger. My voice failed.

The Sacred Blade was buried to its hilt in his chest. Whole Moon light sparkled off the several inches of blade protruding from his back.

His roar did not falter, but in a moment it slowly faded to silence. He took an eternity to fall on his knees. The drums began again, quietly.

Medicine Man stepped forward with his knife ready, but Spirit Wolf put up a paw-hand to stop him, shaking his massive head. Medicine Man stepped back, bowing low.

Spirit Wolf dropped to his hands and knees, blood flowing on the ground. Sitting back on his haunches, he reached a huge paw-hand, talons extended, toward her. She did not flinch away, but stepped forward, ignoring the blood that ran from her wounds. She clasped his paw-hand in both of hers and knelt in front of him. He lowered his head and pressed it against her chest, a soft rumble from deep within him. Sandalio rested her cheek on his head, using her other hand to stroke the back of his neck. Their intimacy was powerful, and I felt my Lady in my heart.

He jerked back away from her, now tightly clutching both her hands in one huge paw. She was startled. This was unexpected. The Chief and Medicine Man were obviously alarmed, not knowing what to do. The drums stopped. The People shifted, moved closer, also afraid.

Looking around, searching, his eyes focused directly on me. I did not know what he wanted. After a moment, without releasing his hold on her hands, he raised his other paw-hand toward me, his eyes pleading for my help, help from his People. From our People.

I quickly stepped forward and knelt beside him, taking his offering into both of mine. I saw again that inner flame of joy in his eyes. All I could do was lower my head to his paw-hand, wanting so much to tell him how I felt and not even being able to find the words. Just my heart breaking.

It was then, while still holding tightly to our hands, he gradually slumped to the ground. We both moved with him. He lay there and, with each breath, blood would flow from around that embedded blade. How I wanted to free that blade and bring my—yes, bring my friend back. He lifted his head toward the Whole Moon and roared in defiance and victory. As his fearless song faded, Spirit Wolf rumbled a deep, long sigh. A sigh of relief and regret. I kept my very tight grip on his now lifeless paw.

A few moments later, the Change ensued. Now we both were holding the hands of Louvel, a mere human Man. Without a signal, Sandalio and I both bowed to rest our foreheads against his chest. I was dimly aware of the softness of drumming and rattle surrounding us.

Night of Leaving Moon

Spirit Wolf Child accepting fully the mantle of Spirit Wolf, and experiencing the first change. This was done on the last night of the Moon cycle to give her the following weeks to adjust from these events.

Sandalio was escorted by the Elder Women, with the Elder Men waiting with the Chief holding the Sacred Blade, and Medicine Man with his Sacred Rattle. I was allowed to participate, to stand beside the Medicine Man, but I could only watch. The Women guided her to the center of the Sacred Fires. The encircling People moved in rhythm to the soft beat of the drums and the Medicine Man's Sacred Rattle.

Leaving Moon slowly emerged from behind the peaks. The drums stopped. The People held in place. Only the dense smoke from the burning Sacred Resin moved, flowing around all the Elders, Chief, Medicine Man, me. The scent was overpowering, exhilarating.

Sandalio stood in the center, watching the smoke wrap itself around her, starting at her feet and sensuously curling up to encase her body and then dissipating at her neck, allowing only her head to be visible. She looked up as Leaving Moon's light illuminated her in that cloud. Her arms slowly rose from her sides, straight out, and then palms up toward the Moon. I wanted to… I didn't know what I wanted, but I felt blessed to be here. I felt Louvel around me, around her.

She opened her mouth but no sound came forth. Then a garbled noise in her throat, and the Change commenced. Her body stiffened, obviously in evolving pain. After a moment, she began vibrating, leisurely at first, then as if the ground was shaking under her feet. Her back arched and she screamed in agony, but that terrible scream rapidly became a savage roar.

The change took a minute or so longer than it did for Louvel. Her body became thicker, more muscular, height rising to just over six feet, not so much body hair but enough. Incredible talons. Long incisors. As it progressed, the drums began a soft pulsation, a heartbeat, attended by the Sacred Rattle. All the People danced in place, in cadence. My feet moved with them.

The Sacred Smoke dispersed. Spirit Wolf stood before us. Spirit Wolf took time to self inspect, to look at arms, legs, and talons. The Moon reflected crimson fires in her luminous eyes.

A tentative step. Another. Finding her footing. A long gaze at the Moon. Then a slow sweep of the People, the Elders, Chief, and Medicine Man. Her gaze stopped at me. Her eyes shimmered with moonlight, drilling into me. I saw her inner hunger pulsing, Spirit Wolf's heartbeat. A snarl seemed to be on her lips. I could not break away from her penetrating gaze.

Spirit Wolf drifted slowly toward me, taloned paw-hands moving to grasp, long fangs bared, drops of saliva falling from those glistening teeth. Finally, Spirit Wolf stood directly facing me, her eyes looking down into my eyes, bluntly, devouringly.

The drums stopped. The Rattle stopped. The People stopped. All sound ceased. This was not what I thought would happen, and certainly did not expect. Nobody moved to protect me. I knew now how Louvel felt that night at his camp. I was a very dead duck. My heart broke, crying out my love to my Lady. My thoughts screamed in my head.

'Louvel, tell her to just get it over with. That's all I ask.'

Her strong paw-hands vise-grabbed me at my waist, holding me firmly in place.

Spirit Wolf slowly leaned down to softly and firmly press the top of her head against my chest. I don't know why or how I knew to do it, but I reached a hand up and touched the back of her head, gently stroking her coarse fur. I heard, and felt, a deep silky rumble in her chest. Only with Lady had I ever felt such an open heart. It was a powerful, intimate blessing. I openly wept.

And then Spirit Wolf was gone, leaping away to vanish into the night. Her howl of pleasure, of the change, the hunt, this new and Sacred Way of Life, reverberated through the meadow and carried to the Moon.

I do not have the strength to talk more. This is enough now. My heart still needs to heal.

I dropped my suitcase and closed the driveway gate just as Christie opened the front door. Lady dashed between her legs and sprang at me. I held Lady close, my face buried in her fur. Christie stepped out, holding a box about a foot square and several inches deep.

"Somebody left this box here for you. I found it on the bed, on the pillows."

I set Lady down and she began dancing on her hind legs.

"Thank you, my Lady. I missed you, too."

I opened the box. A card sat atop Louvel's battered old hat. It was then I remembered I had not seen him wearing it, from the flight out and all through the trip. But when did he get it here? And how? And inside my home?

"Lady, you sweet girl. You were with him." Lady stopped dancing and sat on her haunches, that stub tail the sweetest blur of fur. I put Louvel's hat on my head. It fit.

Home now with Lady, being showered with her joy, I remember the joy and especially the serenity I saw in Louvel's eyes as he died. I know Lady understands, in how she looks at me, how she gently touches me with a paw, gently presses her head against my chest.

Dear Louvel, I only knew you a short time. Yet in those few weeks is a lifetime of knowledge and wisdom that you and your people shared with me. The blessing to be of your People, our People. The offering of Sandalio. Witnessing your change. To touch you, see your peace-filled energy radiating within. Most of all, to hold your Spirit Wolf hand as you crossed. Sleep well with your Spirit Wolf Ancestors. I know you are at peace.

Now, going into the future, your people will survive.

I had done something profoundly valuable for Louvel, for the People. And especially for their eternal guardian Spirit Wolf. For my Self and for my Lady, I am grateful to you for trusting me to be with you during your intense and deeply personal time.

Louvel's card told me: 'Home. The heart and trust of my People are yours.'

Lady and I will be ok, too.

PREDATOR
TINA M. CRUMP

Tina M. Crump is a traditional artist who dabbles in multiple medias including pencil, pen, color pencil, charcoal, pastels, and others. She is a Hot Spring, Arkansas local who subject of choice is that of wildlife, pets, and fantasy. You can follow her wildlife and pet works at https://www.facebook.com/WindSong83/ or all of her works on Deviant Art at http://windsong83.deviantart.com/

Predator. Ink and water color.

A PUP'S NOSE
CHRISTIAN ESCHE

Christian was born on the 17th of June in 1995 in his home town Chemnitz in Germany. All of his life he enjoyed creative things like drawing and later photography as well. He always enjoyed nature of all kinds and is engaged in its protection. Wolves became especially important to him and are very present in his life. After regular school he wanted to become an artist or a photographer, but as both failed, he began to study European Studies with cultural background in his home town, drawing and making photos remained hobbies.

A Pup's Nose. Photography.

REWILDING
STACEY EVANS

Stacey Evans is a speaker and an advocate for laws and policies that promote respect and understanding of wolves and other canids. Stacey speaks about policy, legal, and legislative issues impacting wolves, other canids, and our relationship with them. She also inspires audiences to peacefully coexist with wolves, coyotes, foxes, and dogs. Stacey is a guru in government affairs, nonprofit leadership, and issues impacting wolves and other canids. Stacey uses that expertise to assist organizations in their efforts to improve the welfare of wolves, other canine wildlife, and dogs. Stacey is the incoming chair of the American Bar Association's Animal Law Committee. She enjoys raising her newly adopted Alaskan Malamute dog named Rudi, driving dog teams in the Rockies, salsa dancing, and giving keynotes that inspire people to thrive in adversity.

Wolf paw prints expand

Lightly on the moonlit snow,

Rewilding our hearts.

RUNNING WITH WOLVES
JOHN NOLAND

John Noland has won two national chapbook contests and has published two other chapbooks. He has published in Orion Nature Quarterly, Chicago Review, the Great American Poetry Show, Midwest Quarterly, Coyote Journal, Georgetown Review, *and many other publications and anthologies. He lives on the Oregon coast where there are almost as many wild animals as people. He can often be seen prowling the beaches and checking into sea bird life.*

Run with the wolves, howling
on a summer morning,
Loving long trails,
The spicy odor of deer,
running to fill a hunger
calling in the blood,
a hunger even humans know
on cold October nights
when geese fly overhead
calling, and who we are
mixes with the earth,
the wild and ancient sun
and birds whose cries
echo back to some lost ravine
where those old shamans,
the crows, chanting lightning
cracking limestone
and the dark earth awakens into hope
and desire,
those old sparks
of flint
we all share
just beneath the skin
burning

SILENT WILLOW
CHIARA RENDA

Chiara Renda is a student at Mahwah High School and a resident of Mahwah, N.J. An aspiring artist, writer, and animator, "Silent Willow" is her first published work. Chiara's affinity for wildlife and conservation was cultivated at a young age through trips to the Bronx Zoo, and her love of wolves was inspired by visits to the Wolf Conservation Center in South Salem, N.Y., and the Lakota Wolf Preserve in Columbia, N.J.

The waves of the crystal blue pond were still, a peaceful sort of still. The birds sang their harmonious songs. We sat under the shade of the weeping willow. Its branches were heavy and overheard our one-sided conversations. I wanted to respond. I really did. But I wasn't like you. I never was, and I never could be. I close my eyes and remember. A boy, the age of seventeen you said, with hair the color of the deep red leaves during the fall and eyes blue like the clear sky. You weren't like others, no. You said you wore clothes, but they were colors I never imagined before. Sometimes red, sometimes purple. I remember when you first met me.

"My name's Christian. What's yours?" You asked me. You showed me kindness. No one ever has before. But you were different.

"Tama," I answered silently.

"D-Don't be afraid. Come here." You smiled. You sat beneath the willow, by the base of the trunk. Cautiously, I came near you and sat next to you. You were tall...but so skinny. You put your arm around my shoulders as I sat down beside you. "You know, you're the first friend I've made since I moved here. And that was months ago! How come I never see you...this isn't a big neighborhood."

"I'm a long way from home, too, Christian. This is the only shelter I could find, by the lake." I sighed.

"No friends either, huh?"

"No, Christian..."

"Hey, it's okay. I got an idea: we'll be friends together!" Your eyes were so full of joy when I noticed...they didn't look right. "What's the matter? Oh...Yeah...I'm blind. I always was and always will be."

Your eyes. So blue and clear like the sky, but never empty. They were full of imagination and happiness. You weren't blind, not metaphorically anyway. Every day, you'd come here and tell me about your day at your home and school. Some days you'd come by the willow with a face so red and fists clenched and other days your face was wet with the tears you'd cry. But I'd always be there for you. I'd clean the tears away or make you forget your anger. I wondered if I could fix whatever made you feel this way.

"I don't understand...I'm...I'm not helpless because I'm blind." You cried one day.

"Of course not."

"If only they could understand. Then maybe...maybe those jocks would stop. Maybe they'd finally understand!" You tried to wipe your tears with your sleeve. "But they're stupid and so full of themselves."

"Hush, Christian...It will be okay. Everything will be okay." I tried to assure you. But you couldn't hear me. You were so interested in trying to be accepted you didn't notice me there for you. After that day, you didn't return for some time. I was worried, and I'd wait every day for you. One day I heard you, but with others, so I hid. You were with two other boys and a girl. One boy had piercings on his ears and dyed hair, the color of the grass in spring and his eyes greener still. The other looked much like you except his hair was brown like the bark of the willow and his eyes hazel. The girl had long black hair, soft and beautiful with pale grey eyes that reminded me of storm clouds. You all cheered happily and joked around, and I watched from a distance. I wasn't good with people. I'm still not good with people. Even then, you called out for me. I knew you'd still care. I loved that you still cared. I loved you, but I couldn't say a word because day after day, I saw how much you fell in love with the girl. Soon enough, it was you and her sitting where we used to sit. Talked where we used to talk. And the willow still conversed along with you. My disappearance was silent. Like...Like a camellia blossom. The one I gave to you, you gave to her. My tears scatter the earth like the rain, quiet and tragic. But they proclaim nothing. Like a thunderstorm, I come for some time and leave without another word. I watched you day by day, hidden but always by our willow as you grew up with your friends.

One day, I decided to wait by the willow's trunk. Everything was still, the birds weren't singing and clouds rolled in, warning me about the impending storm. But I still waited for you. The rain came down slowly and pitifully at first, but then the sky opened up and started to sob. Its muffled yells of sadness echoed through the skies. This time, I looked for you. I trotted into the town, so rightfully named Wolfwater. I, through the storm found your house, I remembered your address when you told me, and carefully looked through the window.

You were sitting comfortably on the couch with the girl you loved and your other two friends on the floor. You were watching the television and smiling, enjoying snacks as I sat outside in the rain. I cried with Mother Nature as I went back to the lake. I laid down near the willow tree to protect myself from the rain. The willow wrapped its sorrowful branches to comfort me.

"How could you!" I screamed into the sky. "How could you!"

There was no answer. I fell asleep to the lullaby of the willow, knowing I would never see you again.

I am here now, under that same willow. I lie, old and dying, retelling the tale of how boy and creature became friends. I am reminded because of the storm. It goes on as I remind myself of you. You still live in Wolfwater with kids of your own. My fur, once pure white, is now dull and gray. It sticks to my skin because of the rain showing my fragile figure. My stomach aches for food, but I am too weak, my bones are too old. I have no strength left. The brightness of my yellow eyes has faded. I know this is the end. But I can never give up; I want to find you Christian. I want to say my goodbye. Like a storm I am there for some time, and I disappear without another word. I throw my head back in a final howl and say goodbye under the now dead and silent willow.

STARTLE WOLF & WOLF HOST
ANNE WALSH

Anne Walsh is a poet and a story writer whose work falls somewhere on the border of those two countries. Sometimes, she is a dual citizen, and sometimes she has no country at all. Most of the time, she is illegal everywhere, a local nowhere. Born in Philadelphia, she now lives in Australia. Her poems have shortlisted for the ACU Prize in Literature and The Newcastle Poetry Prize (2014). Her work has appeared in Glimmer Train *literary journal (US, 2011);* Prayers for a Secular World *(Inkerman and Blunt, Australia, 2015),* Reflections of Elephants *(Australia, 2015),* Australian Love Poems *(Inkerman and Blunt, 2013) and in* Sotto Magazine *(Australia, 2013). Her first collection of poems,* I Love Like a Drunk Does, *was published by Ginninderra Press (Australia, 2009).*

Startle Wolf

I am your forest.
    You are my roaming.
Your tongue
out licking
the timbre
of my black cheek.
Your mouth tinder.
    My face burning.

Wolf Host

I am the avé in a nave of trees
the sancta in the sanctuary of snow
                    the place in fire

My hymn is the house red of forests in autumn
the frantic grandeur of an organ gone wild with requiem
                    in an apse of Alders

I am the riot of peace
the fir razed with the cello sound night makes
                    the holy order

CHILDREN OF THE STRAWBERRY MOON
MELISSA LULLABY CABLE

Melissa Faith Cable is 21 years of age and lives in Newfoundland, Canada. She loves to write and explore the worlds of creativity and imagination, showing them to this world for all to see. Cooking and learning are two of her biggest hobbies, and she has a passionate love for wolves and any form of wolf relations in mythology.

Children of the strawberry moon
(a song for the June wolves)

Under June's full moon
Amongst flowers that bloom to midnight's light
That is the place you call home
In with the crickets and cascades
The lullaby of the wild
Do the stars guide your path?
Lead you to where you must go?
Raise your muzzle to the starlit sky
Sing to the strawberry moon
We await your song to reach us
The song of the wolves of June

TRUST IN FATE
RICHELLE GARDNER

Richelle Gardner is 15 and is from Downsville, NY.

Trust in Fate. Drawing. (Text: You'll never know what's out there, until you take that leap of fate.)

WOLF 1
PATRICIA LEHTOLA

Patricia Lehtola is a freelance artist and wildlife conservationist. Her inspiration comes from spending her summers in the upper Peninsula of Michigan on her uncle's farm, listing and watching wildlife in the night. She is a native of Southern California where she currently resides.

Wolf 1. Drawing.

THE WOLF OF JAPANESE AND EUROPEAN FOLK-TALE: WHEN HORKEW KAMUY MEETS THE BIG BAD WOLF
PAULINA ANGELA SZYMONEK

"Some children weaned on fable never inquired deeper into the animals than the stories led them, and so went through life believing the wolf evil, the fox sly, the bee industrious, and the ass foolish," wrote Barry Holstun Lopez in his *Of Wolves and Men* (Lopez, 1978). Certainly that was the case with the wolf in Europe. *Canis lupus* of the European lore was a beast from hell, a devil's dog, a source of evil and a symbol of lust. In Japan, however, the wolf was held in high regard; the wolf for this culture was a revered animal. Although at times dangerous, it was essentially regarded a protective spirit, a guarding dog, and a powerful deity that was willing to help people. All these beliefs survived in the folk tales and fables of these cultures, and it's these tales that I'm going to use for my analysis. Since most of the fables, fairy tales and folk tales have their own structures, and the wolf figure in this kind of stories has its permanent place as a type of hero, I will compare selected traditional tales of aforementioned cultures to prove that in Japanese culture the wolf function in fairy tales is invariably positive, as opposite to the European notion of wolf as a villain. In this paper, I will try to analyze the place and function of the wolf as a character of the story, while attempting to recreate a theory for portraying it in European and Japanese fable and folk tale.

Vladimir Propp studied over a hundred Russian folk tales, and distinguished 31 functions and 7 types of heroes that appear in the plot. Propp also noted that what is important in the structure of the tale is not the characters, but the actions they perform (Propp, 1928). However, identities of the characters are important and depend on the culture. For instance, the sheep and the wolf in the story represent, respectively, people and evil. At least in Christian imagination, it is a strong, yet simple metaphor of "good" and "bad," as the vulnerable lamb is always threatened by the ravenous wolf. Of course, the structure of the tale remains the same, but one should not ignore the social importance of certain characters that are used as symbols.

Although Propp used only Russian folk tales in this study, various authors have successfully applied this kind of structural analysis for other types of stories, as well as tales from other parts of the world. In an approach to apply Propp's methodology to Japanese folk tales, Takenori Wama and Ryohei Nakatsu successfully analyzed 20 of such stories and concluded that "there is no single basic storyline, as in the case of Russian folktales, but four basic storylines" (Wama and Nakatsu, 2008).

There is, however, a certain weakness in Propp's structural approach. It concentrates on the form while ignoring the content, which is, in fact, an essence of the story. Unlike Propp, I'm taking into account cultural, religious, and geographical differences while analyzing the place of the wolf and its function as a character in the tale. By looking at the context of the stories, the recurring themes can be identified: that of the Big Bad Wolf of the European fairy tale, and that of Horkew Kamuy of Japanese folklore. There seems to exist a set of principles according to which the stories about wolves were created in these cultures.

In fairy tales and fables the characters were meant to serve as metaphors, but it doesn't change the fact that more often than not, the wolf was used as a symbol of evil, but not only. Alexander Pluskowski wrote, "in numerous fables the wolf is an object of ridicule" (Pluskowski, 2006).

Perhaps one of the best known and the most widespread fairytales having the wolf as a character is "The Little Red Riding Hood." Already in this tale, the character of the Big Bad Wolf appears. What is interesting is that Japan has its own version of the tale, in which the wolf apologizes to the Little Red and promises to be good from this point on, and is therefore forgiven (Cashdan, 1999). The Big Bad Wolf is also well known from other popular fairytales, like "The Wolf and the Three Little Pigs" and "The Wolf and the Seven Goats." S.K. Robisch has noted that the titles of "The Wolf and the Seven Goats" differ in some editions of Grimm's tales, having the word "kids" instead of "goats," "perhaps a preference for the double entendre indicating the nickname for human children," thus anthropomorphizing the goats for the story (Robisch, 2009).

In Japan, there are no equally recognizable tales that depict wolves, but there is a character, which, as in the case of the Big Bad Wolf, appears frequently in the stories. Horkew Kamuy (also called Large-Mouthed Pure God, from jap. Oguchi no Magami no hara) is a wolf deity in Japanese lore (Walker, 2005). Unlike in Europe, where wolves were highly feared and hated, mountain people in Japan didnot fear wolves. The purpose of the "honorable dogs" (oinu) was to protect, not to prey. People often turned to wolf deities in troubling times for support. Canis Lupus Hodophilax (Honshu wolf) meant "guardian of the way," and so in the folk belief the wolf was guarding travelers through the dangerous mountains. Much of the Japanese folklore presents wolf as a "benign beast" (Knight, 1997).

In "Horkew kotan kor kur," an Ainu tale, the narrator is the wolf-god Horkew Kamuy. He tells a story of how well he is treated by his owner (which, at this point, shows the blurred line between the dog and the wolf in the Japanese tradition; Horkew Kamuy is treated as a dog when in village or in the proximity of people). Each day the wolf-god goes with his master to hunt in the mountains, until one day the other wolves persuade him to hunt with them. When Horkew Kamuy returns home, he is beaten to death by his owner as a punishment for not hunting with him. The wolf wakes up, floating down the river of dreams, and somewhere in the middle of that river he finds himself at another Ainu master, who recognizes Horkew Kamuy as a high-ranking god. Ainu invites the deity to his home and treats it accordingly, until the previous owner shows up with gifts of apology to get his dog back. Horkew Kamuy returns with his master, and the same scenario occurs: instead of hunting with the man, the wolf god runs with the other wolves, and as a punishment he is beaten to death. This time Horkew Kamuy doesnot stop at the house of the second Ainu master, but continues to the third house. When the next Ainu comes out with gifts to welcome the wolf deity, Horkew Kamuy flees across the ocean, where he meets the wolf boss, whom he tells his story to. Although Horkew Kamuy decides not to take revenge on the man who wronged him, the wolf boss gathers other wolf gods and together they kill all the people in the village (Walker, 2005).

The Japanese wolf appears as a provider and donor in a traditional folk tale "A Hair from the Wolf's Eyebrow." In this story, a man on the edge of poverty decides to commit a suicide. He goes to the mountains so the wolf can devour him. However, when the wolf comes at night, it doesn't attack. So the man asks the wolf why it doesn't want to eat him, and the wolf replies that it doesn't eat the real people, but only those who are animals in human disguise. The man asks how the wolf can distinguish between them, since all the people look the same.

Then the wolf pulls a hair out of his eyebrows, gives it to the man and says that if he looks through the hair, he will be able to see the true nature of people. The man accepts the gift and departs. He stops at a house and asks if he can stay for the night. The old man agrees, but his wife rudely refuses. Then the wanderer remembers the strange gift and puts the wolf's hair to the eye and sees that the old woman is in fact a cow. The man returns to be wealthy and happy (Knight, 1997).

The wolf is also a protector. A fairytale "The carved wooden wolf" (Kibori no okami) tells a story of a hunter, who, drawn by magical impulses, finds himself at a small house where a woman with child live alone. Each night an angry bear god attacks the woman, and each time he is stopped by a wolf. She explains that the wolf is in fact a small wooden wolf that she's got as a charm from her brother. The bear returns again and fights with the wolf, but this time the hunter kills the bear with an arrow. The wolf changes back into the wooden charm. Then the hunter has a dream, in which the bear explains that he loved the woman, and so had cast a spell on her father-in-law that made him abandon her. The story ends with celebration, as hunter brings the woman back to the village (Walker, 2005). This tale is a perfect example of how Propp's theory applies to Japanese stories, having at least half of 31 functions.

The wolf of European tale is often put in opposition to the fox and the dog. In folk tales and fables both fox and dog are opponents or enemies of the wolf, while in Japan the fox (kitsune) is a helper, sometimes also a partner of the wolf (okami), and the dog (inu) was not always distinguished from the wolf (Walker, 2005). The wolf of fable is always defeated by a clever fox or a brave dog, even though the wolf, the real wolf, is way more cunning than the fox, and more intelligent than the dog. I will, however, focus only on the wolf-fox relationship.

The wolf and the fox are ever-present in fables and folk tales. "The Fox, the Wolf, and the horse," "The Lion, the Wolf, and the Fox,"

"The Wolf Accusing the Fox," "The Wolf and the Fox" from the fables of La Fontaine, are just to list a few. In this type of tales, usually "fox outwits the wolf by getting him to do something foolish, like sticking his tail in a hole in the river ice to catch fish, only to have it freeze and break off," (Lopez, 1978). Also "Reynard the Fox," based on feud between the wolf Isengrim and the fox Reynard, presents the wolf as fox's fool, although in this tale the fox is the treacherous one. Thomas Bewick, in his publication of Aesop in 1818 in England, presents wolf as "innately evil, irreconcilably and fundamentally corrupt, and not very intelligent," (Lopez, 1978). Interestingly enough, "what passes for cleverness in Bewick's fox is dishonesty in his wolf; and what for the fox is craft is for the wolf cheating," (Lopez, 1978). That alone tells much of how the wolf was perceived.

For comparison, in the folk tale "The White Fox who saved the Wolves" (Okami o tasuketa shiro kitsune), fox and wolf are both positive characters. In this tale, after the famine strikes on the lands of Ainu, the white fox god saves people (Ainu) and gods (animals). Wolf gods, despite being excellent hunters and higher-ranking gods than foxes, cannot catch the game because of the two monsters: Kinaposoinkara, who scare away the deer, and Peposoinkara, who scare away the salmon. The white fox god, the trickster, kills the monsters with yomogi arrows, and so the herds of deer and shoals of salmon return. This allows both people and the gods, including wolves, to feed. Ainu people, in gratitude, send prayers and leave gifts for the fox god. Then the white fox god marries the wolf sister, and they sire several children (Walker, 2005). This is certainly not the picture of the wolf and fox that is known from Aesop fables.

Also themes of ungrateful and grateful wolf are worth mentioning. In the Japanese "Grateful wolf" type of tales, a man helps the wolf either by pulling a thorn out of wolf's mouth, by giving it salt or by simply rescuing it from a pit. The wolf, in return, brings an animal, usually a wild boar, deer or pheasant to the man, or protects him from other wolves (Knight, 1997). In contrast, in Aesopian "The Wolf and the Crane," the wolf is definitely the ungrateful one.

In conclusion, by using Propp's character theory, the wolf can be identified as a specific type of hero: in Europe as the villain (with some exceptions), so the negative type of the character. The wolf as the villain type is found in most of the folk tales and fables, some of which being "Little Red Ring Hood" or "The Wolf, the Sheep, and the

Lamb". In Japan the wolf is the hero (,,Horkew kotan kor kur"), the donor ("A Hair from the Wolf's Eyebrow"), the helper ("The carved wooden wolf"), and the princess ("The white fox who saved the wolves"), so the positive types of the characters. Out of the actions in the story, also a set of recurring motifs can be identified:

In European fairy tale and fable:

1. The Wolf is the Devourer (driven by the hunger, he wants to eat everything that is alive, mostly sheep, horse, human).
2. The Wolf is ungrateful (and bites the hand that feeds him, or rather wants to devour the owner of the hand).
3. The Wolf fights the dog or argues (with) the fox.
4. The Wolf's stupidity or overconfidence let others (usually his would-be victims) fool him.
5. The Wolf loses its tail or teeth.
6. The Wolf is outwitted, beaten, chased away, or killed.
7. The Wolf returns humiliated and hungry (if he's even alive at this point).

In Japanese tale:

1. The Wolf is the mountain deity, a Large Mouthed Pure God.
2. The Wolf is unpredictable, and so feared but deeply revered.
3. The Wolf is protector, and guards the travelers on the paths.
4. The Wolf deity wanders into the village to stay there as a dog.
5. The Wolf helps in various situations (usually protecting the fields and crops from ungulates).
6. The Wolf is a provider, and gives a hair from the eyebrow (through which one can perceive the true nature of the people).
7. The Wolf is grateful, and repays for help.

The common and recurring theme in the European tale is that of the Aesopian wolf: "a base, not very intelligent creature, of ravenous appetite, gullible, impudent, and morally corrupt," (Lopez, 1978). The wolf's role in the tale, then, is more or less consistent, and its function is highly predictable. On the other hand, the wolf (now extinct in Japan) of Japanese lore was more varied, more unpredictable, and portrayed in overall contrast to traditional European wolf-villain.

Therefore, the function of the wolf as a character in fables and folk tales of Europe and Japan indicate the differences in the perception of the real wolf and its place in these cultures. It also shows the discrepancies between the traditional stories of these communities.

Bibliography

Cashdan, Sheldon. *The witch must die: The hidden meaning of fairy tales.* (New York: Basic Books, 1999).

Knight, John. 'On the Extinction of the Japanese Wolf'. *Asian Folklore Studies*, Volume 56, 1997: 129-159.

La Fontaine, Jean. *A Hundred Fables of La Fontaine.* (London, 2008).

Lopez, Holstun Barry. *Of Wolves and Men.* (New York: Simon and Schuster, 1978).

Pluskowski, Alexander. *Wolves and the Wilderness in Middle Ages.* (Woodbridge, 2006).

Propp, Vladímir. *Morphology of the Folk Tale* (Translation 1968, The American Folklore Society and Indiana University, 1928).

Robish, S.K. *Wolves and the Wolf Myth in American Literature.* (Reno, NV, 2009).

Walker, Brett L. *The Lost Wolves of Japan.* (Seattle, WA, 2005).

Wama, Takenori and Ryohei Nakatsu. 'Analysis and Generation of Japanese Folktales Based on Vladimir Propp's Methodology'. In Paolo Ciancarini, Ryohei Nakatsu, Matthias Rauterberg, and Marco Roccetti, editors, *New Frontiers for Entertainment Computing*, number 279 in IFIP International Federation for Information Processing, 129–137. (Springer, 2008).

WOLF IN THE SNOW & A WOLF'S PLEA
DAWN SHARMAN

Dawn Sharman is an artist living in the United Kingdom with her husband Murray. Dawn works as a volunteer in a charity shop which raises money for the local hospice. One of her positions is a window dresser which enables her to use artistic skill and imagination and is often complimented by the customers for her beautiful window displays. Dawn has many creative talents including painting, sketching, crafting, photography, and poetry. Being a great animal lover with a particular love for Wolves, some of her animal designs have been used on coffee mugs, jigsaw puzzles, and calendars mainly through entering and winning art competitions.

Wolf in the Snow. Pastels.

A Wolf's Plea

We live in the forest
my pack and me
we are safe at the moment
running wild and free
trying to survive as best as we can
tired and exhausted
as hunted by man
All we ask is to be left alone
so we can live out our lives
in this place we call home.

THE WOLFISH MIND
NORBERT GORA

25-years-old poet and writer from Poland. Many of his horror, SF and romance short stories have been published in his home country. He is also author of many poems in English-language poetry anthologies around the world.

Inside the wolfish mind,
the continuous pursuit,
the call tears ahead.

The smell of adventure
in the air feeling,
gaining the speed.

They whisk in spite of wind,
in the cold,
in the heat.

Inside the wolfish mind,
secrets deeply hidden,
who knows, what we will find, behind those beautiful eyes.

Inside this mind,
there are love, fun,
uncertainty and fear.

Forepaws crossed the air,
in a joyful dance,
let fortunately to bloom for them.

We can hear the howling,
the recovery time has come,
for the pack of shining eyes, suede noses.

Inside the wolfish mind,
time is a relative term,
inside the wolfish mind, the ember of opposing feelings burning.

LIST OF WOLF VETERANS

Here is the list of contributors who have had works accepted in both the first and second volumes of this anthology. From now on in the series, we hope to continue to honor our ever-constant Wolf Veterans.

A.M. Duvall

Chelsea Dub

Chris Albert

Hannah E. Christopher

Jenny H. Thornton Woodley

Jitka Saniova

John Noland

Katt Reingruber

Kelly Walford

Melissa Lullaby Cable

Michael E. Hayne

Shannon Barnsley